Amo

DONNA GEORGE STOREY

NEON

A NEON PAPERBACK

This paperback edition published in 2007 by Neon,
an imprint of The Orion Publishing Group Ltd
5 Upper Saint Martin's Lane
London WC2H 9EA
An Hachette Livre UK Company

1 3 5 7 9 10 8 6 4 2

A CIP catalogue record for this book is available from the British
Library.

ISBN (MMP) 978 1 9056 1917 7

Typeset at The Spartan Press Ltd,
Lymington, Hants

Printed and bound at Mackays of Chatham plc,
Chatham, Kent

The Orion Publishing Group's policy is to use papers that
are natural, renewable and recyclable products and made
from wood grown in sustainable forests. The logging and
manufacturing processes are expected to conform to the
environmental regulations of the country of origin.

PROLOGUE – Vows

The day I left Japan, I stared at my reflection in the mirror in the airport ladies' room and made the following vows:

I would never tell another lie, especially to myself.

I would never let desire overwhelm common sense.

I would never sleep with a man who was married to someone else, mime fellatio with a complete stranger on a stage, or take money for sex again.

In fact, to cover all bases, I would never have sex again with anyone, man or woman, for the rest of my life.

A tall order given my recent past, but I figured if the Amorous Woman could renounce her sluttish ways and spend the rest of her days meditating in a mountain hermitage, then so could I.

My vows were almost too easy to keep in my first month in San Francisco. I was busy training for my new job teaching Japanese culture to businessmen facing overseas assignment in Tokyo and finding my own place, a sunny townhouse on the Peninsula, absurdly spacious by Japanese standards. I began to feel so virtuous I wondered if I couldn't just go ahead and become a real nun on the do-it-yourself plan. I'd already given up most of my possessions. I was eating spartan meals, although that was partly because I kept forgetting to go to the grocery store. Celibacy?

So far so good, if you don't count lustful thoughts, but those would fade with time, I hoped. I hadn't shaved my head yet, but I did invest in a book on Zen meditation. I liked the idea of spending long hours in a state of serene mindfulness, cleansing away the years of illusion from my soul.

It may seem strange that I wanted to model my life on that of a Japanese courtesan-turned-nun, who existed only in the fantasies of her creator, the seventeenth-century monk Ihara Saikaku. Yet to me, she's always seemed like a kindred spirit.

I remember well the first time I met her. My Japanese literature professor told the class, with a twinkle in his eye, that this week's reading had been banned in pre-war Japan because the main character was a woman of strong carnal appetite and even reading about such behavior was thought to corrupt national morals. I purposely did the assignment on a day when my roommate was away, expecting I would need to slide my hand down my pants to take care of my own amorous urges. To my disappointment, I read the whole book with barely a twinge. True, the Amorous Woman was a nymphomaniac who spread her legs for every man who crossed her path – a common male fantasy that seems to vanish as soon as a guy meets a real-life woman who likes sex – but the act itself was buried deep in the footnotes and Japanese wordplay. I did learn, for example, that in seventeenth-century Japan, if a woman's eyebrows itched it meant her lover would visit her soon. Interesting, yes, but hardly a turn-on.

The true threat of the Amorous Woman, I decided,

and the reason I admired her, was her sense of adventure. She insisted on the freedom to live many lives and indulge her passions, difficult enough to do in this day and age and almost unknown for a woman in old Japan. At one time I yearned for the same thing, and in a way I got it. In my nine years in Japan, I did lead many lives and have a lot of sex – much of it very good indeed.

But as the California winter rains turned to the balmy sunshine of spring, I wasn't so sure I really could follow in her footsteps as far as the total renunciation of worldly desire. How did a woman who once devoted her whole existence to sensual pleasure manage to pull that off?

I know now that the literal translation of 'Amorous Woman' in Japanese was 'a woman who loved colors'. Even for a nun, there was plenty of color to love in a mountain hermitage above Kyoto: the blushing cherry blossoms, the scarlet maples, the writhing golden flames of the summer bonfires lit to welcome dead souls back to earth, the pure white clouds of a spring morning that the old poets called 'the floating bridge of dreams'. Could the Amorous Woman still let herself enjoy the silken glide of spring water on her fingers and the scent of plum blossoms on a cold February morning? Or did the prayers lull her senses into sleep, so that her only yearning was to feel no desire at all? Did she ever tell herself that maybe what she did in the course of her colorful career wasn't so bad – that millions of people have affairs, get divorced, have sex with strangers for thrills or money or both? Was it such a sin that she did her best to 'fuck like a man'? Many women have done that, not to mention most men.

Only after I bought myself a new copy of the book at the local university store, did I remember that the Amorous Woman did not really give up desire. When two handsome young men made a pilgrimage to her hut to ask her advice in matters of sensual love, she soon fell back to her old ways, drinking *saké* with them and singing love songs.

A temptation I could easily avoid I told myself, as I dressed for my class on Japanese business practices one Tuesday evening in April. My gray skirt and blazer — chosen to give a short, slender woman like me at least a suggestion of professional gravitas — were dull enough for a convent. So what if I added a blouse of periwinkle blue, a color that never failed to earn me compliments on the striking blue of my eyes? And so what if my students just so happened to be two young men, and rather good-looking ones at that?

I wasn't that far gone in my fantasy. I knew it was the twentieth century and I wasn't really a nun, and there was little chance they would ply me with liquor and ask for a song.

Part One

THE HERMITAGE OF LOVE
(San Francisco, 1992)

CHAPTER ONE

When those two attractive young men did actually ask me out for drinks a few hours later, I hesitated. They were my students and I'd just finished explaining *tsukiai*, the Japanese custom of bonding over drinks after work. Professional courtesy made it almost a duty to accompany them to the trendy microbrewery just across the street from their office, although I knew it was more in keeping with my renunciation of the world to make an excuse and go home to an empty bed.

I looked at the young men's faces, so fresh and expectant as they waited for my answer. Brad Boyer, the cookie-cutter blonde on the left was in marketing and sales and not my type at all. His more substantial engineer colleague, Tim Monroe, was definitely tempting with his dark hair and creamy Celtic complexion, but I'd learned just today that he and Brad were twenty-six, four years my junior. Even if Tim did entertain fantasies of doing it with a former babysitter, the fact that there were two of them and only one of me made a spur-of-the-moment 'second party' between the sheets highly unlikely.

Besides, how could I get in trouble just having a quick beer with a couple of kids? It was as safe as going to church.

Ten minutes later we were seated at a table in a

9

cavernous room with a ceiling that left the guts of the building – girders, wires, pipes – exposed to view. A very American setting, I decided.

Brad held up his glass in a toast. 'What do the Japanese say again, *Sensei*?'

Although I felt like a fraud being called 'teacher' – I was taking good money to instruct them in Japanese business etiquette and I'd never worked in an office in my life – I was fairly confident in my knowledge of after-hours corporate culture.

'*Kampai*,' I said and lifted my glass while bending forward in a slight bow.

'*Kampai*,' they repeated dutifully.

We all drank. The beer was pleasantly bitter, delicious. It had been a long time since I tasted something so good.

'I've learned too many rules and customs these past few weeks,' Tim said. 'I know I'm going to forget and do something wrong.'

He looked so earnest and appealing; I had to come to his rescue. 'I'll let you in on a secret. The Japanese prefer their foreigners clueless. As long as you don't soap up in the bath or walk in a house with your shoes on, any other mistake gives you a certain endearing barbarian quality.'

'I assume it was different for you since you're fluent in the language and have a Japanese last name,' Brad said.

'Not really. Even if you manage to bewitch some poor native son into marriage, you're still an outsider.'

Brad gave Tim a triumphant smile. 'See, she

married a Japanese guy. That's what I thought. Tim guessed it was a grandfather with weak genes.'

'I said it was a possibility,' Tim corrected him.

When they spoke to each other their voices were low and quick. Comfortable. I felt a pang of jealousy. Would I always be an outsider, even here?

'I hope your husband doesn't mind us taking you away for a couple of hours,' Tim said.

I took another swallow of my beer. Yuji was well past minding what I did. At least I hoped he was.

'My husband's in Osaka. We're not really together anymore.'

This information had a visible effect on my companions. Tim blushed and dropped his gaze to the table. Brad's eyes flickered.

'There's a lot of that going around,' Brad said, grinning at Tim. 'Tim's girlfriend's not so happy about him going to Tokyo. In fact, as of last weekend, he's a free man.'

It was my turn to feel uncomfortable, although Tim didn't seem particularly embarrassed. I'd forgotten how promiscuous Americans could be about sharing their private lives. Of course, this would be good news if I were on the prowl for a bed-warmer. A guy who's recently been dumped is ripe picking for a wild, revenge-fueled one-night stand.

I took another swig of beer and glanced over at Tim. His five o'clock shadow seemed to deepen before my eyes, a subtle promise of tireless masculine vigor. I imagined kissing him, the oddly pleasant friction of that beard against my chin and upper lip.

Brad's voice interrupted my reverie. '*Sensei*? I'm

going to pick up our nachos. Can I get you another beer?'

You'd better take it easy, the saintly Lydia in my brain warned, her rosaries rattling. *You know what happens when you let men get you tipsy*. But the slightly buzzed, happily repatriated American Lydia had other ideas.

I smiled and nodded at Brad, a loose, effortless motion. It's always been so much harder for me to say no.

CHAPTER TWO

After Brad left, I felt my smile widen from polite to genuinely pleased. Without even trying, I'd finally gotten Tim all to myself.

'Are you sure you can't talk your girlfriend into going with you to Tokyo?' I asked, a touch perversely, as if I really did want them to get back together.

'I'm sure,' he said with a small, defiant smile.

Maybe I'd have a little company tonight after all? Perhaps I was being a little harsh on myself with my vow to give up sex for eternity. After all, the Buddha taught we should be open to what life hands us and take the middle way between renunciation and pleasure. I could just tell by the way Tim moved his body and used his hands that he was the attentive, caring sort of lover who would most definitely bring me pleasure. He'd kiss and fondle my breasts for hours until I came just from the sweet tug-tugging of his lips on my throbbing nipples, then he'd gently part my thighs and use his tongue down there with such slow, savoring skill that I'd come again, drenching him with my juices, and he'd swear it was the sweetest nectar he'd ever tasted. Afterwards, he'd wrap me in his arms and we'd float together, not the doomed and melancholy drifting of the courtesan with her lover of the moment, but as twin spirits joined in timeless bliss.

Suddenly I realized Tim was talking to me. Perhaps he had been for some time.

'I do want to settle down, just not quite yet,' he said with surprising firmness. 'So, I'm going to do it. And whatever happens, at least it will be an adventure.'

'Yes, I'd rather do something I regret than regret something I didn't do,' I said with a smile.

'I know exactly what you mean.'

My chest tightened. It was brave of him to give up safety for adventure and suddenly I wanted to give him something to help, something more than tips on exchanging business cards or even a few sweaty rounds of sumo-wrestling on my futon.

And so I told him how living in Japan will give him a leisure no mere tourist has to know the rhythms of the place, a land of tiny poems. In autumn, he'd see the persimmons glowing like huge, orange jewels on their bare branches, then winter's dusting of snow on blue tile roofs. He'd learn why the old erotic pictures are called 'spring prints' – because in that season the air is as soft as a lover's whisper – and he'd sigh at the perfect coolness of iced barley tea slipping down his throat on a wilting summer afternoon. As the year passed, he would become part of it. The neighbors would stop staring and start to nod a greeting, and one day the tiny old lady in the gray kimono at the snack-stand would wrap up his regular order of red-bean-and-rice balls before a word was spoken, and she'd flash him that first gold-toothed smile, and he'd be happy all day. It's like someone's given you a whole other life I told him, an extra life to live for a while.

Tim listened, lips parted, the way men do when they want to be enchanted. And how could I blame him for falling under Japan's spell? Not so very long ago, I was enchanted, too.

CHAPTER THREE

Just then Brad returned holding a tray, jauntily, like a waiter with a better job on his mind. He transferred the platter of nachos to the middle of the table and placed another pint glass beside me.

'What did I miss?'

'*Sensei* was just telling me more about living in Japan. It sounds amazing,' Tim said.

'Too bad. I could definitely use a sales job on the place myself.'

I felt my cheeks grow warm. So maybe I did go heavy on the *haiku* and cherry blossoms, but it wasn't exactly a sales job.

The men started in on the nachos. I sipped my second beer as I watched their capable hands plucking up the chips, which sagged under a mountain of melted cheese and guacamole. It wasn't the direction my appetite was taking tonight.

It would take no more than a flick of the wrist to slip Tim my business card as we said our goodbyes. Perhaps I could excuse myself to the ladies' room and write a little note on the back: 'I'd love to talk more about Japan. Give me a call'? Or would American forthrightness be more effective: 'Interested in a no-strings sport fuck while you're still officially single? How about tonight'?

As if on cue, Tim's trousers erupted in a trill of

sound. I jumped guiltily. He looked embarrassed too, as he pulled out his beeper and checked the caller ID.

'Excuse me, I have to make a call,' he said, rising from his seat.

'Could you pick up a couple of these on your way back?' Brad held up his glass. '*Sensei*'s thirsty tonight.'

Tim nodded and headed over to the public phone near the entrance.

'Oh, and say "hi" to Jenny for me,' Brad called after him, but softly, so that only I could hear.

CHAPTER FOUR

Brad looked different when we were alone. It was his eyes. They'd grown warmer, the soothing, reliable blue of a California afternoon. I didn't fool myself into thinking it was genuine attraction. He was clearly the type who went for arm ornaments — slinky blondes with melon breasts like my cousin Caroline. But the lack of possibility between us had definite advantages. It meant I could relax and have a little fun.

'So, I'm getting the impression you're not looking forward to your new assignment.'

He sighed. 'Not really. To be honest, I don't think the business environment is going to turn around any time soon. Plus they want me to stay over there for at least two years. It could get pretty lonely.'

'Would you like a little advice on how to penetrate the mysteries of the Orient?'

He shrugged. 'I'm not one of those guys who has a thing for Asian women. Of course, I'm not against it either, it depends on the person. But two years is a long time not to have a . . . relationship.'

I was amused to see a blush rise in his cheeks. It was hard to imagine him as a sexually desperate man, but then my mind handed me another image: Brad's handsome face glistening with beads of water, neck arched, and mouth half open in a moan of private ecstasy. The hot spray of the shower would turn that blonde hair to deep gold. I could see it shining wet against his flushed skin as clearly as if I were there with him. Of course, I couldn't resist lowering my gaze for a peek at the real action below – his thick cock rising from the corona of wet curls, the steady jerking of his fist, the plum-colored cock head swelling and straining as he neared release, and finally the jets of semen spilling over his hand into the swirling water at his feet. I even rewound the tape a bit to put myself in the scene, kneeling to catch his spunk in my mouth. When I was turned on cum tasted like a bowl of ceremonial green tea to me, grassy and bracing.

I took another swig from my glass and pretended it was the flavor of the beer that caused the faint sigh of appreciation. Fortunately, when I looked up, Brad was in his designer suit again, hair dry and combed, a faint frown of worry still creasing his brow.

I considered telling him the good news, that outgoing, blonde foreign men can usually find plenty of Japanese women interested in an exotic fling. But Brad brought out my contrary streak.

'Well, you can always pay for it,' I said with a wicked grin.

His frown deepened, which was just the reaction I was hoping for, but a moment later the corners of his mouth lifted in a strange smile. 'Ah, yes, *Sensei*, but don't we all pay for it in the end?'

For a moment, I was speechless. Then we both laughed.

'I'm sorry, it wasn't personal. It's just that most Westerners think all Japanese women are beautiful geisha-girl prostitutes with a menu of exotic sex tricks tucked up their kimono sleeves.'

'Well, I don't believe that and even if I did, that's not what I want.'

'What do you want?' To my surprise, I was curious to hear his answer.

'You'll laugh, but I'll tell you anyway. I want to find true love.'

'Oh, is that all?'

'See, you did laugh.'

It was more of a dismissive snort, but he was right, these days I did find the idea of romance absurd. 'Well, I wish you the best of luck,' I said, raising my glass.

Brad studied my face, his expression softer. 'What do you want, *Sensei*?'

'I don't know. I used to think good sex was all I needed.'

'Oh, is that all? An attractive woman like you could have your pick of guys day or night.'

'You weren't listening.' I shook my finger at him like one of those ancient librarians at my high school. 'I didn't say sex, I said good sex. If you think any sex is good sex, you aren't paying attention.'

'You know, *Sensei*, I've been trying my best to pay attention. Even though I'm not the teacher's pet.'

Once again I was speechless. Had I been that obvious in my preference? It's not that Brad didn't have his charms. All that drive and attention to detail would surely translate into bedroom skill. He'd be one of those octopus lovers who could do four things at once – one hand tweaking my nipple and the other strumming my clit, his tongue circling the other aureole, while his muscular ass drove his cock into me with perfectly timed strokes. He'd have a naughty playful streak too, a taste for bedroom games. He'd tie my wrists and tease me, make me beg for it, then, with equal grace, turn and tilt up his perky bottom to my lusty school marm who had a very special punishment for bad boys. Best of all, I wouldn't have to scrawl come-on lines on a business card to make it happen. I'd only have to glide with the current.

But suddenly I was tired, so tired. 'I can see you're paying attention,' I said, my voice sounding thick and blurry. 'That's the key to good sex, isn't it? At the beginning anyway. But then you cross over to that place where you don't have to think anymore. All the differences between you melt away, and you're totally in the moment. That's when it's good. Beyond good. There isn't even a word for that feeling, is there?'

'It's unusual to find a woman who's so comfortable talking about these things.' Brad leaned closer. I thought for a moment he was going to take my hand.

'Don't get the wrong idea now.' I laughed, but didn't move my hand away. 'Just because we're sitting here talking about sex doesn't mean I'm going to sleep with you.' Although, in truth, it usually did.

'I know,' Brad said, his smooth voice slipping down my spine to pool in my belly like warm syrup. 'On the other hand . . .'

CHAPTER FIVE

Suddenly Tim was standing above us, a beer in each hand. I jerked my hand away. Brad's hand veered toward the nachos, as if that were the plan all along.

'So, did you ask her?' Tim said curtly.

'Not yet,' said Brad. 'We were talking about other things.'

I watched this exchange with mild curiosity. There was no need for jealousy. As I made some headway into that third drink, I began to see the appeal of bringing both of them home with me tonight, the salesman in his designer suit with the spark and glamor, the solid engineer with the staying power. Isn't that what I really wanted? To compare the flavor of their kisses, like different vintages of a fine claret. To watch two different hands caress each breast, side by side, Brad's tapered fingers, Tim's squared, thick hands which, like everything about his body, made me think of that luscious word *big*. In the end – the thought made me shiver – I'd be sandwiched between them, their cocks filling me front and rear, my body stretched and filled so full my head would explode when I came. Filled so completely I would never be hungry again. I always feared that I craved too much pleasure. Perhaps the problem was that I didn't ask for enough?

'I think you should ask her now,' Tim snapped. 'It's getting late.'

'Ask me what?'

Brad turned and gave me a conciliatory smile. 'Well, *Sensei*, Tim and I wanted to ask you a question. We want to know the truth about you.'

All at once I saw everything: Tim's single pint glass, half-full, Brad finishing his first beer quickly, wiping his mouth, and in front of me two empty glasses and one full one, glittering like washed gold.

They are trying to get me drunk.

Or rather, they'd already succeeded. Suddenly I was aware of my teeth sitting in my head, tingling. They could ask the question, but I wasn't sure my tongue could manage a reply.

'The truth?' I repeated stupidly, as if it were a foreign word.

'Well, do you remember when the president of your company introduced you at the first meeting and he said your course would give us an understanding of Japanese business practices that would ensure our success in the challenging international environment?'

I nodded, although I'd done my best to tune out the old windbag. It was pure fantasy that I could teach anyone in five evening sessions what I had failed to do in almost a decade of all-too-earnest effort. I found it amusing, too, that in the eyes of the world this charade was the most respectable job I'd had in quite a while.

'Do you remember after he said that, you did this?'

Brad folded his hands and rolled his eyes in perfect imitation of a surly teenager.

'I did not do that,' I protested, but my voice rose in a damning adolescent whine.

'You did, and not only that. When he said, "Lydia Yoshikawa will provide you with a highly experienced insider's perspective on Japanese interpersonal relations," you did this.' He brought his hand to his mouth as if to stifle a snicker.

I'd been sitting at the back of the room and didn't think anyone would bother to look in my direction. Of course Brad had been paying attention.

Instinctively I turned to Tim for help. All he gave me was a merciless grin, his eyes narrowed as if he enjoyed watching me squirm. Harsh punishment for such a small transgression, a bit of flirting with his friend. The nice ones are always the cruelest in the end. They lull you into thinking you've found paradise then cut you out cold.

'The truth?' I said again. 'That might take a long time.'

They gazed at me, waiting.

What could I tell them? That I knew little of Japanese business practices, but plenty about picking up strangers in hot spring baths, handcuffing guys to beds in tacky love hotels, playing mistress to wealthy playboys, and miming sex acts on stage at a year-end banquet, amongst other activities I had thought best not to mention on my résumé? That if I hadn't had sex with every last able-bodied Japanese male over eighteen, it wasn't for lack of trying? That I was a fraud and a lecher who'd spent every class undressing them in my mind and forcing them to service my insatiable sexual needs?

Suddenly tears sprang to my eyes. Real tears. I had been unprofessional and now I would lose my job, just as I'd lost everything else. What a fool I was to think I could make a fresh start. I was still the same old troublemaker, indulging dangerous whims, sabotaging myself at every turn. I buried my face in my hands and took a few deep breaths. *Clear your mind. Let it go.* Then a stronger voice rose up through the beer-induced fog, older, familiar, the one I always listened to: *Run*.

'I'm not feeling well. I think I'd better go home,' I managed to say. 'I don't think I can drive myself though. If one of you could please call a taxi . . .'

That's how Tim ended up driving me home in my car with Brad following me in his to drive Tim back to the office, and then they both insisted they walk me in to make sure I was OK.

In fact, I couldn't have worked out a better way to get both of them back to my place for a three-way romp if I'd planned it from the beginning.

CHAPTER SIX

My townhouse was, to say the least, not ready for guests. I hadn't bought furniture for the downstairs, partly because of money, but mostly because I liked the spaciousness of it after my cramped apartment in Japan. Now, with two normal American guys glancing uncomfortably around the empty rooms, what had been an abundance of pure possibility seemed to reveal a disturbing lack.

It got worse. Murmuring something about getting me a glass of water, Brad walked into my kitchen and opened the refrigerator door to find nothing but a container of plain yogurt and a phallic-looking package of pickled white radish.

'We need to get you some dinner,' Brad said. 'Is Chinese OK? There's a pretty good place a few blocks from here.'

I waited meekly as Brad called in our order – Buddha's Delight and brown rice for me – and sent Tim out to pick up the food.

What else could I do then but invite him up to my bedroom?

When Brad saw the fireplace and the pile of wood the former tenants had left stacked neatly beside it, he offered to make a fire, which wasn't such a bad idea on this chilly spring evening.

'Thanks for doing all of this. I'll be ashamed to face

you next week in class, but you'll probably get me fired for what I did, so at least I won't have to worry about that.'

'Do you mean because of those funny faces you made? I won't tell. In fact, that's when I decided I liked you.'

I felt oddly moved by his words. I wanted him to like me. I wanted them all to like me. That was the problem.

'Well, I'd like to keep my job.'

'I want what you want, *Sensei*.' He smiled at me for a long moment, then began crumpling newspaper for kindling.

I stretched out on the floor and tucked the meditation pillow under my head. I liked watching him at work. His rolled-up sleeves and loosened tie gave him a fetching vulnerability, a boy playing businessman. 'You must have been a Boy Scout.'

'Yes,' he said, 'but I dropped out.'

I laughed.

The doorbell rang and Brad motioned me to stay put while he went downstairs to let Tim in. With a bag of fragrant Chinese take-out in his arms, my Irish engineer looked even more delicious than I remembered. There it was again, that pang of arousal. Like hunger, but lower.

Yet strangely enough, I wasn't torn between them now. I did have them both here, in my realm, where I could admire them in the firelight, the sharp Caucasian topography of their faces so exotic but nostalgic, too. With my belly full and warm, my lust mellowed into a desire for good company, which they were,

27

telling me funny stories of work, imitating the bosses, explaining movies and fads I'd missed in all those years away, teaching me to be American again.

It might have been an illusion, our sudden friendship, but isn't all human intercourse as fleeting? Strangers become lovers over a few beers; husbands turn to strangers with a single frown. I could already feel the silence of the place when they left, the loneliness.

I wondered how could I get them to stay. It was then I realized what I really wanted from both of them. Or rather, I wanted to give them something, exactly what they had asked for.

For all of those years in my adopted country, I was locked up in silence. There were many things I didn't know how to say, either with words or in other ways, and so many more it wasn't proper to speak of at all. What would it be like to tell my story honestly?

'Do you really want to hear the truth?' I asked.

They both turned to me, chopsticks in hand.

'Remember? The truth about my life in Japan? You might find some of it . . . surprising.'

Tim nodded. Brad mumbled, 'Absolutely. I'm all ears.'

'It's a story of bygone days. In some ways Japan changes so quickly, but many things stay the same. Oh, and there's a lot of sex in it. Too much maybe. Do you think you can handle it?'

They exchanged a glance.

'We'll give it our best try,' Brad said in a soft voice.

Suddenly I saw an image of myself sitting before them in *yukata*, the blue-and-white cotton robe you wear to relax at a hot spring. As they watched, I untied the sash, pulling open one panel, then the other, so they could see me as I really was. Not my nipples blushing dusty rose, or the reddish-blonde curls where my thighs met, but something softer, darker, deeper than flesh.

I took a long, slow breath. I began to tell my story.

Part Two

THE PLEASURES OF A MAIDEN IN SPRING
(Washington, D.C., 1962–1980)

CHAPTER ONE

How did I become an amorous woman? I think this is the best way to describe myself until not so very long ago, although I don't look the part of the sensuous vamp. I'm more of the gamine. Strawberry blonde hair, even features, and an easy smile usually earn me a ranking of second-prettiest girl at the party. And everyone knows we try harder.

I did well in school, a talent not usually associated with the courtesan, but I found that reading books and reading men are not really so different. Being smart meant I was not voted 'most likely to spend her days devoted to erotic pleasure and the fulfillment of male sexual fantasies' in my high school yearbook, but given the course of my career, perhaps I should have been.

My parents played a part in shaping my character, of course, if only by their absence. My father died when I was three, his car hit head-on by a drunk driver. My memories of him are few: a dark shape in an overcoat standing in a doorway – I can see the bluish winter light around his shoulders better than his face – and the salt-and-tobacco flavor of his knuckle, a fleeting taste before he pulled his hand away, 'No, honey. My hand's dirty.'

In my favorite photograph of us together, a round-cheeked blonde girl nestles against a slim man who looks a bit like Humphrey Bogart, his dark hair already thinning, although he would have only been in his mid-twenties. By looks alone we hardly seem related, but I am gazing up at him and he is gazing down at me and our smiles are so radiant we seem to float together in a circle of golden light. Dark, silent, eternally smiling, made mostly of dreams, if I were searching for a lover like my father – and what woman isn't? – there was no better place for me to look than Japan.

My mother, on the other hand, was a very real presence in my childhood, constantly shifting her look and her mood, the Princess of a Thousand Faces. In the mornings she had the blank, blonde prettiness of a princess in my books of fairy tales until she put on the dark skirt and sober face befitting an executive secretary in the law firm of Reed, Garner and Woodson – 'Don't forget to lock the door when you leave for school, honey, Mr Woodson needs me at work early today.' After work, when she changed into pedal pushers and clingy sweaters, she was suddenly younger, an older sister and ally who always took my side against other adults, the teachers who seemed annoyed I knew all the answers, a shopkeeper who scolded me for lingering over a magazine I couldn't buy.

The biggest change, of course, was when she went out on a date with a gentleman friend. I loved to lie on her bed and watch her get ready, knowing I was witnessing a preview of my own future. Years later, when I read descriptions of Japan's great medieval warriors ritualistically donning their armor to prepare for battle, I thought of my mother at her dressing table with her lipsticks and powders and perfume.

When she was finished, she was no longer the weary mother I knew. Her chin held high, her shoulders back, she was a model in a fashion magazine come to life, ready to vanquish the large, foreign creatures called men, who arrived promptly at eight to take her away from me and into the night. As far as I could tell, her victory came the moment they saw her, dreamy smiles spreading over their faces, their eyes dancing with a strange light. My mother had a power over them I didn't understand. I only knew some day I wanted it too.

On the evenings my mother had a date, Mrs Muller from the apartment below us would come and stay with me. Mrs Muller was a different kind of widow from my mother – gray-haired, pink-faced and doughy – but I loved her and was sorry when I grew too big to snuggle in her soft lap. After the click-clack of my mother's high heels faded from the stairway, she would give me a wink, and then make a show of checking out our refrigerator for the makings of 'a wee snack'. As if she ever expected to find anything but skim milk, cottage cheese and lettuce. 'This won't do at all. Why don't you go down to my kitchen and bring up the little treat I made for us, Lydia dear? I swear she must be starving you, you poor girl.'

I always found something wonderful waiting for me in her kitchen: squares of sticky gingerbread that filled the room with the fragrance of cinnamon and cloves, butter cookies that turned to sweet vanilla sand on my tongue, a pyramid of brown sugar fudge that made my teeth ache. But first, before I carried our feast back upstairs, I indulged in a secret pleasure of my own. I opened Mrs Muller's refrigerator, full to bursting with jars of cream, slabs of butter and packages of bacon, and eased out one of the jars of her strawberry preserves.

Hoisting myself up onto the counter by the narrow window, I gazed out into the darkness and dipped a finger into the cool jam. Night transformed our block of low brick apartments into a mysterious wonderland. Golden squares of window floated against the sky, streetlamps glowed blue, shadows of trees stirred like veils in the wind. As I licked the essence of berry-and-summer languidly from my finger, my own flesh began to tingle. I always felt a little like Rapunzel, trapped in a tower in a foreign country, longing for her true home. I yearned to slip down the fire escape – a pretty name, I thought, for that rickety, rusting ladder outside the window – not to escape a fire, but to dive into my own heated adventures with dark and faceless men, who would do to me all those things men did to women, although of course I wasn't quite sure what that meant.

What would it be like to have a lover? I settled on images harvested from movies, distilled in the strange heat of my fantasy, a thick-fingered hand fumbling at the buttons of my blouse, a pair of eyes glittering in the dim lamplight, a husky voice murmuring that I needn't be ashamed to show myself as I really was, not a pretty girl like me.

This, I later discovered, is not so different from the way it really happens after all.

CHAPTER TWO

If my mother and Mrs Muller were my first teachers in the secrets of sensual pleasure, my cousin Caroline was high school, college and graduate school all rolled up in one. My apprenticeship began one Saturday evening in late February. My mother and I had been invited to a party at Aunt Jean and Uncle Bob's new house, or rather, mansion, in Potomac. Uncle Bob had just been transferred to his company's national headquarters in Washington, and my mother told me Caroline was so furious about having to leave California to spend her senior year in a new school, she demanded her own saucy red MGB GT and a shopping spree in Europe as her just compensation.

'I'm glad you're nothing like her,' my mother said as we headed up the long path to their columned front entrance.

'Me too,' I said, wrinkling my nose at the very thought. Dutiful daughter that I was, I tagged along to the party for her sake, bringing along a thick book to read while I holed up in some deserted guest bedroom. I planned to avoid blonde surfer-girl Caroline like the plague, as I always did at our rare family gatherings over the years. But Caroline, and life, had different plans.

My cousin snagged me as I was wandering around looking for a hideout. She waved a bottle with a fancy

French label at me. 'I lifted some champagne from the bar. Come on up to my room, Lydia, and you can meet my friend, Marybeth. She's wild.'

'Caroline, you didn't tell me your cousin was cute!' Those were Marybeth Leary's first words when we met. She was stretched out on my cousin's queen-size bed like Cleopatra, eyes hooded with marijuana and worldly ennui. She looked like an Egyptian queen, too, with blunt-cut raven hair and luminous skin she later confided was a result of regular moon-lit nude bathing. To give credit where credit is due, she was to play an equally important role in my imminent corruption.

Caroline gave me an appraising once-over. I was used to men looking: construction workers or the dads in the neighborhood who followed me with their eyes as they watered their lawns with leaky hoses. Those stares embarrassed me, but made my insides feel warm and tingly. From a girl, however, it felt more like a chilly finger sliding down my spine.

'You're right, M.B. But in my defense, she's changed a lot since we were kids. She was always reciting some endless poem or waving around her straight-"A" report card so she could weasel a silver dollar from Grandpa. I thought she was revolting. But since the hormones have kicked in, I do see more of a family resemblance. She could use a little more up top though.'

'You know what they say — more than a mouthful's a waste,' I said cheerfully.

Caroline studied me for a moment, then seemed to

decide she would find me amusing. 'You *have* changed, haven't you? Well, make yourself at home in my boudoir, Cousin. Have some champagne.' Caroline handed me the bottle. Apparently, the preferred method of consumption was swigging it down like soda pop. I took a swallow and immediately felt dizzy.

'Tell me all about yourself, Lydia. Do you have a boyfriend?' Marybeth asked, her eyes suddenly wide and innocent.

'Yes.'

Harris and I were perfectly matched by the social standards of our high school: two smart kids comfortable enough with Shakespeare to play the fairy king and queen in the class production of *A Midsummer Night's Dream*. We read Stanislavsky together, sharpened our wit by mocking the popular kids behind their backs, and made plans to travel the world together. Not boring places like France or Hawaii, but heroic spiritual adventures like trekking in Nepal or purifying our souls under freezing waterfalls in the mountains of Japan. I knew none of this would give me much boyfriend credit with my present company, but at least I could say I had one.

'Is he good in bed?' That was my cousin.

I shrugged and took another gulp of the champagne. With the skill of expensive attorneys, the girls quickly established that Harris and I had had a few tepid make-out sessions in the five months we were together, and his date of choice was the ballet, when he could get cheap tickets.

'Oh Lydia,' Caroline said, shaking her head, 'it's

very cool to have a gay guy as a friend, but I'm afraid he's holding you back from your full potential. I mean, don't you ever get the itch?'

I felt a blush rise on my cheeks. I did get a secret feeling *down there* now and then – OK, pretty much every night – and I knew exactly how to relieve it in my bed under the covers, but no torture could get me to divulge that secret. They did, however, get me to confess that I'd never had sex even though I turned eighteen a few weeks before.

'Lydia, I cannot allow you to go to college a virgin. The honor of our family is at stake.'

'Besides, you're too pretty to be a virgin,' Marybeth drawled.

The champagne made another round, and Caroline patted the bed for me to sit down. 'Marybeth and I can help you. We know a lot of foxy guys who'd be more than willing to be your first. We could have a party and you could pick the one you like.'

The idea was so absurd, I just grinned foolishly. They seemed to take my silence for agreement, however, because Marybeth reached over and pulled me back on the bed beside her. Caroline kept her perch at the edge of the bed, gazing down at us with a strange little smile.

'We'll take care of you,' Marybeth cooed. She ran her fingertips over my forearm, as if she were stroking a kitten. Part of me wanted to jerk away, but to be honest, the champagne was making me horny and it felt nice. As I lay there, Caroline's warm, soft bed seemed to suck me in even deeper. Could it really be that easy to get laid – throw a party, pick your favorite stud, and bye-bye virginity?

'So what kind of refreshments will you serve for a lose-my-cherry party?' I asked. 'Lots of maraschinos and cherry pie?'

Caroline's smirk stretched into a genuine smile. 'That's the spirit. But we'll have to wait until spring break so we can invite the college boys. They generally know what they're doing – like how to find the right hole – which is better for your first time. Who do you think will be best for Lydia, M.B.? How about Todd?'

Marybeth cringed. 'He's too big for the first time. Ouch!'

'Sean? He's the literary, sensitive type. Lydia might like him.'

'I think Doug is the cutest.'

'Mr 69? He'll be so busy eating her, he'll forget to fuck her and that's the whole point. But some day you have to get together with him, Lydia. An experience not to be missed.' She and Marybeth exchanged a private look. 'He'll want you to blow him, though. Do you know how?'

'I think we've already established I'm clueless when it comes to sex.' I was familiar with the concept of oral sex from discussions with my own friends, but whenever I heard the words 'blow job', I couldn't get beyond the image of huffing and puffing at some guy's crotch as if I were blowing out birthday candles to make my wish come true. This was my chance to get some expert advice.

Marybeth nuzzled my shoulder. Her hair smelled of

peaches and her breasts pressed against my arm like hot little pillows. I felt sweat rise on my skin where we touched. 'Oh Cousin Lydia, you are too cute.'

Caroline narrowed her eyes. Her gaze was more like a guy's now, all glittery and full of schemes I didn't quite understand. 'What do you say we give you a little blow job lesson tonight, Lydia?'

I laughed nervously. This was getting far too strange for an innocent virgin like me. But at the same time a small voice inside my head whispered — *go ahead, do it, go along for the ride.*

'Sure, I guess so,' I said, 'but where are you going to get the penis?'

They both erupted in gales of laughter, but I rather liked making them laugh with me rather than at me.

Of course, I should have known such resourceful girls would have a handy substitute for the real thing. That's how I found myself sitting at the edge of the bed with Marybeth kneeling before me, her lips wrapped around the base of my thumb.

I'd never felt anything like it before. Her mouth was warm and soft and liquid and my thumb seemed to float there. Next I felt a firm, undulating pressure along the bottom: her tongue. Then she began to move, squeezing with every stroke. I watched her top lip stretch out thin and smooth when she glided down, then grow full and pouty as she pulled back up, her cheeks hollow with the suction.

I giggled.

'OK, your turn.' Marybeth sat on the bed and presented her thumb to me. I glanced quickly at Caroline. She was watching us with great interest, as if she were challenging me to prove our bond of blood.

I knelt and tried my best to mimic Marybeth's movements. Soon my jaw began to ache.

'Good. Very good for the first time. I think you're a natural.'

'I just have to point out that most guys are bigger than your thumb, M.B.'

'She's doing great, it'll translate,' Marybeth insisted. 'But, Lydia, you do have to remember each guy is different. What I do is pretend it's my first time and ask him to teach me what feels good.'

My cousin snickered. 'I'm sure they all fall for that line, M.B. By the way, are you going to tell Lydia about the grand finale?'

Marybeth nodded and proceeded to do exactly that.

'In my mouth?' I squealed.

Again they doubled over in laughter, but I was well past minding.

'What does it taste like?' I asked.

Marybeth cocked her head. 'It's hard to describe. Grass maybe. Warm, gooey grass.'

'I'd say more like Clorox mixed with snot,' Caroline said in a matter-of-fact tone. 'But here's the deal, Lydia. There are two kinds of women in this world. Those who swallow and those who don't. Naturally, Marybeth and I do.'

'You have to if you want to be the crème de la crème,' Marybeth said, with a twinkle in her eye. 'It's worth it though, Lydia. It's kind of pathetic how grateful they are. And if you swallow it quickly, you don't even really taste it.'

I sat there in silence, taking it all in. I really did feel that I was standing at a crossroads in my life. One path led into the dewy morning sunlight where I would be the girl all the grown-ups thought I was — serious, pure of mind and body, safe and reliable. The other road was shadowy, hidden by curtains of moist foliage, fragrant with musk and intoxicating spices, the path of The Kind Who Swallowed.

'Hey, Caroline,' I said, 'did you really mean it when you said you'd throw a party for me?'

'I always mean what I say. Put it in your calendar — the first Saturday of spring break. I'll take care of everything. You just come and pick out your favorite guy.'

'What if no one wants to do it with me?'

Caroline shook her head. 'Don't worry about that. Guys are the real sluts, you know, no matter what they call us when they get mad. They'll get it on with anyone, especially after a couple of beers. Not that you're just anyone. You're supposed to be my cousin, right?'

I smiled and took the last swallow of the champagne. 'What if I want them all?'

Caroline gave a low, witchy laugh that almost made me like her. 'You know, Lydia, I'm beginning to think we *are* related.'

CHAPTER THREE

Over the next month, Caroline and I actually became friends in our own way, after a lifetime of rivalry and mutual disdain. Sex deserves the credit for bringing us together, because it's pretty much all we talked about during our party-planning phone calls.

At first I tried to back out of it, but Caroline was determined that the party would happen just as she'd planned, and she had answers for every excuse I offered.

Of course I didn't have to be in love with the guy, she argued, it was my duty to explore and experiment first so that when I did find a guy I loved, I could appreciate him. And no, we weren't exploiting her friends by planning it in advance. After all, wasn't it a time-honored tradition for an experienced relative to take a young man to a brothel where he learned his first lessons in pleasure? Why couldn't women do it, too? Besides, she'd bet her new car that whichever guy I chose would welcome the exploitation.

Finally I confessed my real fear. 'Suppose he freaks out when he discovers it's my first time?'

'Most of them will probably be flattered, but I guess there could be the odd throwback who still thinks the first time should be special. So, if he asks – and he probably won't – you should just lie.'

'But he'll be able to tell, won't he?'

'Absolutely not, Lydia, because you're going to do "homework". And we both know what a good student you are.'

'What do you mean?'

'I mean that the next time you play with yourself – and I know you do, so don't try to pretend you don't know what I'm talking about – you should put something bigger than a finger inside. That way it won't hurt much at all when the guy puts his dick in.'

'Caroline,' I said, a nervous laugh bubbling up in my throat, 'I don't think I can go through with this.'

But the truth was, the more we talked, the more I wanted to do it. Caroline was offering me more than an A-list group of Ivy League boys from a rich D.C. suburb, a keg of beer to put them in the mood, and the free run of her house, with Aunt Jean and Uncle Bob tucked safely away in a country inn on Maryland's Eastern Shore for the weekend. She was giving me something even more precious – the freedom to travel to a foreign land where I could do anything and be anything I wanted, if only for one night.

It was a gift I'd have to travel halfway around the world to find again.

CHAPTER FOUR

Caroline was clever to call it 'homework'. She knew I couldn't resist the chance to get an A, even if it was in the art of masturbation. And so I told my mother I had to study for a test and retired to my bedroom early that night.

I lay in the darkness, my hairbrush beside me, the handle carefully washed with mild soap and dried with a clean towel. My heart was pounding in my throat. I played with myself all the time, but I'd never put anything inside, not even a finger. Would there be blood? Would I scream out in pain? Would my hairbrush respect me in the morning?

My hands wandered under the covers and I slowly hiked my nightgown up to my waist. I slid my hands down over my belly, tracing feathery circles with my fingertips as I went. My right hand dipped between my legs, the left settled on top, protectively. This was my usual position for self-pleasuring, but it suddenly seemed funny, as if one hand were trying to keep the other from escaping. This time maybe it was.

I touched my middle finger to my clit. I was already wet, and in fact, I'd been tingly down there since my talk with Caroline. My heart was a taiko drum, hammering louder and faster, and I feared for a moment that I might come in a few strokes and blow the assignment.

I took a few deep breaths and forced my finger into a lazier rhythm, teasing flicks rather than a desperate, home-stretch strumming.

And then, suddenly, I knew I was no longer alone. My eyes were closed, but I could feel him walk into the room. I smelled him too, Old Spice aftershave and a hint of male sweat. He didn't visit me every time I touched myself, but he'd been coming regularly almost from the beginning. I never saw his face, but I knew he was an older man from his voice, a bit hazy, as if he were calling through a door, but deep and smooth and utterly confident I would do everything he commanded.

'Pull down the covers, Lydia,' he said softly. 'You know I like to see your naked pussy when you play with yourself. Much better than watching a twitching little lump of hand jiggling away under the blanket.'

I felt a sweet stabbing sensation low in my belly, lust and shame all twined together. Obediently I pushed the blanket down so that anyone standing at the bottom of my bed would have a fine view of my lower half, thighs parted, vulva exposed.

'What's this I see beside you? Are you going to do something naughty with that brush?'

Reluctantly I nodded, my eyes squeezed shut.

'You have become a bad girl since you started listening to your cousin. But of course I'm very glad you're taking her advice. The world would be a happier place with more women like her.'

'I'm not sure I have the nerve to do what she said,' I confessed. My lips weren't moving, but I knew he understood.

'Of course you do. I want you to do it and you don't want to disappoint me. Why don't you pick up that brush and press it against your virgin hole?'

With a quivering hand, I reached for the brush and held the rounded end of the handle against my secret lips.

'Very good. Now push. Gently. Very gently.'

Ever the star student, I probed myself gingerly with my makeshift dildo. There was a mild stinging sensation, but with steady pressure I managed to coax it in a few inches. I pressed my other hand to my chest to keep my heart from jumping free of my rib cage.

'A little farther now,' the voice urged.

'I don't know if I can.'

'Try, Lydia. For me. Show me how brave you are.'

I pushed. The entire handle slipped inside.

'Very good. I knew you could do it. Now move it in and out slowly. I know you want to open yourself for your lover. And for me.'

This is indeed exactly what I wanted. Somehow he always knew just what to make me do, as if he could see desires inside me I myself didn't understand. He knew when it was time to stop the fucking movements and ease the brush out, knew I could soothe the lingering soreness by touching my clit again and coming on my hand, while he watched and murmured words of approval and even snapped a few photos for his collection along the way. And then, as quickly as he'd come – and I'd come – he vanished into air.

Afterwards, I curled up under the blankets, hugging my extra pillow to my chest like a lover. Could any real man know me so completely? Especially if, as Caroline said, I had to lie to him to lie with him?

Sex and honesty didn't fit together so easily. Even as a virgin, I seemed to know this was true. Which is why it was so funny that I ended up telling the guy who popped my cherry the truth from the beginning.

CHAPTER FIVE

Mike wasn't even on Caroline's list. He was the cousin of her boyfriend of the month and stopped by before the party to help deliver the keg. Caroline told me he was cool enough to put the deposit required by the liquor store on his credit card so she didn't have to pony up the cash.

I could tell he was older – twenty-three, I found out later, a Brown graduate, already working at a non-profit 'saving the world', as his cousin put it with a good-natured sneer. Mike wasn't cute in the good cheekbones way Caroline liked, but I liked his dark curls and the way he filled his jeans. What really got me were his sturdy hands clutching that keg and that suggestive grimace of exertion as he bent over to set it down. Lust made me bold and after I thanked him for his help, very nicely, I asked him if he was coming to the party.

His frown made me realize what a stupid question it was. Why would a genuine adult like him want to party with a bunch of high school girls and college sophomore boys? But then a tiny golden flame suddenly sprang to life in his dark eyes.

'Will you be there, Cousin Lydia?'

'I'm the guest of honor.'

'Is it your birthday?' He smiled and I caught a glimpse of a snaggle tooth, like a fang, which made him still more attractive.

'Something like that.'

'Well, I've got something to do around eight, but I'll try to stop by after.' He winked at me and was gone.

Mike did show up around eleven, which was a good thing, because after the initial interviews, I wasn't too keen on Caroline's college boy offerings. Their smiles had the twinkle of perfection, and their pedigrees were flawless, but all they seemed to be able to talk about was their new cars or how clever they were to arrange their college schedules so they didn't have classes on Friday.

When I spotted a tousled Mike on the patio by the keg, I made a point to saunter by while he was filling his cup.

'Another beer, Lydia?'

Slightly tipsy and reckless as only a girl determined to lose her virginity can be, I went for the direct approach. 'Thanks, but just a little. I'm going to have sex tonight and I want to be in top form.'

He laughed. 'Who's the lucky guy?'

Did they all fall into the trap so easily? I leaned closer. 'Why, you, of course. You're the most interesting guy here by far. So maybe,' I jerked my chin at his beer, 'you might want to take it easy, too.'

Amusement, disbelief, and a glimmer of hope played over his expression like flickering lights. 'Don't worry. I can probably handle a few more of these before my powers are seriously compromised. By the way, if you don't mind my asking, when are we going to have sex? Is this an immediate thing or do we have time to dance first?'

'Dancing sounds good. We can establish a rhythm for later when we're in bed.' I looked into his eyes and smiled.

'You'd be good at poker.' Mike smiled back and hooked an arm around my shoulder to guide me downstairs to the 'dance floor' Caroline had set up in the rec. room.

As we joined the crush of bodies, I managed to wink at Caroline who was perched on the wet bar surveying her domain, while her boyfriend nibbled her ear. I saw her say something to the guy filling in as DJ and one song later, Mike and I were glued together in a slow dance, his hard-on pressing against me.

I stood on tiptoe and whispered in his ear. 'Should we talk and get to know each other better before we have sex or wait until after?'

He drew back and gave me another searching look.

'Do you think I'm kidding?' I flashed him a smile.

'Damned if I know,' he said, but apparently it didn't matter because when we came together again, we were kissing. It wasn't my first kiss, but it was my first nice one. Harris used his tongue with the desperate athleticism of a salmon swimming upstream. But Mike's kiss was as slow and melting as the first hot day in June, tasting of strawberries, sugar and dreams.

Caroline winked her approval as we headed up the stairs, bound for her bedroom. We'd made her bed beforehand with her dark-green Chinese print sheets, in case there was blood, and she'd showed me where the condoms were hidden in the nightstand drawer.

'Are you sure it's OK if we use your cousin's bed?'

Mike said, frowning at the 'Do Not Disturb' sign on the doorknob, which I ignored.

'Oh yes, she knows we're going to have sex. She reserved it especially for us.'

He shook his head and laughed again.

And then, well, I don't remember exactly how we got naked, or who pushed whom down on the bed, or when exactly we stopped kissing and started doing other things, but there were more than a few firsts that night.

It was the first time a guy kissed my breasts so softly and slowly that I learned that lips tugging gently on my nipple could make me wet between my legs.

It was the first time I tried Marybeth's lesson on a real penis – thank you Marybeth for a gift that keeps on giving. It was bigger than a thumb, but far more interesting. I loved the way it twitched when I stroked it, the way it grew even harder in my mouth, the way Mike moaned softly as he watched me do it, eyes glowing.

It was the first time I heard my favorite sound on earth – his sweet groan of homecoming as he slid inside my cunt.

And then, somehow, it wasn't new any more. It was as if I'd always known this: his warm weight pressing me down, his musky boy's smell, his soft lips and slick, snaky tongue, his satin-tipped hard-on and the taut curve of his ass. Then of course, that moment when he bucked and groaned and went crazy because of me just being there, just *being*.

I didn't come that night – that first would happen

thanks to the persistence and skill of the justly famed cunnilinguist Doug – but I was happy enough to take my ecstasy once-removed. Mike, bless him, didn't ask too many questions.

I was the one who decided to confess as we lay together afterwards, just like on T.V., with my head resting against his shoulder and his arm around me like we were a real couple. 'That was the first time I've ever been with a guy, you know.'

'Lydia, you can stop kidding around now,' he said, but gently. Didn't he notice that, of course, all my 'jokes' turned out to be true?

'Why do you think I'm kidding?'

He frowned. 'First of all, you give great head. There's no way that was your first time. You're a pro. Well, I didn't mean it that way, you know, just that you knew exactly what to do.' He laughed, embarrassed, and stroked my hair. 'And then, well, you were really into it.'

'I do like to joke around. It's an old habit.' It wasn't exactly a lie.

'You know what? You're fun. It's easy to be with you.' He pulled me on top of him. 'Wanna do it again?'

I nodded. Back in my high school, a million years and a billion miles away from where I was now, naked and straddling Mike's hard belly, it was a bad thing for a girl to be 'easy'. Now I knew the secret.

It was good.

Part Three

A DANCING GIRL OF
EASY VIRTUE
(Kyoto, 1984)

CHAPTER ONE

At first, my love affair with Japan seemed just as easy, a feast laid out for my pleasure, not the keg beer and pizza of Caroline's parties, but icy *chuhai* cocktails and *okonomiyaki*, a savory pancake of cabbage, egg and smoky fish sauce 'fried as you like it'.

I was twenty-two, fresh out of college and hungry for new flavors of every kind. Each day of my first year in Kyoto brought some wonderful new discovery – a mysterious fox shrine tucked away in a winding alley, the beguiling sweetness of bean jam wrapped in soft rice pastry, a lovely boy bowing nervously as I ushered him into my apartment. Even in the recollection there is magic. The whole year seems to fold in on itself like a dancer's fan, leaving one perfect day in high summer.

I awoke that August morning with a naked young man snuggled against me, his hard-on pressing into the cleft of my ass. This was not an uncommon event, but I was relieved that this time I remembered his name. My bed partners were almost always college students, the only Japanese males with the leisure for impromptu flings with the English conversation teacher, so exchanging business cards was not usually part of our courtship ritual. A quick cup of Nescafé Gold Blend would usually shake loose a surname from my sleep-fogged brain, although I still found it strange to call a man 'Mr Aoki' or 'Mr Nakamura' after we'd spent the night doing it in every which position on my futon.

But Hiroyuki had been staying over regularly for a few weeks now, so I even knew his first name, too.

'Hiro-*kun*. Wake up,' I said in Japanese. 'Tuesday's my busy day, you know.'

He mumbled something and slipped his arms around me, warm hands cupping my breasts.

'I have to get the train at nine.'

He made one of those little Japanese sounds I loved, a musical grunt, rising into an unspoken question.

I rolled over to face him and gave his cock a gentle squeeze. 'Yes, we have time, but it'll have to be fast.'

Hiroyuki smiled sleepily and eased my cotton kimono over my shoulders to take my nipple between his soft lips. I stroked his thick black hair and sighed. I was still amazed at how beautiful these boys were with their velvet eyes and luminous skin that would put moon-bathing Marybeth to shame. In Japan I'd become *menkui* – a 'face eater' – which meant I liked them handsome, and plenty of the handsome ones liked me, too.

Hiroyuki was special though. We seemed to have a relationship blessed by the Japanese gods, which I attributed to my habit of stopping by Kyoto's many shrines to offer the *kamisama* a ten-yen coin in return for a cute lover. I was sitting in a coffee shop on Kawaramachi Street, devouring a book I'd just found in the English corner at Maruzen book store – *Look Ma, No Hands: A Woman's 8-Step Program to Satisfying Sex Every Time* – when Hiroyuki sat down at the next table and ordered an American coffee. We started talking. He wanted English lessons. I wanted a warm body on which to practise the exercises the book recommended. Both of us got what we wanted and more.

I couldn't have ordered a better partner than this nineteen-year-old virgin who was eager, trainable and completely without preconceptions in bed. He wasn't like my boyfriend at Princeton at all. He didn't expect me to pretend to come in the missionary position, he had no ego issues with me playing with my own clit or doing it for me while we fucked, and he was genuinely curious to know what felt good for me. What felt best of all was his pure and heart-felt gratitude. After our first time, Hiroyuki wrapped his arms around me and whispered, 'Ree-dee-ah, I want to do everything for you.'

For the last few weeks, he'd been doing exactly that.

Now his fingers crept down between my legs and began the patient, teasing come-hither strokes over my clit that drove me wild — when we had time to linger. Unfortunately, we didn't. The clock said seven-forty and I knew I had to be in the shower by eight. I wasn't about to settle for a morning-boner charity quickie like I used to do in college. Thanks to the thoughtfulness of the book buyer at Maruzen, I was converted to the *No Hands* philosophy of female pleasure every time.

Girl-on-top was the quickest route to satisfaction, the book promised, so I swung a knee over Hiroyuki and settled down for the ride. My robe was still tied at the waist, but with my breasts and shoulders bare and the lower portion gaping open wantonly, I felt like one of those floating world prints of a courtesan impaled on her samurai lover's over-sized member. Hiroyuki was definitely enjoying the view.

I started by squeezing his long, thin cock with my secret muscles, bringing on a nice glow. *No Hands* women were active, they squeezed and wriggled and moved at their own pace. But I was still working on step seven which was decreasing my dependence on direct clitoral stimulation. Could I jump on to step eight – 'Any Time, Any Position: Now You're Really Fucking Like a Man' – and graduate early?

In this land of so many unexpected successes, why not give it a try? I leaned forward so my pussy lips were pressed just so against Hiroyuki's firm belly and began rocking my hips to get the right friction on my clit. Hiroyuki was helping nicely by twisting one stiffened nipple between his fingers and flicking the other with the tip of his tongue. But the clock was ticking and the book suggested fantasy as a way to turn up the heat to a quick boil. It was time to call in the reserves.

I closed my eyes and silently called to him. My old friend, the mysterious stranger who liked to pop in now and then to watch me masturbate, had followed me across the Pacific. Over the years he'd lost his domineering tone though. Sometimes I told him what to do, like this morning, when I pulled him, rubbing his eyes and dragging his feet, from the closet where I kept my futon the few times I managed to put it away properly.

He yawned. 'It is rather early, Lydia, my dear. I haven't even had my tea. Why don't you just let that fine young man ejaculate in your pussy and get on with your duties?'

'Because I don't want to be horny all day. Come on, help me out. You always know just the right thing to say, you dirty old man.'

'Please, you flatter me. Although I am aware that you respond well to a challenge. Today's is quite simple. The clock says you have five minutes to come on that boy's cock. Or as the Japanese prefer to say, 'go', which is an interesting shift in perspective, don't you agree? At any rate, if you don't come, or go, as the case may be, you'll have to suffer through a long, hot day as a very unsatisfied young lady. Oh my, now you only have four minutes.'

I let out a moan of desperation and worked my ass harder. Hiroyuki began to bite my nipple gently. A jolt of pleasure bordering on pain shot straight to my groin.

'The second hand's racing forward on that clock, Lydia. The Japanese say a busy life is best, but your schedule is so packed today you won't even have time to slip into a restroom later to finish yourself off. But you'll still be turned on. Every man you pass on the street will see your nipples poking through your blouse, that I-want-it-bad wiggle in your hips. But you'll just have to endure – *gaman*, *gaman*, as the Japanese do – until you can get home and ease that throbbing hunger in your cunt.'

'Faster, yes, faster.'

I must have said those particular words aloud, because Hiroyuki dutifully quickened his thrusts.

'One minute left now, my dear. What will it be? A nice orgasm to start your morning or a whole day of aching frustration?'

His taunting words made my skin tingle and burn. I'd show him what I could do, the bastard. I jerked my hips, slamming down hard until I felt my orgasm rising, cutting through my belly, bursting up into my throat as a low, quivering groan.

Hiroyuki followed soon after, his moans an echo of my own pleasure.

'Congratulations, Lydia dear, I'm off to breakfast now,' the voice said with his usual insouciance, but I could tell deep down he was proud of me.

My other lover, the one in bed with me who had a body, pulled me down and hugged me to him, a gesture that needed no translation.

I lay in his arms for a moment, reveling in the applause as they handed me my diploma. 'Lydia Evans earns her first completely *No Hands* orgasm with Hiroyuki Kawakami, Kyoto, Japan.'

It was indeed a great way to start the day. And from there it would only get better.

CHAPTER TWO

Gaijin — foreigners — in Japan are often told they look like movie stars. I got Brooke Shields, Audrey Hepburn, Jodie Foster and the occasional Marilyn Monroe, a list varied enough to suggest I might not have a future as a celebrity impersonator after all. However, it is true that the life of an ordinary *gaijin* is a lot like that of a celebrity. Strangers approach you, bowing nervously, to ask you if you will pose for a photograph with them. You are invited to cherry-blossom viewing picnics and *karaoké* parties and even weddings of people you barely know. On occasion, your fame also makes you the target of heckling gangs of country boys who troop through Kyoto on their school trips. And guys who get off masturbating on train platforms tend to pull their trench coats open in front of your window for that extra frisson of international exposure. Everywhere you go you are noticed, watched, even devoured, by curious stares.

It may have been that 'hey-everyone-I-had-my-first-no-hands-orgasm-this-morning' glow, but I seemed to get more star-struck attention than usual as I criss-crossed the city from my English conversation classes at a construction equipment company to my Japanese dance teacher's villa in the eastern hills. I was riding the bus to my last appointment, a private lesson with a wealthy dentist's wife on the west side, when some mutual staring turned into my second conquest of the day.

Everyone's eyes turned to Jason as he climbed onto the bus at the Philosopher's Walk stop and asked the driver in loud, but serviceable, Japanese if this bus went to Kyoto Station. I myself couldn't help staring at his chiseled nose, green eyes, and curly brown hair, light enough to be called 'blonde' in this part of the world. I had grown so accustomed to the eye-soothing planes of Japanese faces, the restful repetition of black hair and golden skin, that I sometimes jumped when I glimpsed a foreign devil's face in a train window at night, realizing in the next moment that I was gazing at a reflection of myself.

In Jason's case, it was more his body that got to me: solid, sturdy, the perfect build for practising my newfound riding skills. He was definitely a big man. I had to wonder as my eyes grazed his jeans, the brawny thighs and ass – *how big*? Of course, I wasn't really planning to find out the answer. I didn't come to Japan simply to fuck white guys. I'd done plenty of that back home.

Just then Jason's eyes lit on me – a fellow countrywoman who'd obviously had great sex that morning. He made his way past the giggling junior high school girls in their summer sailor blouses and asked if the empty seat next to me was taken.

I could hardly lie.

I was immediately dizzy from the smell of him, the slightly sour, cumin scent of American male. Japanese men smelled of shampoo or tobacco, always something other than themselves.

Jason introduced himself and I nodded back, Japanese-style.

'You look like you live here,' he said cordially, taking in my loose jumper and blouse, which was the current fashion for Japanese girls in their twenties, and my fraying book bag with the words 'Men's Volcano, Men's Good Up Down Good Feeling' silk-screened across the front.

'Your powers of observation are exceptional,' I said with a smile. As much as I claimed to spurn fellow foreigners, it was fun to dust off advanced English vocabulary. 'And you look like you're taking a character-building trip through Asia before you go home and start law school at Harvard.'

Jason blushed and corrected me – he was starting law school at Stanford in the fall. He then asked if I could recommend any off-the-beaten-track tourist sites, which made me like him again. I was always intrigued by a man who wanted to probe deeper. So I told him about my favorite temple, a place called Rengeji, where the curator would serve him thick green tea on a veranda by a stream that ran straight through the temple grounds. It was hidden away in a quiet neighborhood in the northeastern part of the city, and chances were he'd be the only visitor there.

'Now, if I were back home,' he said with the assurance of a future litigator, 'I'd try to get your phone number and wait a civilized day or two to call, but circumstances being what they are, I'll just blunder ahead and ask if you're free tonight. I'd swap a dinner for a few more tips on how to make the most of my visit.'

67

'I'd like to, but I've been invited for *kaiseki* by one of my English conversation students. Did you see those fancy restaurants in Gion with the terraces overlooking the river? I never thought I'd get the chance to eat there, but tonight I'm parting the curtains and going inside.'

'How did you finagle an invitation like that?' he asked, clearly envious.

'My irresistible charm, I guess. It just started happening as soon as I got here. Dinners, cruises on the Katsura River to see the cherry blossoms, tea ceremony parties, I'm always booked with something, because it's just so hard to say no. That's one advantage to being small and female. I'm *kawaii*. You're such a big, scary brute, they're afraid you'll rape their daughters. No one seems to mind I'm raping their sons left and right.'

Jason stared at me with amused disbelief, though at what I was claiming to do or at the fact I was talking about it so freely, I wasn't sure. 'You could meet me after dinner, couldn't you? Unless you have plans to rape another Japanese guy?'

I also liked a man who didn't give up. Maybe I could make an exception to my I-don't-fuck-foreigners policy after all? 'No rapes on the schedule tonight, so I guess I could meet you. Maybe about ten in front of Takashimaya department store? But I can't show you any fancy hostess clubs, I only know the cheap watering holes in that part of town.'

'I have a feeling I'll learn a lot from whatever you show me, Lydia,' Jason said.

'I sincerely hope so.'

My bus stop was announced by the chirping, recorded female voice. I stood and Jason shifted his knees into the aisle so I could squeeze past.

'Ten at Takashimaya then?' he said.

I nodded and gave him a little wave as I stepped down into the narrow artisan alleys of the western district of the city. A nine-course Japanese feast, followed by a creamy hunk of American dessert. It was shaping up to be a very indulgent evening indeed.

How could the *kamisama* grant me any greater bounty than two cute guys in one day? But they did.

CHAPTER THREE

A mere two hours later, I was falling head over heels in love with a Japanese dentist.

I know my passion is a hard sell to someone who's never been to Japan. I might be allowed my dalliances with pretty college boys, but in the world's eyes, middle-aged Japanese men are by definition the opposite of sexy. They dress in bad suits, their feet are small and they're constantly clicking away with expensive cameras as they follow the tour guides with flags around Westminster Abbey or swarm the red light districts of Manila and Bangkok.

Only when you come to the country do you learn the secret – they keep the best ones hidden safely away in Japan as living national treasures.

I was sitting with my friend and benefactor, Dr Matsumoto, on the spacious terrace of an exclusive restaurant overlooking the Kamo River. Dr Matsumoto and his wife treated me as a daughter, a spoiled one, and all I had to do in return was help the cheerful dentist keep up his very good English over dinner at some of Kyoto's best restaurants. On this particular night, Mrs Matsumoto was meeting high school friends for their annual reunion at a French restaurant a few blocks away, leaving me to enjoy the local cuisine with her husband and his colleague visiting from Himeji.

The sun had set and the sky stretched over us like a bolt of blue-gray silk. Yet the heat of day lingered — it was hard to tell where the summer air ended and my body began. Seated on a cushion with my legs tucked under me in the formal position, I felt a sense of deep contentment, in spite of the inevitable tingling in my feet. I was closer to the secret heart of Japan than ever before, soon to experience culinary delights many Japanese themselves would never know. Not to mention I had a gorgeous *bishônen* of a boyfriend and my sex life was fabulous. What more could I want from life?

A few moments later, the kimonoed waitress ushered an older man to our table.

Dr Matsumoto rose and bowed and the two men exchanged the greeting of longtime friends. *'Hisashiburi ya ne.'*

'This is Lydia-*san*. My wife's English teacher,' Dr Matsumoto said in English. 'My old schoolmate from dental college, Dr Shinohara.'

'Very pleased to meet you,' Dr Shinohara replied. His amber eyes took me in, but the fading light masked any glint of pleasure or disappointment. Sitting down across from us, he let out a volley of Japanese, from which I picked out some good-natured complaints about a meeting going on too long.

I took the opportunity to study Dr Shinohara's hands. His fingers were thin, graceful, the color of old parchment. His face, too, was lean, with high cheekbones and a slightly weathered look around the eyes.

I realized I did want something more from life now.

I wanted this man to find me interesting. And not as a daughter.

The problem was that I didn't know how to proceed. I was pretty good at picking up American guys with flirtatious banter and Japanese boys with a simple invitation for an English lesson back at my apartment, but how could I charm an older man, a *sensei* no less, oozing otherworldly wisdom and refinement?

Three waiters appeared, setting large black lacquer trays before each of us at precisely the same moment. Each tray held five small dishes with bite-sized seasonal delicacies, a diamond of pressed sushi, a square of fish paste, fresh vegetables sculpted into the shape of flowers. A miniature glass goblet occupied the right corner of each tray and at the left glowed a small lantern, painted with a scene of a mountain rising above a tiny city. On the side of the mountain burned a red-ink '*dai*', the Chinese character for 'big'.

Dr Matsumoto explained the theme was chosen especially to suggest Kyoto's upcoming Daimonji festival, when bonfires were lit on five mountains surrounding the city to welcome dead souls back to earth. I'd heard of the festival, one of the highlights of summer in Kyoto. Dr Shinohara added that it was an impressive sight, but the downtown could get very crowded.

'Some of the hotels have special Daimonji dinners where you can watch from the roof terrace,' Dr Matsumoto said. 'Perhaps you would like to join my wife and me this year, Lydia-*san*?'

I nodded, blushing at my benefactor's never-ending bounty. I was grateful, but the invitation would remind

Dr Shinohara I was his friend's surrogate daughter, something I was hoping to make him forget.

I took a sip from the goblet. It was some kind of chilled cordial, faintly sweet with a tang of fruit, cherry or plum perhaps. Like all sweet liquor, it went to my head immediately. After a few sips, I decided that Dr Shinohara was actually one of the most handsome men I'd seen in quite some time, in spite of his austere, monkish air. Or maybe because of it.

It was then I hit on my strategy. I'd impress him with my aesthetic sensibility and my knowledge of old Japan – something that didn't play well with the younger crowd. All that reading I'd done to score an 'A' in my Introduction to Japanese Culture class in college might actually help me score in a different way.

'I saw the preparations for the bonfire on Daimonji Mountain from my dance teacher's house today. The clearing is so wide, you can't even see the shape of the calligraphy,' I said in my best Japanese. I gestured to the flickering miniature version. 'I think Japanese artists are skilled at making grand things into something very small and beautiful.'

Dr Shinohara raised his eyebrows in mild surprise. 'I agree, but I wonder which you will prefer? The real bonfire or the one the artist painted?' He answered in Japanese – real Japanese, not the condescending foreigner's version – a compliment rare enough that my attraction turned to adoration right then and there.

'Yes, which is better, the real or the imaginary? I think each will have its own kind of beauty. I wonder

73

if I could choose both?' I gave him the mischievous smile of a child angling for two servings of dessert.

Dr Shinohara smiled back. This time I did see a flicker of interest in his eyes. My ploy worked. I'd become more than just Dr Matsumoto's adopted *gaijin* girl. One point for the culturally sensitive foreigner.

The waiters brought the next course: a small boat of sculpted ice upon which was arranged slices of sea bream and snow-white conger eel, fluffy as curls of fresh butter.

'What brings you to Japan, Lydia-*san*?' Dr Shinohara asked. I'd heard that question so often it usually made me yawn, but the way he asked it made me feel warm and tingly, *seen*.

The honest answer was that I came because I craved adventure, a life of surprises, a non-stop feast of exotic sensual pleasure, anything but a job in investment banking like most of my college friends. But at this point it was probably better to give the doctor my safe, standard line.

'I came to Kyoto to learn traditional Japanese dance.'

'I see. Do you enjoy wearing kimono?'

Should I tell him the truth now – that it feels unspeakably sexy to wear one and I loved being bound by the column of cloth hobbling my legs and the *obi*'s snug embrace at my breasts? It probably meant I was a sexual masochist, but I didn't really want to admit it. More exciting was the promise of transformation through that bondage, the chance to shed my foreign awkwardness for the Japanese dancer's gliding grace.

'Yes, I do like wearing kimono, but it's a challenge, too. I have to move my body in a different way, so maybe I can understand, just a little, what it's like to be Japanese. I think it is the Japanese way, in dance and in life, to transform . . .' I pulled my English-Japanese dictionary from my book bag and quickly leafed through it for the right word.

'Constriction,' Dr Matsumoto read out for me.

'To transform constriction into art.'

'Lydia-*san* understands Japan very well,' Dr Shinohara said to his friend, who nodded, as proud as any real papa.

'No, I just study too much. You see, I'm a Kyoto-style foreigner. We come here to study a traditional art so we can try to understand the heart of Japan. Foreigners who live in Tokyo only care about money. Isn't it the same for Japanese? In Tokyo, money is the most important thing. In Kyoto, it's heart.'

Both men laughed loudly. I definitely racked up a few points with that one.

'I do believe you must have been Japanese in a past life,' Dr Shinohara said with his Buddha's smile.

I bowed my head, my cheeks burning with pleasure. I'd not only been seen, but embraced. How could he have known that was my secret fantasy – the fantasy of all true Kyoto *gaijin* – that our wandering spirits had reconnected us with our lost home?

CHAPTER FOUR

In Japan, almost every social occasion continues with a *nijikai*, a smaller, more intimate second party. In this case, it would not have been unusual for Dr Matsumoto to send me home in a taxi so he could take his old friend to a hostess bar for some male bonding. We were all having such a good time, however, he invited me along as well.

I was supposed to meet Jason in less than half an hour, but I'd never been to a hostess bar and was dying to see what it was really like. Should I go deeper into the mysterious neon canyons of Gion with Dr Shinohara? Or trade predictable banter followed by equally predictable sex with an American tourist I'd never see again?

When ten o'clock rolled around, I was sitting in a hostess bar tucked away in the basement of a narrow high rise a few blocks from the restaurant, agreeably tipsy on whisky and compliments. Sorry, Jason, but in my place, you'd probably do the same.

The room was tiny, no bigger than my eight-mat apartment, and papered and upholstered all in red, like a womb. The *mama-san* seated us at a small table and brought out more snacks and a bottle of imported whisky wearing Dr Matsumoto's name on a necklace resting on its shoulders. I wondered what picture we must make to her: a twenty-two-year-old Western girl with a middle-aged dentist on either side. Back home my dentist was just a silver-haired guy with stale breath and hair on the backs of his hands, coming at me with metal probes and a water pick. If he had a private life, I wouldn't imagine it was taking young Japanese women to dinner at fine restaurants followed by drinks in the company of ladies who made a living from their charms.

As if on cue, a slim hostess, no more than a few years older than me, slipped onto the free seat at the end of our table. I wouldn't call her beautiful, but her sleepy eyes and full lips gave her an undeniably seductive air. She greeted Dr Matsumoto with a pout and a flutter of her eyelashes – it had been such a long time since he'd visited and she'd missed him. He smiled and made introductions. Her name was Yukiko and she shook my hand in the American fashion. Her hand was faintly moist and as soft as padded satin.

With a perceptiveness I would appreciate later when I was in her shoes, Yukiko immediately sensed that Dr Matsumoto was the customer in need of her attention. She invited him to sing a duet at the elaborate karaoke machine set up near the bar, leaving me and Dr Shinohara to entertain ourselves.

'I would like to see you dance some time, Lydia-*san*,' he said, bending close. I got the impression he meant what he said.

'No, I'd be too embarrassed. I'm not very good. The lessons are so different from ballet. My teacher never explains anything. She just walks through the steps and I have to try my best to follow her. We do the same thing over and over again until I get it right, which often takes a long time.' Rather like sex, I thought, remembering my morning's lesson with Hiroyuki.

'That's the Japanese way, to learn with the body.'

'Yes, but it's hard for me. Americans don't really trust the body.'

'That is unfortunate. The body has many wise things to tell us.' His eyes twinkled and I thought for a moment he might touch my hand, but instead he merely reached for his whisky glass and took a polite sip.

Dr Matsumoto had finished his first song. To my relief, my 'father' had a pleasant bass voice, and I could applaud with genuine enthusiasm.

'Please sing a song in English,' I called out merrily, although my motives weren't exactly pure.

Nor were my thoughts. In spite of my protests, I realized I did want to dance for Dr Shinohara, in an elegantly appointed *tatami* room, just like the geisha of Gion. I could picture the scene perfectly: the doctor seated on a cushion, me standing before him in the opening pose of the tea maiden dance I was practising for my concert in the fall. Except, at his request, I wasn't wearing a kimono. I was wearing nothing at all. *I want to see you as you really are*, he whispered, and I wanted to show him. Everything. And so I dipped and turned and twirled my fan, my skin flushed pink under the warmth of his steady gaze. Could he hear the click of moist flesh between my legs as I moved? Could he smell my arousal? Of course he could, he knew it all, and when the dance was through, he would come and lift me from my low bow, and – here my desire took a strange dental twist – in my gratitude I would take his finger in my mouth and suck it, like a cock, to taste the complex, ancient flavor of his skin.

I was sure his body would have many wise things to tell me. With the way things were going, I might even have the chance to hear them this very night.

My reverie was shattered by the return of Dr Matsumoto after his creditable cover of Frank Sinatra's 'It Was a Very Good Year'.

After a few more pleasantries, Dr Shinohara checked his watch and said, 'I'm afraid I must be going soon. I have an early train tomorrow.'

Suddenly things were not going in the direction I hoped at all. 'Yes, I'm afraid I have to go too,' I blurted out. 'I promised to meet a friend at a disco near here at eleven.'

And so, in another twist of the usual custom, the two guests bowed our host off in his taxi home. Then Dr Shinohara chivalrously offered to walk me to the meeting with my friend.

It was now or never. 'Dr Shinohara,' I said, my voice sounding bolder than I felt, 'I don't really have to meet anyone.'

He gave me a puzzled, but genial look.

I preferred subtlety, but time was running out and the direct approach had always gotten me what I wanted in the past. Besides, indecent proposals are always easier in a foreign language. I took a deep breath. 'What I was hoping to do is go back to your hotel with you.'

A change came over his face, although I wasn't

quite sure how to read it. Then he smiled. 'There is a certain place I'd like to take you, Lydia.' He hooked his arm in mine, and led me down a narrow street, the neon lights twining up the buildings as thick as jungle vines.

CHAPTER FIVE

Unfortunately, the place Dr Shinohara had in mind was not a love hotel or restaurant with private booths for postprandial amour, it was a coffee shop with a traditional Japanese theme, the tables looking out over a small rock garden atrium. It was a rather classy way to say 'no, thank you.'

He ordered us coffee, then leaned toward me and said in English, 'Lydia, you are a very lovely and intelligent young woman, and I am flattered by your offer. Perhaps this will be hard to understand, even for a person with a wise heart like you. You see, in my youth I was a hungry man. Many times I gorged myself on delicious food until my stomach ached. Only now do I understand that there is just as much pleasure in standing outside the restaurant and breathing in the delicious fragrance.'

I frowned. His fancy words didn't really ease the sting. Now that he'd rejected me, I didn't need to play games any more.

'But I'm still young, Dr Shinohara. I want to eat the delicious food. I want to know Japan, but sometimes I think Japan doesn't want me.'

'That is not true. All Japanese feel *akogare* – desire, I think you say – for the West. If you stay here for very long, I think you will have the chance to taste many new flavors, many loves. Perhaps you will even grow tired of it?'

I shook my head. I'd never stop wanting more.

Dr Shinohara studied me, a sage's smile playing over his lips. 'May I share with you a poem, Lydia, a favorite of mine? The poet's name is Teika, a famous poet who lived more than seven hundred years ago.'

I wanted his cock, but I got a fucking poem instead. I almost laughed, but thought better of it. 'Sure, I like poetry.'

He smiled and gave me a slight bow before he began. The brief stream of words was mostly incomprehensible to me – I caught 'spring' and 'dreams' and 'sky' – although there was a definite rhythm to the flow.

'Do you understand?'

'No, I'm sorry.'

'The poet speaks of a "floating bridge of dreams". In *The Tale of Genji* these words mean human life and desire, and sadness for how quickly both pass. But Teika makes the dream into a cloud floating in the mountains like a bridge from earth to sky, something so beautiful you will remember seeing it for your whole life. But then the cloud breaks, cut by the mountain peak, a thing that is very sharp and real.'

In spite of myself, I could almost see the pearly white bank of clouds and the jagged mountain peak floating before my eyes.

'It is sad that the beautiful bridge of cloud and dreams is broken, but the *yokogumo*, the new shape of the clouds, now slender and more delicate, is also very beautiful.'

Wisps of cloud, a dinner of fragrance alone, could I ever be satisfied with such meager nourishment? Perhaps some day I would be so wise, but now my whole body ached with disappointment. Just when I thought I'd gotten deeper into the heart of this country, there was another sliding paper door, another chamber of secrets before me.

'Perhaps we should be going now, Lydia? I'll see you to a taxi.'

I nodded.

But Dr Shinohara had another surprise for me. He took my hand, bowing as if he were about to kiss it in the old-fashioned European manner.

His skin was warm and slightly rough and I held my breath, expecting the touch of his lips. At least I'd have that to remember.

Instead Dr. Shinohara inhaled, slowly, his eyes closed, like the Heian aristocrats who trained their noses to identify hundreds of subtle scents and tested their skill in elegant contests.

Oddly, I felt lighter, almost buoyant. And when he let go of my hand, it seemed to float between us for a moment, as if it were separate from me, weightless as air.

CHAPTER SIX

As I glided along Shijo Street toward home, the whine of *enka*, Japan's country music, drifting from the taxi driver's radio, I spotted a familiar figure on the sidewalk ahead. Oversized, slightly aimless. Obviously foreign. Jason.

He looked different than he did on the bus. His shoulders sagged and he wore a tired frown. And why not be gloomy? Japan was no longer the Western bachelor's dream it once was. The pan-pan girls were long gone and even the slutty expatriates threw you over to sample the local charms.

As I drew closer, I noticed Jason had changed his T-shirt into something nicer, for me, no doubt. I felt a pang of guilt, which was immediately followed by a twinge of longing. Of course, I'd only be using him to get over my thwarted dreams of communion with old Japan. If I were a compassionate and enlightened being, I would content myself with the lingering fragrance of our flirtation on the bus. I told the driver to pull over and rolled down the window.

Jason's head jerked sharply in my direction at the sound of his name.

I smiled.

He didn't seem exactly thrilled to see me, but I sensed there was room to make amends.

'I'm sorry I couldn't make it at ten. My Japanese

friends took me out to this really fancy place and I couldn't get away. Duty's always getting in the way of pleasure in this country.' Little did I realize then how right I was.

I thought I saw the beginning of a smile, but then it was gone. I held out my hand. 'Come on, get in. I'll make it up to you. I promise it'll be better than going back to the youth hostel.'

The smile finally broke through, and I knew I had him then.

'One more passenger,' I told the driver.

The automatic door of the taxi swung open and he climbed inside.

We fell into each others' arms, my mouth opening to his tongue, his hand laying claim to a breast, my palm pressed to his crotch to feel the last twitches of his growing hard-on. He *was* big.

I pulled away from the kiss, just for a moment, to whisper in his ear, 'Jason, I feel awful about what happened, so the first thing I'm going to do when we get back to my place is get down on my knees and suck your cock. I can't wait to feel it hard and hot between my lips. You can come in my mouth if you want to, or save your jizz for another warm, wet place, because then I'm going to get on top and ride you. I've wanted to do that since I first saw you this afternoon.'

He sighed in assent, like a Japanese boy. I was glad it didn't take much for all to be forgiven.

If my dream was broken, it was almost as sweet to be part of his. Wasn't that the fantasy of every lonely heterosexual male traveler, to have a young woman pull over in her car, hold out her hand, and whisk him away to her apartment for some wild and sweaty no-strings-attached sex on a warm summer's night?

Jason seemed to understand, because he said, as I pressed myself against him, 'Are you sure I'm not just imagining you?'

I shook my head, but I wondered, too, if he was right after all. Tomorrow, after the instant coffee and the goodbyes, I would be just a memory for him, which is not so very different from a dream.

Part Four

MARRIAGE MEETING
(Osaka, 1985)

CHAPTER ONE

As I settled into my second autumn in Kyoto, the magic moments weren't coming quite as fast. Suddenly Japan wasn't Disneyland anymore. Or maybe it was, but I was an employee now, sweating inside the Mickey suit.

I was twenty-four. Soon I'd be 'Christmas Cake' by Japanese reckoning, on sale at a bargain rate to prospective husbands after my twenty-fifth had passed. Hiroyuki and I had parted after he told me his friend insisted he was still a virgin because he hadn't slept with a Japanese woman yet.

'Do you believe that, too?' I asked.

He denied it, but he didn't say the things I really wanted to hear either – 'you do mean something, you do matter.'

I was tired of flings with college boys anyway. My eyes were following the men in their late twenties hurrying along with the serious, battle-weary expressions that were as much a part of the salaryman's uniform as a suit and tie. I liked to imagine I could bring magic to their lives, make them smile. In return they could offer me what no college boy could – the chance to go deeper into the heart of this country and make it my home.

Meeting eligible men of the right age was difficult enough for Japanese women and I figured if that's what I really wanted, I had to do it the Japanese way. That's why I agreed to an *omiai*, an arranged marriage meeting, an 'honorable once-over'.

I'd observed many *omiai* in the atrium coffee shops of the city's high-class hotels. It was quite a production with the matchmaker couple, two sets of parents dressed as if they were already going to a wedding, and the pampered youngsters who studied the carpet, cheeks tinted the color of maple leaves in October. As I sipped my milk tea and pretended to chat with my Japanese girlfriends, I would furtively watch the bobbing and blushing with a mixture of pity and envy. I knew the rules had relaxed since the samurai days. The prospective bride or groom could always refuse a second meeting, but some, no doubt, would glide on into a lavish wedding at the same hotel, then children, and even possibly a lifetime of happiness together with someone else making all the hard decisions for them.

My *omiai* was not quite so formal. My matchmaker was another American named Nancy Anderson, one of the in-house English teachers at the Shiga office of the electronics company where I taught supplementary conversation classes on Wednesday afternoons. She was engaged to a Japanese guy she'd met in the States and when she learned I was interested in dating a 'real' Japanese man, she told me she knew just the candidate. This Yoshikawa-*san*, for that was his name, worked at the head office in Osaka and was nice, attractive, smart, and funny. His English was decent. He was twenty-seven and had traveled to France and

Italy, but not following a tour guide with a flag like a duckling. Mr Yoshikawa had done it all on his own.

I wiped the drool from my lips, discreetly, but I couldn't resist some American cynicism. 'He sounds perfect. On the other hand, if he's so gorgeous, brilliant and worldly, why doesn't he have a girl-friend already?'

Nancy laughed. 'I don't know. Maybe it's the same reason you're still looking?'

She had me there. So I told her I would appreciate it if she could arrange a casual get-together. What did I have to lose? If I didn't like him it would make a good story, a blundering *gaijin* girl attempts *omiai*. If I did like him, it might make an even better one.

CHAPTER TWO

A little over two weeks later, I was standing at the north exit of Kyoto station where I was to meet Nancy, her fiancé, Shinji, and that paragon of Japanese manhood, Mr Yoshikawa. The golden autumn light was edging into gray and the air had a tinge of wood smoke and loamy decay – my favorite season in Kyoto – but on this particular afternoon I was too nervous to enjoy it. Now that the meeting was so near, it was hard to delude myself that this was anything as romantic as a genuine rich-kid *omiai*. All I'd really done was consent to a good old-fashioned blind date.

Nancy promised she'd come early so she could make the official introduction, but she was already ten minutes late. As I scanned the crowd of Saturday commuters and college student couples, I realized that all she had really told me about Mr Yoshikawa was that he was a little bigger and stockier than most Japanese and that he was 'attractive'. What else would there be to say? If she'd told me to look for a young man about 5' 9'' with dark hair and glasses, that would describe pretty much every male waiting in the plaza.

I, on the other hand, was the only foreign young woman in sight who was clearly waiting for someone. Mr Yoshikawa would know who I was, although he might find it awkward to approach me without Nancy here. Was he watching – and judging – *me*? I certainly hoped he'd get the wrong impression from my demure wool skirt and pink sweater, the virginal make-up and downcast eyes, all promising the sort of modesty and chastity you'd want in a wife.

Another wave of bodies poured through the ticket gate, all the men about 5' 9", with dark hair and glasses.

'Sorry we're late!'

I turned to see Nancy rushing towards me. 'He's not here yet. He's coming right from work, so maybe he was held up.'

I let out a quiet sigh of relief. I hadn't yet been 'looked over'.

'This is Shinji.' Nancy gestured to the man standing behind her. He had a bit of Charles Bronson about him, or maybe it was just his black leather biker's jacket. He stepped up and shook my hand firmly with the ironic smile I associated with Japanese men who've been tainted by long stays abroad.

'Thanks, both of you, for doing this. You probably have better ways to spend your Saturday afternoon,' I said.

'Nervous?' Nancy asked.

'What do you think?'

'Ah, there he is.'

I followed Nancy's gaze to the crowd of passengers rushing through the ticket gate from the latest arriving train. A man who was indeed about 5' 9" tall with black hair and wire-rimmed glasses was walking toward us. He was wearing a stylish grayish-green suit and had that vaguely worried look I loved, but then he saw Nancy and smiled. His eyes shifted to me.

That's when I looked into my husband's eyes for the first time. I wouldn't quite call it love at first sight, but I saw my own surprised pleasure reflected there. Nancy was right. He was attractive, not art-poster pretty like most of my college-boy crushes, but definitely easy on the eye. His face was very Japanese – a harmonious blend of broad cheeks, almond eyes, and a sensual mouth with a hint of five o'clock shadow at the upper lip. At least I wouldn't have to struggle back from the disappointment of visual dis-taste. With the first hurdle cleared, we could move on to discovering things about each other we couldn't see.

'Nancy, hello.' He turned to me with a quick bow and a smile. 'I'm Yuji Yoshikawa. Very nice to meet you,' he said in English.

'Lydia Evans.' I bowed and smiled back. 'Nice to meet you, too.'

'We'd better get going if we want to do a little sightseeing before dinner.' Nancy started off toward the plaza. The rest of us followed.

Yuji and I walked together. 'I'm sorry I was late,' he said softly. 'My work . . .'

'Oh, that's OK. I was a little late, too.' It was a lie, of course, but it seemed like the right thing to say.

Shinji said something in gruff Japanese and Yuji answered amiably. Far from being jealous of their easy camaraderie, I was glad for the help. As always, I found myself suddenly tongue-tied when I actually wanted the guy to like me.

Nancy dropped back and lifted her eyebrows at me in an unspoken question. I nodded, ever so slightly, letting the corners of my mouth curve into the beginning of a smile. Who said Westerners can't communicate without words?

CHAPTER THREE

When I arrived at Tsukaguchi station, halfway between Osaka and Kobe, Yuji was waiting for me by the ticket machines, just out of the steady December rain. I recognized him at once in his sea-green sweater and black jeans, his weekend uniform. Even though I had spilled steaming hot *saké* all over his hand when I tried to pour for him at the restaurant on our first date, he asked me on a second date, and a third and within a month we weren't going out anymore. We were staying in. Not that anyone would guess it from the way he acted in public.

'Hi,' I said in English, instinctively dipping my head.

'Hello.' His smile was guarded, even downright formal. It was hard to believe this was the same man whose voice had slipped like warm syrup through the telephone the night before – *When I get you back here, I'm going to lift you up on my kitchen table and spread your legs and lick you down there until you come over and over again.*

Part of me was still confused, and even hurt, by his coolness, but I had to admit it excited me too. Before long, this daunting stranger would have his cock inside me, his face twisted in orgasmic release. Or would he?

We headed to his car, parked across the street. The

windshield wipers slapped the rain away as we drove through the shopping district, decked out in sprays of white and pink ping-pong balls, the sign of winter in mercantile plastic land.

I noted his quiet sigh of relief as he turned into the garage under his apartment building. The ritual here was always the same, too. We eased the car doors closed and muffled our steps as we crept up the concrete stairs to his apartment. In the weeks I'd been coming here, he had yet to introduce me to a neighbor.

Yuji turned the key in the lock of his gray metal door. My pulse quickened. I knew what lay on the other side.

His apartment was nicer than mine, but sparsely furnished, with a Western-style dinette set in the kitchen-dining area and in the *tatami* room beyond, some pillows, an impressive black-and-chrome stereo system, and a tall, tightly packed bookshelf. We'd done it in every room: stretched out on the *tatami*, pressed tightly together in his bachelor's single bed in the dark, narrow bedroom, sliding our soapy bodies against each other on the tiled floor of his roomy Japanese-style bathroom. But not on the kitchen table. Yet.

In fact, the table looked different today. Usually it was neat enough, with a soy sauce dispenser or a box of cake he'd bought for us from a local European-style bakery. Today it was completely cleared away except for some kind of nappy tablecloth. Then I realized it was a towel.

He took off his glasses and set them on the kitchen counter. It seemed he would keep last night's promise.

He took three steps toward me, took me in his arms, waltzed me back against the table. We were already kissing, his tongue soft and warm, opening my lips. His fingers brushed the top button of my blouse. He unfastened the first button, then the next and the next. I could hear his breath, in and out, above the hiss of the heater, and the rain too, spattering against the windows.

'I was looking forward to this,' he whispered in Japanese, pulling my blouse and bra straps over my shoulders.

'Me too.' The words slipped off my tongue so easily. We always spoke Japanese when we glided into lovemaking. It was the only time I didn't care if I got it wrong.

He cupped my breasts. I glanced down to watch him flick my nipples with his thumbs, almost guiltily, although he'd told me he loved to watch me watching. My eyes looked so dreamy, he said, as if I'd traveled someplace far away, above the clouds.

Today he wasn't watching. Eyes closed in a dream of his own, he bent to kiss my breasts, one, then the other, then he began to suckle. I arched back with a sigh and my thighs fell open. Hiking up my skirt, he leaned into me and I wiggled forward so I could feel his erection through the jeans. This is what he'd been hiding beneath that stiff mask of formality, another kind of stiffness I liked very much indeed.

'I want you,' he whispered.

In translation it might be hokey, but in his husky Japanese the words alone brought another gush of wetness between my legs. I was glad for the towel beneath my ass.

'I'm going to take you right here, but first we have to do what you're supposed to do on a table. Eat, right?'

I sighed assent, lifting my buttocks as he inched my panties down, crouching to pull them over my feet. Then he eased me back so I was lying on the table, arranging my body carefully so my pussy just cleared the edge. My chest was heaving and already flushed with arousal. Gentle as he was, it thrilled me to submit to Yuji, to be taken just as he'd planned it in the weekday fantasies he'd used to bewitch me every evening on the phone.

Yuji knelt and parted my legs. The first lick was always long and slow, like a bolt of hot silk unrolling, undulating against my nether lips.

I moaned, then covered my own mouth with my hand. The walls were thin and, in truth, I'd discovered it excited me to muffle the music of my pleasure. My orgasms seemed all the more intense when I turned the moans inward, my own personal transformation of constriction into art.

Yuji found my clit and began teasing it, circling, flicking, batting it from side to side lightly with the tip of his tongue.

'*Kimochi ii*,' I whispered. It feels good.

'*Oishii*,' he replied. You taste delicious.

He stood and brushed my lips lightly with his fingertips so I could have a taste too. He dipped his fingers in my mouth then, and I closed my lips around them and sucked desperately. I wanted him inside me bad, anyway, every way, but he told me on the phone he wanted me to come on his mouth this first time so he could lap up the gush of sweet juices after my orgasm. Then, if I was a good girl and didn't make too much noise to disturb the neighbors, he'd fuck me. And make me come again.

I knew it was unlikely I could manage that twice, on a kitchen table, but it sounded good as I sat huddled in the hallway of my student apartment building, clutching the pink receiver of the public phone in one hand and pressing my fingers between my legs under the Japanese-English dictionary lying open on my lap.

The first part was going as planned anyway. Yuji was back to feasting on me, except he'd stop now and then, just to make me squirm.

'Are you going to come for me, Lydia?'

'Yes, oh, yes.' I spoke in English now. I always did when I was close and Yuji said he liked that, the real me. He pushed my legs up, opening me further, stretching me so tight my ass seemed to lift off the table and my thighs shook like an earthquake. Relentless now, his tongue lashed at my clit. I rolled my head back and forth, biting back the scream rising inside me, swelling, throbbing, pounding. My body thrashed on the table and the roaring in my head was so loud I thought my skull might burst, but in the end only a few soft squeals leaked from my lips as I came all over his face. Then he was kissing me, his lips and chin slippery.

'Fuck me,' I whispered. 'You said you'd fuck me. I was good, wasn't I? I hardly made any sound at all.'

'Yes, you were good,' he said, smiling down at me.

He moved back to the edge of the table, unbuckled his belt and struggled out of his jeans. Then he pushed my knees up again and entered me, slowly sliding in full length.

I gasped. I'd never fucked on a table before and his cock seemed to fill me deeper than ever before. It seemed to have a similar effect on Yuji. His eyes were closed, his head thrown back, and he was moving inside me, as if against his will. I always liked it better when he was as crazy as I was, bucking and grimacing. My real goal was to make him come so hard he couldn't help groaning out loud, so the neighbors would know everything he did with the foreign girl in his apartment on Sunday afternoons. I liked it when he was bad because of me.

But Yuji seemed intent on carrying out the story just as planned, to bring me to a second climax. Now his hand was on my nipple, tweaking and twisting. His other hand snaked between us to tease my clit.

Could I come again, so soon, in this strange new position? I'd never managed it before. It was certainly worth a try.

I thought of those neighbors again, crowded all around us. In spite of his precautions they probably already knew what we were doing. They probably planned their Sundays around it. Next door, the housewife in a frilly apron had her ear to the wall, straining for the sounds as her hand crept beneath her skirt and slipped under the elastic of her panties to find her swollen, pink clit. Downstairs sat a bright-eyed grandma and grandpa, peeling tangerines around their *kotatsu*. With each thump and groan from above, they shared a lewd and knowing glance. *Do you think that horny foreigner spread out on the table like a whore will have another orgasm, Grandma? I hope so, Grandad. I do like to hear her scream.* They wanted me to come. All of Japan wanted me to come. They were waiting. To the other side of us, a student with one of those victory headbands was begging me: *Please, honorable Miss Foreigner, have an orgasm so I can get back to my studies and enter a national university.* How could I let them down? They were crowding into the room now, watching, reaching over to pinch my nipples with their chopsticks, spreading my legs to make my pussy grip Yuji even tighter. *Come for us, come for us, the whole nation wants you to come. Do it for Japan!*

Yuji was waiting for me, too. I could tell by the slow, careful thrusts. The head of his dick was knocking against some sweet spot up there, something I'd never felt before, a pleasure just short of pain. *Do it for us, Lydia-san. Do it for Japan.*

I moaned — too loud — but the thrill of transgression pushed me higher. We were bad, so bad. Even Yuji was losing it. He was grunting now as he worked his hips faster, his cock taking charge, selfish in its urge for release. But I was selfish, too. Now I was crying out with each thrust. The housewife had collapsed to the floor, thighs spread wide as she strummed desperately. The grandma was fondling her husband's cock, a thick purple stalk sprouting from his kimono. The student was already coming, tissues poised to catch the white banners of jism arcing from the swollen head of his uncut tool.

Yuji was coming, too. I could tell by the 'oof' and the sudden shift to long, rhythmic strokes as he emptied himself in to me. *Go along with the group, Lydia-san. That's what we do in Japan.*

Arching back, I hammered my ass up to meet his last strokes, and yes, it was coming, I was coming, we all were coming together in one sighing, trembling mass of flesh and fire.

Yuji stayed with me until the shudders subsided, eyes closed, his hands resting on my hips as if he were engaged in some blissful meditation. I sat up and rested my arms on his shoulders. 'That was good. It's always good,' I whispered.

He smiled and opened his eyes. They melted into me, like chocolate, something sweet and comforting that a child liked to eat.

He'd never said he loved me. He didn't have to. In this place, we didn't need words.

CHAPTER FOUR

I knew we'd make love again before he took me back to the train station, back to the real life that started for us both bright and early on Monday morning. But in between stretched the lazy hours of lounging on the *tatami* together, drinking good coffee and listening to Oscar Peterson or Paul Desmond. He'd be in jeans and a T-shirt, but I always wore his bathrobe, knotted loosely so he could slip his hand casually inside to stroke my breasts or trace messages in Japanese on the sensitive skin of my inner thigh, as the spirit moved him.

I learned a lot of new Japanese characters 'through my body' on these languid afternoons. There was the frilly, girl-shaped *bijin*, for 'beautiful woman'; the gliding strokes of *yawarakai*, or 'soft'; the reassuring repetition of cross-strokes in *shiawase* which meant 'happiness and good fortune'. Sooner or later, he would say a word I didn't know at all, and I'd have to reach over to the bookshelf for the dictionary. This was as much a part of our ritual as the coffee, the cake and the caresses. Sometimes we even consulted it when he was inside me.

On this day, as I pulled his well-thumbed Japanese-English dictionary from the shelf, a magazine that had been shoved into the narrow space above it slithered out onto the floor.

'What's this?' A silly question since the title was plain enough: *Penthouse*.

Yuji blushed, but he recovered quickly. With lifted eyebrows and a sly smile he asked, 'Isn't it an American magazine?'

'Is this where you get your ideas, by the way?'

'Not really. I get my ideas from you.'

A good answer, but I decided to tease him a bit more. I leafed through the pages, hoping to get another blush from him. There were lots of bare breasts and buttocks and an even mixture of Japanese and foreign women, but all of their genitals were shaved and carefully, if scantily, covered with panties or well-placed hands in accordance with Japanese law. Back then, men's magazines imported from abroad were subject to the attentions of little old ladies with razor blades who scratched out any hint of pubic hair.

'Don't you get bored with Japanese magazines? You can't see anything really naughty.'

Yuji shook his head. 'I like imagination.'

'I do, too,' I admitted.

'I know.' He reached for the belt of my robe and pulled the knot loose. 'But sometimes real is best.'

I allowed him to stroke me, but I kept turning the pages. 'Which one do you like? Do you like blondes or redheads or . . .' I stopped at a slender Asian woman with breasts spilling over a corset, the nipples as big as demitasse saucers. 'Gee, do you think those are real?'

He laughed. 'No. Not real. This magazine is all a dream.'

'A fantasy,' I corrected.

'Yes. A fantasy.' He lifted the magazine from my hands and set it back on the bookshelf.

'Have you ever done those other things they say salarymen do in Japan? You know, those places where the women soap you up with their naked bodies or you can pretend to be a pervert on a subway car and touch a woman dressed like a schoolgirl?'

Yuji tilted his head and frowned. Had I offended him or just spoken too fast? It was a big leap from a run-of-the-mill porn magazine to connoisseur of the 'water trade', but I was curious.

'You mean soaplands? No, I don't go there. But I think you know my friend Mr Nakamoto, from the Shiga office?'

'Masaru?' I did know Nakamoto-*san*, although he wasn't in my conversation class because he spoke English fluently after doing postgraduate work in the States. But we usually ran into each other after class in the employee lounge and ended up chatting. He was attractive in a hawkish way, with a high-bridged nose and piercing eyes. I'd considered trying to seduce him – they way he smiled when he saw me made me think it wouldn't be too difficult – but he had an edge that put me on guard. Japanese men who had lived abroad really were different, not so easy in their skins.

'Masaru, yes. He goes to soaplands and places like that.'

'Really?' I was certainly glad I'd met Yuji before anything happened on that front, but part of me was thrilled to know a man who did such perverse things.

'Yes. His family is rich. They have many kimono

shops. A merchant family, do you know? I think it's tradition for the men to be with ladies you pay.' He wrinkled his nose. 'But I don't like old-fashioned Japanese ways so much.'

A sentiment I shared, in this particular case. We lay together for a moment, gliding on the smooth current of Paul Desmond's alto sax.

'But I like this,' Yuji said. 'Talking with you.'

'Me too.'

'In English I feel I can speak my mind freely.'

'Me too.'

He laughed.

We kissed again, slowly, eyes open. Both of us knew the hour of parting was drawing nearer. We would make love again, Yuji would cook a simple dinner for us – fried soba noodles or chicken curry on rice – then drop me off at the station in the cold rain with a nod. He would never even touch my hand after we stepped outside. I'd have the scent of him on my skin, the taste of him on my lips, but that would fade after a few days. All I'd have then was his voice through the phone, murmuring dirty things in a strange tongue that would send me straight to my futon for relief on my dancing fingers, but the hunger would never really be satisfied until I was back here again on our little island of warmth and golden light.

Thinking of that hunger and loneliness, I pulled up his T-shirt and shimmied down to kiss his chest. I liked the mild salty flavor of his smooth, almost hairless, skin. I circled his right nipple with my tongue. He watched me with narrowed eyes and an indulgent smile, the way most men do when you tease their nipples, but I knew his secret. His other nipple, the left one, was sensitive to the slightest touch, like mine.

I pushed him onto his back and straddled him, then bent and took the magic nipple between my lips. He stiffened and shook. I knew exactly what he was feeling – the electric shot jolting straight from nipple to crotch. Maybe this was the closest I'd ever come to fucking like a man, to making love to myself. I always wondered how a man could get so turned on just by touching me, even when I was doing nothing for him in return, but with Yuji's trembling torso caught between my thighs, each flick of my tongue sending a new shudder through his body, I suddenly understood.

The doorbell rang. We both jumped guiltily. I slid off and wrapped myself quickly in the robe. 'You expecting anybody?'

'No.' He sat up and yanked his T-shirt back into place. The lump in his jeans would be hard to miss, but he headed for the front door anyway, pulling the sliding door of frosted glass closed behind him. To shield me or hide me, I wasn't sure.

A male voice, servile and polite, floated into the room with a gust of damp, chilly air. *'Yoshikawa-sama de irrashaimasu ka?'*

'Hai,' Yuji answered in a deep voice, so different from his soft, hesitant English.

The man said something I didn't understand. Yuji replied. He always talked so quickly with other Japanese, and part of me worried he was grateful to be speaking his own language after the strain of being with me.

When I heard the door close, I got up and peeped into the kitchen. The entrance was piled with packages, all wrapped in brown delivery paper from various department stores.

'Wow, it's too early for Christmas, isn't it?'

I expected a laugh, but his expression was blank. It was the first time I'd seen his outside face in here. 'These are year-end gifts. I'm sure you know the custom.'

I had indeed seen the displays in the department stores: boxed sets of soap, soy sauce, dried seaweed or oil, with the price prominently displayed on a card beside each one. I myself dutifully slipped an extra month's tuition into my dance teacher's December payment envelope.

'Who are they from?'

'Business associates,' Yuji replied.

'What do you think is inside?'

'Whisky probably.' His voice sounded weary.

He stepped over the packages, walked back into the living room and rubbed his hands in front of the heater. Apparently he wasn't going to open the goodies in front of me.

'Why did they send it here instead of your office?'

'You ask too many questions, Lydia.' In spite of his words, he smiled and lay down on the *tatami* again, patting the space beside him.

I stretched out next to him. 'Are they bribes?'

He gave me a sidelong glance. 'Not exactly. But maybe you didn't see these things.'

I was about to make another joke, but instead I nodded. It was a rare chance to show him he could trust me with matters out there in that other world.

'Now, where were we?' Yuji said, lifting me on top of him and unknotting the belt of my robe again.

'I think I was about to give you my year-end gift to thank you for your kindness in the year past and beg for your good favor in the year ahead. It's not whisky, though. I hope you're not disappointed.'

He wasn't.

CHAPTER FIVE

I had high hopes for the New Year with Yuji. Of course I wanted those X-rated phone calls and sex-drenched Sundays to continue, but I was hungry for wilder transgressions. I wanted to wander among the cherry blossoms hand in hand, have him actually smile at me in public and maybe even go so far as to introduce me to his parents. Like a fairy tale, my dreams had the odd habit of coming true. Just not the way I planned.

The phone call came in late March. It wasn't Yuji this time, it was my mother's boss, and for some time now her lover as well, Frank Woodson. *Lydia, your mother is ill. Very ill. How soon can you get home?*

Then came the travel to Hospital Country, a strange, fluorescent-lit land lurking inside the America I remembered. There the men were hulking and hairy, with pointy noses and name tags pinned to their white coats, always rushing away to some new crisis. The women were enormous, too, their bosoms like brows, their hands pink and busy poking needles into bruised flesh.

Only my mother was shrunken and quiet, wearing a bandage on her shaved head where they took out the tumor. The doctor gave her a year to live. Mercifully, he was wrong. She died of a heart attack two days after the surgery. At least I had the chance to say goodbye.

The dream dragged on into the nightmare of packing her clothes to give to charity and filling trash bags with make-up and potions, all weapons in her arsenal that were useless now.

After the funeral, Frank Woodson stopped by to discuss the estate. I smiled and thanked him for his help, marveling in a numb sort of way that this man was the closest thing I had to a father here. I often felt the outsider in Japan, but here I was even more alone. I couldn't wait to go back home. To Kyoto.

CHAPTER SIX

Yuji picked me up at the airport on a chilly Saturday evening in cherry blossom time. He scooped up my luggage with a half-smile and headed off to the parking lot. I followed, a few steps behind, grateful for the protective mask of public manners, although I sensed beneath it a new softness.

Once we were in the car, however, he reached over and hugged me, hard.

'I'm all alone in the world,' I whispered into his shoulder. The words would be far too self-pitying to say to another English speaker, but I knew Yuji wouldn't mind.

His arms tightened around me. 'No,' he said. 'You have me.'

With our future settled in those brief words, we drove straight back to his apartment. He carried my luggage up the stairs with no effort at discretion. For dinner he made me my favorite Japanese comfort food, omelet wrapped around white rice, and some milky black tea. Afterwards he suggested we take a bath and offered to wash my back, which meant, I knew, no sex required. But sex was exactly what I required.

After we rinsed off, I turned and rested my elbows on the edge of the sunken tub, lifting my ass in offering. His lips lifted into a smile. He understood.

Part of me wanted him to jam himself into my hole with no preliminaries at all. Part of me wanted that shock, so I could scream out my pain. But of course, that wasn't Yuji's way. He stroked my body gently, running his hands over my hips, my flanks. That's how I felt, like an animal on all fours, wallowing in sensation and instinct. The words 'in heat' spiraled through my head, but after that I tried not to think anything. Thinking was what I wanted to escape.

I wanted Yuji inside me so badly I was shaking. '*Irete ne*. Put it in now,' I whimpered.

He probed my slit with the head of his cock.

'Now!'

He pushed inside, knocking against the neck of my womb. I gasped. It had been a month since we made love and my walls were as tender as a virgin's. Yuji held himself still, except for his finger still dancing over my clit, and left the movement to me. I rocked forward slowly, then back, swinging higher, ever higher into the starry night sky, far above death's muddy grasp. All I wanted now were the fireworks, his gush of white cream against the darkness, the fountain of new life.

I rocked faster, like a girl on a swing, up and back, but the sounds I was making were not a girl's. They were an animal's bellows and brays, cresting then falling as my pussy milked his cock. Yuji came too, right behind me, shooting into me with helpless cries of release.

He fell over me, wrapping me in his arms. I was in a hammock now, buoyed up, far above the darkness and pain. He whispered something very softly in English. *My wife*.

But the words in my head at that moment were different, a sign perhaps of the very different paths we would travel, though I didn't see it that way then. I was only glad and grateful to say it, silently, sure he would know and understand. *I'm alive.*

Part Five

PICTURE BRIDE
(Osaka, 1987)

CHAPTER ONE

I began my wedding day as a foreigner in a shiny pink smock, seated on a chair, gazing at my own pale face in the full-length mirror of the hotel dressing room. Could this blue-eyed *gaijin* possibly be transformed into a Japanese bride?

'Did Lydia-*san* use the restroom? It'll be at least five hours until she has the chance again.' The kimono-dresser, a perfectly round, cheerful lady named Mrs Komatsu spoke these words not to me, but to my future mother-in-law.

Yuji's mother made a sound of assent. In fact I'd had to work to squeeze out a few drops. When I'd had my breakfast at dawn, Mrs Yoshikawa had permitted no coffee or tea, only a few sips of water and a piece of dry toast. I knew it would be a day of following instructions, of obedience. My skin tingled. For a Japanese bride suffering brought beauty, surrender, bliss.

'Well then shall we begin?' Mrs Komatsu brushed my hair back from my face and slipped on a hairnet. The snug white band over my forehead made my head look shorn, ugly rather than bridal. Mrs Komatsu studied my face with a frown, as if she shared this evaluation, too. Suddenly a razor flashed in her hand, one of those pink, single blade types they sold in the ladies' section of drug stores. I jumped in my chair.

'It's OK,' Mrs Komatsu said genially. 'The skin has to be smooth or it looks bad.'

'Ah, yes. I'm sorry. I forget to tell you about that, Lydia,' Mrs Yoshikawa said, placing a reassuring hand on my arm.

'Some of the Japanese girls who come in here have hair like a wild boar. Yours is very fine.' As she spoke, Mrs Komatsu attacked my upper lip, my jaw and chin, and the skin between the eyebrows. Then she was behind me, pushing my head forward and running the razor along my hairline at the nape of my neck with practised speed. She wiped my face with a warm towel, then, as if by magic, produced a bowl in one hand, a paintbrush in the other.

'Close your eyes,' she said.

I obeyed, tilting my chin up trustingly.

At first the make-up was cool and wet, very wet as Mrs Komatsu slathered it on my face, chest, arms, neck and shoulders. But when it dried it was lighter than I expected, not oily like the pancake make-up I used to wear in school plays, but powdery and soft, like a caress. When I opened my eyes, a foreign ghost – her face dead white – stared back.

Next came the red powder around the eyes, the black eyeliner, the penciled-on eyebrows, the bright red mouth painted on with a tiny brush, smaller than my own mouth. My lips had a prim, static look, and I remembered Mrs Yoshikawa's warning that I wasn't to smile more than a fraction of an inch while I wore the bridal kimono. Toothy, radiant smiles were for the Western wedding dress.

The finishing touch, of course, was the wig, rolls of

black hair to frame the face and a lavishly decorated topknot. I closed my eyes as Mrs Komatsu adjusted the cumbersome, almost architectural, creation on my head. Fortunately, my round face was as suitable to Japanese costume as my small bust. Now the mirror showed me the magic I'd been waiting for: a geisha with sky-blue eyes, head bowed at the proper angle.

I understood now, too, that the elegantly drooping head was not just modesty. The wig was damned heavy. But I loved it, the weight of tradition, the intoxicating hit of camellia oil and secret storehouses of old.

Mrs Komatsu asked me to stand now to be fitted in my first kimono, three layers of pure white robe with a padded train for the ceremony in the hotel's shrine room, the symbol of my rebirth as a Yoshi-kawa. I would later put on a lavish orange version of the outer robe for the first part of the reception, followed by a white Western wedding dress, the usual custom in Japan, but doubly symbolic for an international couple. Yuji would change only once, from formal kimono into a tuxedo, but I didn't feel even a twinge of envy. In Japan, the hero of the day is the one who endures the most.

The door slid open and Yuji's sister, Akemi, stepped inside, followed by my cousin Caroline, who had flown in for the wedding.

'Ah, how pretty!' Akemi had a soft voice, like velvet. She wore a loose, pale pink dress that hid the gentle curve of her belly. Married a year ago, she was expecting a baby in the New Year. She had been as kind and welcoming to me as Yuji's mother, although his father still terrified me, a cool man with a perpetually disapproving frown.

'Very pretty,' Caroline echoed. She also wore a modest silk dress, and I noticed she stood with her toes pointed slightly inward, Japanese maiden style. To my surprise, Caroline had made a serious study of the customs and language before her trip and was putting all her knowledge to good use. The word from Yuji's family and friends was that Caroline was 'gentle' and 'well-mannered', and that she had a 'Japanese spirit just like Lydia'. I didn't have the heart to tell them what she was really like. Or perhaps she had changed as much in the past few years as I had?

Mrs Komatsu lifted a white hood over my wig, then stood back and nodded her approval.

'That's the *tsunokakushi*,' Akemi explained to Caroline. 'To hide the bride's horns of jealousy.'

Caroline frowned. 'Lydia doesn't need that, right? Yuji's so nice and gentle. Now, my fiancé is terrible. He has many girlfriends. I may have to borrow that white hood for my wedding.'

Caroline had told me about her fiancé – a super-rich lawyer she'd met through work who, she said, was old enough to be her father if he'd knocked up his girlfriend in high school. Although it would be his third marriage, he was so madly in love he wasn't even making Caroline sign a prenup. Privately, I didn't give them more than a year, but she'd asked me to be a bridesmaid and Yuji and I were using the wedding as an excuse for a California honeymoon.

Akemi giggled. 'He sounds like a Japanese man.'

'I wish he were,' Caroline said. 'Some of the men I've met are very attractive. Yuji's friend, Masaru, for example. If I weren't spoken for . . .'

'Caroline-*san* likes playboys, I think,' Akemi said. Now her soft eyes took on a knowing, mischievous air. 'Masaru-*kun* is — how do you say it?'

'Trouble,' I chimed in.

'Then I'll be sure to keep the proper distance.' Caroline gave me a sidelong glance and I knew, at that moment, she hadn't changed at all.

'It is very interesting that two cousins are getting married at the same time,' Mrs Yoshikawa said with a smile. It was Yuji's smile, transplanted onto a middle-aged, female face.

'Maybe not so surprising,' Caroline said. 'We've been together for many important events in our lives. I've helped Lydia get ready for parties before, but I have to say she has never looked so beautiful.'

'Yes, very beautiful,' Akemi and Mrs Yoshikawa agreed.

I have at times looked in the mirror and thought myself pretty, especially after sex. There's nothing like an orgasm to make the eyes sparkle and the complexion glow. But this was different. The figure in this mirror was completely transformed — slim, elegant, draped and bound in blinding white — a beauty transcending myself alone.

The best compliment of all came from Mrs Komatsu, the expert. 'She doesn't even look like a foreigner. If she closed her eyes I'd swear she was Japanese.'

CHAPTER TWO

I'm not sure what happened to our wedding album, but I've kept snapshots of highlights of the day in my memory. Yuji looking so handsome in formal kimono and *hakama* trousers, smiling encouragement as we waited to go into the shrine room for the ceremony. The beaming sea of faces as the guests rose to applaud us like celebrities each time we entered the banquet room in a new costume. The endless speeches by the older men in their sober suits, especially Yuji's father intoning the word *kurô* over and over – in your life together you will face many troubles, trials, hardship and pain. Sliding the ceremonial sword into the groove of the towering plastic cake, my hand resting on Yuji's, and noticing a small dust ball lodged under the foot of one of the decorative cherubs. Bowing and chanting *arigatô gozaimasu*, 'thank you for coming, thank you for your good wishes', like an automated doll in the window of a souvenir shop.

But by far the most vivid memory was walking in on Caroline and Masaru having sex on the floor in our wedding-package honeymoon suite at the hotel. Strictly speaking, they weren't fucking at the moment I joined them. The shirtless Masaru was bent over her, his face buried between her slim, tanned legs, which were tied together at the knees and ankles with strips of some sort of silky black cloth. Her wrists were tied together too, and secured to the leg of the writing desk.

They must have been too caught up in their game to notice me come in, but my involuntary cry of surprise brought Masaru up on his knees, reaching for his suit jacket on the bed to shield Caroline's not-quite-nakedness. When he realized who it was, his eyes narrowed and his wet lips melted into a predatory smile.

'Lydia,' Caroline cried out, half shocked, half pleading.

I just stood there, my jaw hanging open.

Masaru was the one who got the clever line. 'Hey, Lydia. Want to join us?'

I turned and fled, slamming the door behind me.

Now I stood in the hotel corridor, my chest pounding as if I'd been the one caught doing something wrong. It was wrong – wasn't it? – to use our honeymoon suite for their kinky game. Or was I just being a prude? After all, Caroline had loaned me her room on many occasions for similar purposes.

The real problem was I'd had an encounter with Masaru myself a few days before. We were having a little party for out-of-town friends and he'd gone with me to get more beer while Yuji stayed back at the apartment to play host. *I can't believe Yoshikawa got the pretty English teacher. If I'd known you liked Japanese guys, I'd have tried harder myself.* Masaru was clearly drunk, which is always a good excuse in Japan, but I still felt slightly soiled by the comment, and even more troubled by that sexual twinge between my legs, as if my body were filled with a similar regret. I loved Yuji, we were getting married, and I would never even think about another man as long as I lived. Right?

Somehow I managed to get myself back to the sky lounge and our group of friends crammed around the tiny tables, the requisite shopping bags filled with souvenir gifts from us and a small box of an edible version of our wedding cake tucked at their feet.

'Did you get the aspirin?' Yuji whispered as I slipped onto the seat beside him.

'Yes. I could probably use something to drink now.' It was the first lie I told as his wife.

'You need some food. I know you haven't eaten anything all day.'

'Sure, what do they have?'

'The usual over-priced hotel snacks. Seafood salad. Sandwiches. How about your very favorite corn pizza?'

Yuji's teasing always cheered me up. I'd used the example of corn pizza to teach him the phrases 'abomination' and 'perversion of nature'. The only thing more unnatural was the Japanese practice of sprinkling corn flakes on ice-cream sundaes.

'Corn pizza actually does sound good to me now. It's as if a mysterious change has come over me in the last few hours.'

Yuji smiled. 'Can someone get the waiter? Lydia-*san* wants the corn pizza.'

His request was met by loud hoots of laughter from our friends.

'You can't call her Lydia-*san* anymore,' one of my

English conversation students scolded. 'She's your family now.'

'You know wives get no respect. She's just a plain old Lydia from now on,' Nancy added with a laugh.

Yuji blushed. It was the first of his many mistakes as a husband.

Just then Masaru sauntered in, impeccable in his formal black suit. He walked right up to me and leaned over, hand resting on the back of my chair, to whisper in my ear.

'Caroline's in the ladies' lounge outside the restaurant. She needs to talk to you.'

I fought the urge to spit in his face. 'I have to get some aspirin for Caroline, too. Jet lag,' I murmured to Yuji and slipped away, careful to avoid brushing against Masaru, as if his treachery were contagious.

CHAPTER THREE

'Oh, god, Lydia, I'm *so* sorry. Masaru said you and Yuji would be on duty with the other guests for hours.'

The moment I stepped into the lounge, Caroline threw her arms around me in an American hug. She smelled funny, shampoo mixed with sex, and was noticeably flushed and bright-eyed in her contrition. Apparently she wasn't so sorry that she and Masaru didn't bring things to a satisfying conclusion first.

'How did you get the key?' I pulled away.

'He got an extra one from the front desk somehow. I didn't ask.'

Caroline nudged me over to the sofa in the anteroom, an absurdly ornate piece of furniture that was probably supposed to evoke the luxury of Versailles.

'I know I'm not thinking straight, Cuz. I'm pretty mixed up, actually. I didn't tell you this, but when we started going out, Taylor had three regular girlfriends — mistresses, really, it was almost that old-fashioned. He swore on his stock portfolio he'd give them all up if I married him. But I'm positive he's taking advantage of my trip to Japan to say "goodbye", if you know what I mean. So who says I can't have a little fling, too?'

'Taylor sounds like an asshole, Caroline. Are you sure you aren't making a terrible mistake?' I was too angry to be diplomatic about it.

'Excuse me, but haven't you just signed up for a lifetime of bowing and serving tea and calling your husband "master"?'

'I don't think you could possibly understand what Yuji and I have.'

Caroline looked at me beseechingly. How many men had she beguiled with those blue eyes? 'I didn't really mean that. You two are very sweet together. And I'm certainly learning the appeal of Japanese men. Oh, go ahead and glare at me, but Masaru's very sweet, too. Taylor is definitely not sweet.'

'Then why do you want to marry him?' My voice was softer. In fact, I was genuinely curious.

She shrugged. 'I don't know that I do. But he wants to get married. And I want to be like him. I want to be that sure of something. If that makes sense.' She touched my arm. Her hand was warm. 'Don't you have any doubts, Lydia?'

I shook my head. 'Maybe I should, but being with Yuji is great. It's like living in a dream.'

Caroline's lips lifted into an indulgent smile, but I noticed her eyes were wet. 'I'm glad for you, Lydia. I really am. And I am sorry too. Will you accept my apology?'

The forbidden scene flashed into my head once more: Caroline trussed up, the inky darkness of the bonds against her white flesh, the bulge in Masaru's black pants. In my imagination I picked him up, like a puppet, and laid him on top of her, his hips thrusting rhythmically. Could he actually fuck her when she was all tied up like that?

In the next moment, I was back in the ladies'

lounge, my thoughts bridal and pure again. Couldn't I afford to be generous on my own wedding day? Caroline had always had everything she wanted and more. For a change, I was the rich one. I smiled and held my arms open for another American hug, although the custom was beginning to seem rather strange to me already.

It was another moment in my life when I thought I had so little in common with my cousin, with her troubled marriage doomed from the start. Once again, in all too short a time, I would discover I was wrong.

CHAPTER FOUR

But even Yuji and I were allowed our Japanese honeymoon. The morning after the wedding we boarded the bullet train for Tokyo, then took the local train north into the mountains to a hot spring famous for its grand cedar bath. I'd seen it in a guidebook full of luscious photographs of feasts and naked girls lounging languidly in steaming water. Yuji agreed it was romantic. The north was a foreign country for him too, he told me with a smile.

The inn was a low building of weathered wood straddling a silver mountain stream. The kimonoed maid guided us to our room in the oldest section of the inn and set out cotton *yukata* robes with thicker woolen *haori* coats, the uniform of the hot spring resort. I'd been to hot springs a few times before with Dr Matsumoto and some of my housewife English students, so I was familiar with the ritual: shed your ordinary clothes and your ordinary life to indulge in endless baths and a table groaning with gourmet food. With a new husband, there would be even more delicious pleasures.

Dinner at the inn was exactly as promised, a feast of carp, mountain vegetables and the season's *maitaké* mushrooms. For me, the most delicious part was presiding over the rice caddy, sculpting each serving into a perfect mound with the wooden rice paddle, the way Yuji's mother did. When the maid called me

Mrs Yoshikawa and praised my Japanese, the tingling thrill in my body was not too far short of an orgasm. And unlike our *omiai*, when I poured *saké* into Yuji's cup, I didn't spill a drop.

After she cleared away the dishes, the maid laid out our futons, lined up suggestively side by side, and left us in the semi-darkness of a single rice paper lamp. I lay down on one of the mattresses, clutching my stomach. 'I ate too much. I think I'm too full to take another bath.'

Yuji joined me on my bed, wrapping his arms around me. 'You'll feel better in a little while. We have time. We have lots of time.'

I snuggled against him, sliding my hands under the collar of his robe to his warm, firm chest. 'The Japanese do know how to have fun sometimes. This place is positively decadent,' I said in English.

'Decadent?'

Both his English and my Japanese had improved to the point we seldom used the dictionary anymore, but this word seemed worth explaining.

'It means being totally selfish and indulgent like the Roman emperors, doing nothing but eating fine food, taking long baths . . .'

'Making love?' His hand wandered down between my legs. The ever-convenient robe parted willingly beneath his fingers, as did my legs.

'Especially that.'

He began touching my thighs with soft, feathery strokes. I was getting ready for further indulgence sooner than I thought.

'Yuji, I have a question . . .'

'You always have questions,' he said, but he was smiling.

'Well, I've watched a lot of dramas on TV, you know, silly shows, but the people in the stories always have such a hard life. They can't be happy for longer than five minutes, it's all *gaman* and endurance. And your father, at the wedding, he kept talking about marriage and suffering.'

His eyes softened. 'I hoped you weren't listening to that. But he only knows his own life. He doesn't know what we have. I'm different. When I'm with you, I'm always happy.'

How did he always know the right thing to say? 'I hope so. But your father doesn't like me, does he?'

'He's afraid of you. He only likes things he knows. He must have power – how do you say it – control?'

'That's how I say it.' I laughed. 'How about you?'

'I told you, I'm different.'

' "Different" means wrong in Japanese.'

He laughed. 'Maybe. But not in English.'

His hand moved higher, to my belly, circling, teasing. Then he whispered, 'Lydia, do you want to try to make a baby tonight?'

I caught my breath. Again Yuji seemed to have read my mind. As a good Japanese wife, it was almost a duty to prove my fertility as soon as possible. I thought of Caroline's latest delivery of contraceptive sponges from the States, a handful stashed in my luggage. It would be a pleasure to let them languish to expiration, to fuck Yuji naked, inside and out, to carry our beautiful child inside me.

'How many babies do you think were made in hot spring inns?' I asked.

'Many. Very many.' He tugged on the belt of my robe, and it fell open, as if by magic.

I closed my eyes.

We weren't alone. I knew my old friend was watching us from the shadows, his eyes glittering. I hadn't meant to pack him for this trip, but he must have slipped in my luggage with the contraceptive sponges.

'A very romantic setting for a honeymoon if I do say so myself, Lydia, dear.'

'What are you doing here, old man? Can't you see I'm busy?' I sighed and arched up. Yuji's hands and lips were doing some very nice things to my breasts.

'Very busy indeed. I see from the shameless way you're rocking your hips that you're quite aroused already. But I never know when you might need me. It is my duty to be ready when you call.'

'But I haven't called you in a long time.'

'Oh I know you've been spreading your legs for that Japanese salaryman every chance you get, but I might still be useful on occasion.'

'Not tonight. Not ever again, actually. I don't need you anymore,' I told him, and at that moment I believed it.

'Ah, Lydia. I expected you might say that to me tonight.' He bowed, Japanese-style, but his smile had a touch of Western irony. 'Congratulations on your marriage and I wish you the very best.'

And then he was gone.

'Goodbye,' I whispered, although I wasn't really all that sorry to see him go. I actually thought it would be that easy to banish fantasies from my life forever. A fantasy if there ever was one.

Part Six

A MONK'S WIFE IN A CITY OF WORLDLY TEMPTATIONS
(Osaka, 1989)

CHAPTER ONE

When I woke up, Yuji was gone. The sheet of his futon was pulled back and the pillow had a head-sized indentation, reasonably convincing signs he'd been here for some part of the night.

I rolled out of bed and stumbled down to the WC. A plate with some crusts of toast and a half-empty coffee cup sat on the table, more evidence I had a husband, especially if you added in our wedding photo on the bookshelf in the hall. But to tell the truth, I was no longer really sure.

Still groggy, I sank back onto my mattress, kicking aside the cotton sheet that served as my summer blanket. Lemon sunlight filtered through the gap in the curtains and the breeze from the open window was sweltering. It was going to be another August day under the broiler.

The sound of children's voices drifted in from the hallway. Our condo was close to Umeda Station, a new two bedroom-dining-kitchen unit still smelling of construction glue. Our neighbors were mainly office worker husbands on the fast-track and stylish young wives who had at least one baby, if not the full complement of two.

Our plan, at the beginning, was to be just like them. We'd tried to get pregnant seriously and enthusiast-ically for a year, then with resigned determination for six months and then apparently, he'd given up, although we never talked about it.

We didn't really talk about anything anymore. I wish I could say it was because we understood each other so well we didn't have to speak. Unfortunately, our silence was more of the 'I know we'll have another fight if I say anything, so I'll keep my mouth shut' variety.

Still, Yuji was doing his part to blend into the neighborhood, up early and off to work to keep the Japanese economy churning full steam ahead. I was the odd one out, of course, lazing away the morning in bed.

Today I actually did have a reason to get up for a change, a lunch date with my friend Chieko, but I still had a few hours before I had to meet her. I pulled open my sleeping robe and shrugged my shoulders from the sleeves, naked but for a fine film of sweat. I'd lost weight in the past year. I touched the knobs of bone between my breasts, the hip bones jutting up from my flat belly. Now I was as slim and fragile as any Japanese woman. At least I managed to fit in that way.

My hands glided lower.

'Good morning, Lydia, my dear.'

Yes, my voyeur friend was back as cheerful and gracious as ever. He didn't even hold a grudge that I'd once sent him into exile.

'I've brought you some presents I know you'll enjoy. Let's see, we have these very interesting black scarves with which to tie you up. And, of course, a handsome young gentleman to do the tying. I hope you don't mind if I stay and watch?'

I recognized his companion immediately. The lean, sculpted arms the color of honey. The strong shoulders tapering to a narrow waist. The compact little ass you want to grab and pull in tight. The high-bridged nose and graceful almond-shaped eyes, a compelling mixture of the Japanese and foreign. Masaru, of course.

'Just relax, Lydia, I'll take care of everything,' Masaru whispers and he does, tying my wrists together, then my ankles, lashing my thighs together right above the knees, then winding more cords in a criss-cross pattern between my breasts. When he's done he gazes down at me to admire his work.

'Oh, one more thing,' he says and ties a gag around my mouth. 'Let's try wordless communication today, Lydia. A little *ishin denshin*? After all, that's the Japanese way.'

Eyes narrowed with lust, a wicked smile playing on his lips, he runs his hands over my body, tickling the exquisitely sensitive skin between my wrist and elbow, raking my quivering belly with his fingertips, teasing the inside of my thighs, touching me in every place but the good parts. Masaru always likes to make me beg for it, and I'm already mewing and shaking with raw sexual need. Finally he takes a nipple between his lips and bites, gently. I moan into the gag.

'You really want it today. Your skin is on fire. You're so hot and hungry, I'm not sure one man can handle you. You mind if I bring in a friend?'

I'm gagged – what can I say?

Another figure appears. He doesn't have a face, but he and Masaru seem to know each other well.

Their voices are low and quick as they divide up the territory of my flesh. Masaru takes the right side, his friend the left. I watch helplessly as the two different hands stroke my breasts. The stranger's hand is larger, the fingers square and sturdy. He licks his palm and glides it over the taut nipple in mesmerizingly slow circles.

Masaru's fingers are longer and tapered, more subtle in bringing pleasure – and inflicting pain. He strokes the aureole with the utmost delicacy, then takes the stiff point between his thumb and forefinger and twists, hard, until I bleat out a muffled cry for mercy. Then, for a moment, he is gentle again.

When they've got me squirming and panting, they renegotiate the terms. The stranger continues to attend to me above the waist, suckling one nipple, tweaking the other. Masaru strokes my labia, teasing the lips, but refusing to go any deeper. I'm grunting and rocking my hips, hoping to trick his fingers into the slippery crevice.

'What do you think she wants now?' Masaru asks.

'With these foreigners I'm never really sure,' the other says.

They laugh.

'It's too soon to fuck her yet, right?'

'Not necessarily,' the stranger says with a proprietary air. He tests me with a quick dip of his finger. '*Mô nureta yo.* She's pretty wet.'

He's right. To my shame my thighs are drenched, as if my body knows it has to make enough juice for two.

'Too bad we'll have to take turns,' the stranger murmurs.

'What do you mean?' Masaru grins. 'She has two holes down there. One of us takes her in the front, the other takes the back.'

'Can we do that if she's tied up?'

'Oh, yeah, it's an interesting sensation. It puts pressure on different parts of your dick. And if you haven't tried going in the back door, I recommend it highly. What do you say, Lydia? Think you can handle both of us?'

I whimper through the gag, 'No, please,' but my body has other ideas, in spite of, or because of, the restraints. My cunt and asshole clench, then flutter open, like mute, hungry lips beckoning, confessing my desire.

Masaru pulls me toward him, the stranger spoons me from behind. Masaru pushes into me in one quick move, my thighs stretching open as far as they can against the bonds to accommodate his entry. The stranger is gentler – I'm glad he's taken the rear. He teases my tight opening with a wet finger, then the head of his cock, before easing himself inside.

I gasp, the gag filling my mouth. I'm surrounded now, totally enveloped by male flesh and desire. Cocks invade me, pushing up into my torso all the way to my skull. The stranger's hand reaches around to cup my breast. Masaru's finger finds my clit. They both begin to thrust, and I know they can feel each other moving through the thin wall of my flesh. The man in my ass starts grunting as if his orgasm is near. 'It's time to cut loose, Lydia,' Masaru whispers, his finger dancing on my clit, and I do just as he says, straining against the bonds, pushing and groaning until they burst in the white-hot explosion of my climax, finally freeing me from captivity.

The men's bodies fade into nothingness.

'Good show, Lydia,' my old friend says from his perch at the bottom of the futon. 'I must say it's quite generous of you to let your husband's best friend join in the festivities. If only more women were as open-minded as you, my dear.' The voice, too, ripples away into the sultry air.

I rolled onto my back, panting, my sheet drenched in sweat. In my post-come daze, I thought idly of another threesome. A half-naked Masaru bent over Caroline's bound body, myself as unwitting voyeur, gaping at the obscene show before me. The past two years had brought changes for us all.

Caroline had recently divorced husband number one and was fending off proposals from Silicon Valley's up-and-coming entrepreneurs — *I'm not sure if they want me for my blow jobs or my venture capital*, she joked over the phone.

Masaru's life was very different now, too. He'd finally given in to family pressure to take over his uncle's kimono business and find a 'suitable' wife, which meant traipsing off to hotel lobbies to meet blushing girls nearly ten years his junior. In just a few months he'd been transformed from a carefree younger son to a dutiful scion of the Nakamoto dynasty at last.

The third player in the little drama in my honeymoon suite had come to view the scene in a different light as well. Now I wish I had stayed and joined them.

I was certainly watching Masaru with a friendlier eye, collecting his yearning glances and secret smiles like fragments of shell glittering in the sand at the seashore. Only last Sunday, when he and Yuji came back to the apartment after their tennis game, I had a special snack waiting. Homemade, all-American chocolate chip cookies. It was worth all the trouble to bake them four at a time in our toaster oven just so I could watch Masaru eat one and sigh — *mmm, just like my homestay mom's in Seattle*. He was standing so close I could feel the heat of his body and breathe in his scent of soap mixed with a hint of spicy male sweat, tempting me to take a bite.

But Masaru and I had done nothing in real life that I needed to hide from Yuji. Yet.

CHAPTER TWO

As I rode the elevator up to the fourth floor of my friend Chieko's 'mansion' apartment building for our lunch date, I consoled myself with the thought that Japan was still handing me unexpected gifts, even in the face of disappointment. Chieko, a real friend, had come into my life just as Yuji had, for all practical purposes, disappeared.

We met at tea ceremony class, one of the many ways I filled my days besides screwing my husband's best friend in my fantasies. Chieko's cropped hair, broad shoulders and boyishly handsome face made her stand out from the rest of the students, mostly giggly women in their early twenties who were taking lessons for their marriage résumé. Chieko was thirty — my senior by three years — married to a journalist, and childless. She was just the kind of odd duck to befriend a foreign wife like me.

She first invited me to an exhibit of fine tea ware at a department store gallery and soon we were taking daytrips to Ise and Nara, shopping in Kobe's Chinatown or Kyoto's pottery shops by the Kiyomizu Temple. I learned with each meeting that she loved Japanese art and history, but liked to poke fun at them, too. She had an earthy streak that delighted me as often as it made me blush. She didn't quite fit in with Japanese ways, and beneath her bravado, I think this did cause her pain. In short, we were very much alike indeed.

Over a summery lunch of thin chilled noodles spiked with ginger and shiitake mushrooms, Chieko and I indulged in our second favorite pastime – complaining about our husbands.

Today it was my turn. 'I don't mind it so much when he's at the office working, it's the hostess bars that bother me.'

'Don't worry, Lydia. This is not so dangerous. It's only part of his work.' Chieko took on her mildly bossy *sempai* tone, and I couldn't deny she was my 'senior' in all aspects of Japanese culture.

'That's what Yuji says, but I know these young, sexy women are flirting with him. It's their job. Meanwhile, I'm stuck at home alone watching bad TV dramas and feeling very angry.'

'Maybe it is better not to be angry,' Chieko suggested. 'The hostess just talks. It's only words. Pretend. A Japanese man knows this.'

Except talk was exactly what scared me. I could only imagine how soothing it must be for him to speak his own language with a woman who was nothing but understanding.

'But I want to be the fun one,' I whined. 'I used to be. Now it seems all I do when Yuji is around is nag and complain.'

'That is not so different from a Japanese wife,' Chieko said with an impish gleam in her eye. Then her expression turned serious. 'Do you feel he has a girlfriend?'

'A gut feeling? Not really. But I imagine things. I worry.'

'Lydia, you are his wife. Marriage is real. The rest is only play.'

I nodded and forced my lips into a smile. Chieko meant to reassure me, so it didn't seem right to tell her that she'd just touched on the real problem. If I preferred fantasy over our real life together, how could I blame Yuji if he did the same?

CHAPTER THREE

What happened next was my fault. There was really no other way to see it. Chieko couldn't have planned for me to wander into what she called her study and snoop around while she was clearing the lunch dishes. Naturally she had refused my help and insisted I relax while she set out the green tea cream cake on the proper plates and poured us iced coffee with sugar syrup and thick cream.

The shelves of art books lured me in, thick, gorgeous volumes on Modigliani, Renoir, Ingres, masterpieces of Greek and Roman sculpture, and of course the Japanese masters of the woodblock print, Hokusai, Hiroshige, Kawase Hasui.

Then I turned and glanced over at her desk. There, on a large open sketchbook, was a drawing of a naked woman – obviously a foreigner – her legs spread wide, knees bent up to her chest, her head thrown back in a cry of ecstasy. Between her legs was an odd shape, dark lines swirling wildly like tangled vines, and instinctively I stepped toward it to make more sense of this strange vision. With a jolt, I realized it was another woman's head, her cat-like tongue poking out toward the empty space that would have been the first woman's exposed vulva, but for Japanese censorship laws.

This was, without question, a picture that belonged

in a pornographic comic book. There was even dialogue bubble. I leaned closer to read it.

Oddly, it was in *katakana*, the syllabary the Japanese used to write foreign words, although the sentence was in Japanese. 'Ah, wow, yes, that feels so good. You are much more skillful than my Japanese husband.'

Heart pounding, I backed out of the room – and straight into Chieko. A voice cried out in dismay, an oddly sexual sound. It was my voice.

Chieko glanced toward the desk with a nervous smile. 'Are you surprised your friend is so *sukebé*?'

Horny, lustful, dirty-minded? I'd had an inkling, but never dreamed my friend was a professional pornographer.

'No, I'm not surprised,' I said, my cheeks burning with embarrassment. We both knew it was a lie.

Then as if she read my mind, Chieko said, 'Don't worry, Lydia-*san*. The foreigner isn't you. I wanted to draw a beautiful, sexy woman, so I thought of you a little bit. But I would never give the real you to the men who read these stories.'

'Oh, I didn't think it was me,' I said with a false cheerfulness, 'my breasts aren't nearly as big as hers.'

Chieko laughed, then her expression grew cautious again. 'If you like, we can pretend this didn't happen.'

'Oh, no. I think it's great.' My poise was returning and I wasn't lying now. If Chieko had a *sukebé* secret life, this only made us more alike after all. I glanced back at the drawing. It was, in fact, a beautiful piece of work. 'I think you're very talented. By the way, what happens in the story?'

'Are you sure you want to know?' Chieko's eyes glittered.

'Of course.' I sat on the edge of the desk in an intentionally casual pose, to convince myself as much as her that I was the type of person who took porno comics in my stride. Could it be any worse than the raunchy things I dreamed up in my free time? Still, I felt a prickle of fear low in my belly, a feeling not so different from lust.

'Then I will show you.' Chieko turned back the pages of the sketchbook. 'This is very early. Just ideas.'

However, the first part of the story seemed finished enough. An American named Sara tearfully complained to her friend Natsuko that her husband's boss had invited her to lunch and hinted that he would make life very hard for her husband if she didn't let him sample her exotic charms for himself. The Japanese woman put a consoling arm around her friend and said that of course it would be wrong to sleep with another man, to which the foreigner replied, 'Yes, but not with another woman, perhaps?' The two women exchanged a starry glance, followed by a kiss and a series of thought bubbles: 'Her lips are so soft.' 'I feel like I'm floating.' 'I wish this could go on forever.'

And then, of course, came the picture I'd seen, the Japanese woman pleasuring the wide-eyed foreigner with her agile tongue.

By the time Chieko turned to the last blank page, my heart was pounding in my throat and I seemed to have forgotten to breathe for a good minute. So much for my cool, worldly, connoisseur-of-porn act.

'How does the story end?' I managed to say.

She glanced at me shyly, then looked away. 'I don't know. I'm still thinking.'

I swallowed. 'Is that what it's like to kiss a woman?' The words came out before I could stop myself. My cheeks felt hot again, and a new, ticklish sensation between my legs was making it hard not to squirm right there on the desk.

'For me, yes,' she replied. 'You have never . . . ?'

'No, never.'

'Ah.' Chieko nodded, a quick, bowing movement.

I found myself staring at her full lips, her one feature that wasn't boyish at all. My own lips began to tingle, and suddenly I flashed on that long ago February evening in Caroline's room, the champagne bubbles stinging my nose, Marybeth's breasts pressing against my arm, and a new road opening before me, forbidden, dangerous, and thoroughly irresistible.

Chieko must have felt my gaze, for she turned and looked me full in the face, then smiled, as if she knew exactly what I was thinking.

I tipped forward, an invisible hand pressing me toward her. I found her lips and closed my eyes. We stayed like that for a moment, barely touching. I could go no farther myself. Chieko was the one to open and welcome me into her. Her lips were very soft indeed. Our tongues met. I tasted *somen* noodles, the sweetness of the dipping sauce, a hint of her saliva. Chieko brought her hand to my cheek and we melted closer, but then she seemed content to linger, just as we were.

This isn't a man, what the hell do I do? What are the rules?

The words swirled through my head, but strangely, I sensed didn't have to *do* anything but *be*. It was, in fact, not like kissing a man at all. There was no face stubble, no tongue snaking deep as a preview of coming attractions, no conquest, no yielding. All boundaries gave way to the softness. Even the desk under my ass seemed to dissolve into a cushion of air leaving my body suspended, just like Chieko's story with no ending.

Except there was the growing wetness in my panties and the tingling in my pussy gaining heat and fierceness as it rose inside me, a dark, smoldering hunger. Suddenly I did want more, if not an ending then a struggle. I wanted to push Chieko to the floor, crush myself against her breasts, kiss her hard and deep, just like a man would. Or maybe I wanted something altogether different, to fall back beneath her, part my legs and surrender completely to her liquid, knowing tongue. I was soaring and sinking at the same time, a weird, dizzying sensation that made me pull away from Chieko with a low moan.

'*Daijôbu*?' Chieko asked – are you all right?

'Yes. Yes, of course,' I whispered, aware of my chest rising and falling quickly under my cotton dress. Then I added, too politely, 'That was nice.'

'Lydia.' Chieko touched my shoulder. 'Please, this is only play. Not serious. OK?'

I nodded, but the flicker of concern tinged with sorrow in her eyes made me wonder if she was the one lying now.

'We are still friends, Lydia, yes?'

I nodded again. If I lost her friendship, what would I have left but dreams?

'We can forget this happened,' she said firmly, closing the notebook and turning to put it away in a cabinet in the far corner of the room.

I gave my mouth a furtive swipe with the back of my hand. Could we really forget, or pretend to forget, something like this? Of course, since I'd come to Japan, I'd gotten good at pretending all kinds of things. Maybe I was turning Japanese after all?

CHAPTER FOUR

After I got home from our lunch, I curled up on the sofa with a glass of iced barley tea and the comics Chieko had sent home with me. Flustered by the kiss, I'd asked to see published samples of her work out of courtesy, but now I realized I was truly curious to see more of her work, and more of her.

This wasn't my first exposure to Japanese porn comics. I'd picked a few from the racks at Seven-Eleven in my first year in Japan, more for language study than their intended use. I learned that *omanko* means 'pussy' and *chimpo* means 'dick'. I learned that the women spend most of the time saying *iya* – 'no, I don't want to' – or *damé* – 'no, that's naughty', but they go on to have rocketing orgasms anyway. After a few issues I had the vocabulary mastered and my interest waned, especially after Yuji and I started cooking up plenty of erotic drama of our own.

I leafed through the first thick comic book and found Chieko's pen name under the story 'Housewife Confessions: The Call-in Erotic Massage'. I giggled, but then bent closer, studying the drawings more than the words now that I knew the artist wasn't some perverted guy in thick glasses, a pencil in one hand, his cock in the other. Instead it was Chieko bending over her desk, surrounded by books on the great masters, lips pursed, pink kitty slippers on her feet.

The first page showed a young wife preparing a salad as she waited for her salaryman husband to come home from work. In the next few frames, she tried her best to fight off the troubling urge to make love to a cucumber, for, as she admitted to herself, it had been a long time since her husband had done his marital duty. Suddenly there was a knock on the door. Who should it be but her section-chief husband, slumped drunk in the arms of his underling, a handsome fellow named Mr Yoshida? After the soon-to-be cuckold was deposited in the bedroom, the housewife expressed her sincere thanks to the young man who somehow managed to let slip he was skilled in massage and would be happy to perform this service for the *okusan*, clearly tense with worry for her husband. Setting down the cucumber, the wife peeled off her pantyhose and stretched out on the sofa for her treatment. Yoshida began with a foot rub so satisfying the woman arched back and moaned, beads of sweat – or was it tears of delight? – coursing down her cheeks. Slowly Yoshida's magic hands worked their way farther up the housewife's shapely legs. His technique was so adept, she didn't even protest when he pulled up her skirt and proceed to take the most intimate liberties with his boss's wife's body. Chieko's close-up of the woman's thighs dripping with the nectar of her arousal provided clear evidence of its welcome effect. In the next frame, it was she who begged young Yoshida to take her there on the sofa, her legs twisted around him like a pretzel, while her husband snored away in the next room.

I must admit I felt more than a few lustful twinges

154

as I read, but I also couldn't resist a bit of analysis as well. Clearly Chieko was appealing to her readers' desire to challenge the existing social hierarchy, if only in secret. What better protest than to roger the grateful wife of the guy who made your life hell for twelve hours a day, six days a week, not counting the 'optional' bonding time after work? As for the neglected housewife, I personally could vouch for the allure of adultery with your husband's attractive colleague. Did it make me more Japanese if I got turned on by a fantasy so drenched in culture-specific imagery?

Eagerly I pulled out the next comic, the cover adorned with a drawing of a foreign woman, her enormous tits spilling out of a bustier with cups so pointy they could function as a deadly weapon. The stories in this volume were kinkier, with elaborate *shibari* bondage and writhing women stuffed with double-headed dildoes. I blushed, glad Chieko wasn't here to see my reaction. Since I'd come to Japan, my fantasies had definitely wandered into S&M territory, one of my many adaptations to the culture.

In this story a curvaceous young receptionist at a construction company shared a few cold beers with her gangster-like boss at day's end, then headed off to the co-ed restroom to relieve herself. When she opened the door of the stall she discovered to her dismay, that the man was lurking by the sink with a wicked grin. *What a naughty girl you are, to let a man hear you go pee-pee. Now that you let me listen, I have a right to see what you've got down there, too.* Pushing her down on all fours beside the squat-style toilet, he yanked up her miniskirt and examined her pussy and asshole with a penlight, demanding she describe her own private parts to him. She protested – *I can't say it, I've never looked at myself down there* – but the boss refused to believe her and threatened to fuck her with the penlight if she didn't obey orders. Delirious with arousal and shame, the receptionist stuttered out the words: *My pussy is red and slick with my juices, the lips are quivering with excitement and when I push myself open they're all puffy and swollen, oh, please, I can't go on. I'm so embarrassed I could die.* As a reward, the boss soothed her with his tongue and the tale ended happily with the couple screwing doggy-style on the restroom floor.

I rolled my eyes, but I also felt I'd gotten a glimpse into a couple of other Japanese sexual taboos. I'd noticed over the years that my Japanese women friends always flushed immediately when they entered a toilet stall and, in fact, I'd never once heard the sound of urination. Even the easygoing Chieko was careful to preserve this custom. With the cleanliness fetish in this country, fucking on the floor of a public restroom would surely be the height of depravity. More brazen still was the young woman's courage in speaking the unspeakable. She actually described what the Japanese censors wouldn't allow us to see, the visible evidence of her sexual desire, not to mention her tacit admission that she'd studied her own pussy in a mirror when she masturbated.

Now I was definitely turned on. But what really got my mind racing was the thought that my own friend had imagined and created these stories. In her presence I hadn't allowed myself to think about what it meant to her to draw these pictures day after day. Now the questions swirled through my mind like the wild serpentine locks of her lesbian lovers. Did an editor assign the stories or did she make them up herself? Did she ever feel dirty catering to men's fantasies for money? Was she excited by her own work? Did she imagine me – us? – in the throes of sexual bliss as she drew the two women together? Did she masturbate at her desk, legs spread wide around the chair, finger wiggling as she gazed at the lewd image that had sprung from her own head?

I jumped up from the sofa, determined not to masturbate again today. It was time for dinner, although I wasn't hungry, not in that way. A salad seemed right for such a hot evening. I pulled a package of cucumbers from the refrigerator and removed one from the plastic wrapping. I washed it under cold water, rubbing its slightly nubby length with my palm.

I thought of the housewife in Chieko's story and her vegetal yearnings. Japanese cucumbers were smaller than the American variety, just the right size for a little self-comfort on a lonely evening. Already, the saintly intentions were fading.

Clutching the vegetable in my fist, I headed for the bedroom. I flopped down on Yuji's unmade futon and held the cucumber to my chest, running my fingers up and down its length, with particular attention to that sensitive area right below the tip.

Was that a sigh of pleasure drifting through the room? It wasn't my old friend this time. It was definitely a woman's voice, husky with arousal. Tonight was ladies' night.

I wriggled out of my sundress and set the cucumber beside me. Exactly as she ordered. 'Very good, Lydia. Now close your eyes,' she whispered. 'Give yourself to me tonight. I won't disappoint you.'

A hand, as soft and moist as the thick summer air, closed around mine.

CHAPTER FIVE

The new American employee had been sleeping with the company president for a month now. Actually, 'sleeping' was the wrong word. Even when they stayed all night at a luxurious traditional inn, they were too busy fucking to sleep. More often he called her up to his office to take his pleasure with her right then and there – sprawled on his desk or doggy-style, her hands pressed to the picture window for the whole city of Osaka to see, her breasts swaying rhythmically as he thrust into her. But this afternoon he had sent his secretary down to her cubicle with an envelope of thick, expensive paper. The quickly scrawled note instructed her to meet him at an exclusive restaurant near the old pleasure quarter at eight. He promised their evening together would be 'slow'. The very word made her panties wet.

When she stepped into the designated private dining room that evening, however, her smile vanished. The president was indeed waiting, seated in the place of honor by the elegant hanging scroll – and so were three young male colleagues who worked in the international relations section with her, as well as an imposing, but handsome, woman she had never seen before, whom the president introduced as 'Director of Special Projects'.

Still, Lydia knew it was politic to pretend to enjoy

herself, so she poured *saké* for her co-workers, made polite small talk with the mysterious, and decidedly butch director, and praised the lavish spread of sashimi, pink and glistening, like an aroused woman's pussy lips. She had all but abandoned her hopes for any indulgence of a non-culinary nature when the woman, Ms Inoue, bent close and suggested Lydia accompany her to the powder room. Something in her cool smile made the request impossible to refuse.

Once inside the restroom, the woman locked the door and turned her glittering eyes upon the young foreigner. 'The president has a favor to ask of you. As you may know, he is a collector of fine antique scrolls and tea ceremony utensils, but he also maintains a collection of a more private nature.' The director glanced meaningfully down in the direction of Lydia's thighs and arched an eyebrow.

Lydia cocked her head, confused.

'The boss collects women's panties, of course,' Ms Inoue snorted. 'Worn at least a day. Two is his preference, but on a hot day like this, the fragrance should be strong enough by now. He's asked me to inquire if you'd be willing to give him the panties you're wearing now. If I may add my personal opinion, this token gift is the least you can do for him.'

Lydia's stomach clenched in anger. The least she could do? How about letting the old guy fuck her in every obscene way possible inside the office and out? However, she couldn't deny that the perversity of the idea excited her. In fact, given the fresh gush of arousal between her legs, her panties would surely emit the depth of personal perfume the *shachô* treasured. She wondered how he stored his collection – in a special drawer? Or displayed on hooks on the wall of a secret chamber to sniff as the spirit moved him? Why not add her own contribution to the gallery? Brazenly, the foreigner yanked her pantyhose and underwear down. Accustomed to the etiquette of the country, she stepped carefully out of her restroom slippers one at time so her feet never touched the dirty floor and presented the damp white cotton panties to the surprised go-between with a flourish. 'Will these do?'

'Very nicely,' the woman said gruffly. Stuffing them in her purse, she exited the restroom without another word.

That left Lydia alone to struggle back into her pantyhose, which admittedly were scratchy against her bare vulva. However, the secret chafing seemed less penance than a promise of more surprises from her lover before the night was through.

She had no idea the next surprise would come so soon.

'Let's have some entertainment,' the president suggested merrily, when Lydia returned. 'Unfortunately, I'm sure the best geisha have been engaged by other parties at this hour.'

'I have an idea,' Ms Inoue said in her commanding tenor. 'I suggest the gentlemen play a guessing game. Did you know our colleague, Lydia-*san*, had something in her possession when she left the room that she no longer has now? Whoever can guess what this is will win a very special prize.'

The young men turned to Lydia, who blushed furiously. The crafty Ms Inoue had betrayed her, although, to be fair, there had never exactly been a bond of trust between them.

'Did she take off her earrings?' a shy, moonfaced fellow named Fujii offered.

'She doesn't wear earrings. Don't you pay attention to anything?' his senior by a year, the hawkish but handsome Masaru Nakamoto said, poking Fujii with an elbow. 'I'd guess she took off her stockings.'

'Stand up, Lydia, and show Mr Nakamoto if he is correct,' Ms Inoue said.

Lydia stood, too flustered to protest.

'I'm afraid you're wrong, Mr Nakamoto,' the woman sneered, running a possessive hand over Lydia's calf. 'These pretty American legs are covered up quite properly.'

'She left her handkerchief in the lavatory?' offered the third and youngest salaryman, Hamada, a cherub fresh from college.

'Wrong again,' snapped Ms Inoue. 'President Takada, would you care to take a turn?'

Takada smiled. Lydia felt her heart pounding in her throat. Would her lover betray her in front of her colleagues? How could she possibly face them in the office tomorrow?

'I have an idea of what might be missing,' the boss said slyly. 'But modesty forbids me to put it into words. Perhaps if Lydia could lift her skirt and show us. How do you say it in English – "a picture is worth a thousand words"?'

Standing before them, her face on fire, Lydia hung her head. She knew she should march from the room immediately to keep the final tatters of her reputation intact, but a reckless, defiant part of her knew the opinion of these men meant nothing. The game was rigged, as it always was in Japan. It was Ms Inoue who mattered, and Lydia wanted nothing more than to show this goading woman she could stand anything she dished up, even take her one better.

Slowly she grasped the hem of her skirt and hiked it up over her thighs. The men's eyes followed the rising movement of the skirt, inch by aching inch. A collective gasp filled the room.

'Lydia-*san* doesn't wear panties,' breathed Hamada.

'Not exactly, Mr Hamada,' Ms Inoue said, unzipping her purse and pulling out the limp, soiled panties. 'She was wearing these until a moment ago. I was surprised at how quickly she agreed to take them off.'

Lydia scanned the faces of her colleagues, hoping for an ally among them, but she could tell by the glowing eyes focused squarely on her naked mons that Ms Inoue had won them over to her side.

'Now that the game is decided, I propose our American colleague reward each man according to the merit of his guess,' Ms Inoue continued. 'Mr Fujii comes in last with earrings because the ear is the farthest in distance from the correct location. Since a handkerchief is carried in the pocket, Hamada earns one point, but Nakamoto earns two for pantyhose, which consensus would surely hold comes closest. And, of course, our wise president guessed correctly, so he wins the grand prize.'

'Could you elaborate on the prizes you have in mind, Director Inoue?' Takada asked softly.

'With pleasure, Boss. In this contest, the third runner-up earns the privilege of fondling Lydia's bare breasts and rubbing his penis in her cleavage if he so desires. The second runner-up wins the right to caress her between the legs and have her pleasure him with her hand until he reaches satisfaction. The first runner-up may use his mouth and enjoy the skills of her lips and tongue in return. And the winner?' Here she smiled at the *shachô*, whose face was flushed with titillation. 'The winner may do whatever he desires with our naughty little Lydia.'

'You have a very creative mind,' the president grunted in admiration. 'But as a man who values consensus, I must insist the evening's entertainment may only proceed if Lydia agrees to these terms.'

Ms Inoue sighed. 'Naturally, Takada-*sama*, you are a man of the highest honor. I suspect this means our party has come to an end. Lydia surely lacks the guts to provide each player with his due reward.'

'Oh yeah? Don't speak too soon.' With an audacious grin, Lydia quickly stripped off her clothes. She wasn't ashamed of her body. Why else did she jog and lift weights if not to stand nude before an audience of awe-struck men at least once in her life? 'Mr Fujii? It's your turn.' She knelt, took her full white breasts in her hands and held them out in offering, glaring defiance at Ms Inoue.

The blushing young man crawled over the *tatami* to the naked foreigner, the bulge in his trousers painfully evident. Hands trembling, he took a breast in each hand. Soon his awkward caresses took on a more confident rhythm as he teased and sucked

Lydia's rose-pink nipples. Her eyelids fluttered closed, the other woman's challenge momentarily forgotten in the pleasurable sensations shooting all the way down to her belly.

'I would like . . . very much . . .' Fujii stuttered through slick lips, 'I would like to do that action Director Inoue described.'

'Fuck her tits until you come on her chest?' Ms Inoue said with a sweet smile. 'An excellent idea. Perhaps you would like to borrow some of this?' She pulled a bottle of personal lubricant from her purse. The woman was clearly prepared for all eventualities.

Fujii took the bottle and squirted a puddle of lube in the valley of Lydia's breasts, now mottled pink with arousal. Swinging his leg over the supine foreigner's waist, he pressed his erection between the pale demi-globes.

'Mr Fujii needs your cooperation, Lydia. Hold your breasts together for him,' Ms Inoue ordered.

Woozy with a lust incited not only by Fujii's hungry lips, but the longing eyes of the other three men and the cool, appraising gaze of Inoue, Lydia did as she was told. Fujii didn't take long. After a half-dozen thrusts into the slick, makeshift tunnel of flesh, the young man ejaculated with a cry, his spunk spraying beads of pearly white all over Lydia's neck and chest.

From her voluminous bag Ms Inoue produced a hand towel, perfect for mopping it up.

Second runner-up Hamada was already in place, trousers and underwear at his knees. Coaxing Lydia to a seated position, he snaked his hand between her legs. The sound of her wet flesh clicking under the dance of his fingers echoed through the room.

'More lube, Lydia dear?' Ms Inoue asked sweetly.

Nodding, Lydia accepted a quick squirt in her palm, the better to stroke Hamada's swollen member.

This, too, didn't take long. Groaning with frustration as much as desire, Hamada came in her hand within moments, a few stray shots spattering on Lydia's thighs. Again Ms Inoue produced a fresh towel.

'Mr Nakamoto, I'm wondering if you would consider an amendment to your reward?'

Nakamoto bowed stiffly and waited for his orders.

'I had no idea Lydia would become aroused so quickly. I fear that if you take a few nibbles, she may reach her climax too soon. Perhaps you can be satisfied with more selfish pleasures this evening?'

Nakamoto nodded and began to unbuckle his belt. Still in her erotic daze, Lydia knew exactly what she had to do. She rose to her knees to take his ruddy, swollen tool in her mouth. Nakamoto had more experience than the others, second only to the president in his skills. He was clearly savoring her efforts, murmuring instructions on how hard to suck, how best to stimulate his frenulum with her tongue. Deprived of his chance to explore her pussy with his mouth, he claimed a share of Fujii's prize, flicking and tweaking her nipples until it seemed she would indeed climax before the president had his turn.

A sharp smacking sound interrupted Lydia's dizzying climb to her peak. It was Ms Inoue, slapping Nakamoto's buttocks. 'Don't be *too* selfish, Nakamoto-

san,' she warned. 'You'd best finish up now. Our president is patiently waiting his turn.'

With a grunt, Nakamoto jammed his cock deep into Lydia's throat, filling her with his cream. She swallowed, but the resourceful Ms Inoue was ready with another towel so she could dab the last remaining drops neatly from her lips.

'And now, Takada-*shachô*, what service may Lydia-*san* perform for you?'

All eyes turned to the older man.

The company president cleared his throat. 'As you know, my policy is always to include my workers in the decision-making process, as is the Japanese way. I would like Lydia-*san* to choose which act she would like to perform.' He paused and smiled. 'And with whom.'

'Sir?' Lydia asked uncertainly.

'I thought you might like to sample the undeniably powerful charms of your new friend, Director Inoue?'

Lydia swallowed hard, struck dumb by her lover's outrageous suggestion. And yet she felt an undeniable stirring in her loins at the thought of the cocky woman's embrace.

'President Takada,' Inoue chimed in. 'I would be most honored to have the chance to bring our friend her own reward. She has worked much harder for the company's morale this evening than I ever thought possible for an American.'

'What do you say, Lydia? Would you prefer Director Inoue or myself to make love to you this evening?'

Lydia whispered her reply.

'I'm sorry,' Ms Inoue snapped. 'We didn't hear you.'

'I would like Ms Inoue to make love to me,' Lydia repeated louder, her voice cracking.

The president broke into a broad smile. It was, it seemed, the correct answer.

The powerfully built woman squared her shoulders. 'Lie down on the table then, Lydia. I'm very glad I saved room for dessert.'

Her chest heaving with fear mingled with desire, Lydia draped herself over the low dining table. She tried to stop the trembling in her thighs, but she knew it would only be harder to hide her excitement once this formidable lady used her lingual skills directly on her most secret place.

Ms Inoue slipped her hands between Lydia's knees and spread them wide, then pushed them high, up against her chest, so she was totally opened and exposed. There was a shuffling as the men gathered behind the dominatrix for the best view of the action.

'Now I'm going to kiss your soft, pink lips down there. Isn't that what you want, Lydia? Isn't that what you wanted since you took off your panties for me in the restroom?'

'Yes,' the American whimpered.

'Then beg me for it.'

'Please, Inoue-*sama*. Please, Mistress. Do me the great honor of licking my womanly orifice,' the American squeaked in her most proper Japanese.

'With such a polite request, how could I possibly refuse?'

Lydia let out a sigh as the woman's tongue brushed

168

against her cleft delicately, then picked up tempo. She was good, very good — better than the president, better than any American she'd ever slept with. Swirling, stroking, lapping, Ms Inoue's tongue instinctively found the right spot, the perfect rhythm. Lydia's entire being centred on that single point of contact between the tip of Ms Inoue's knowing tongue and her own taut swollen clit, standing obediently to attention. The remarkable sensation lasted but a few more moments, for suddenly she felt more hands upon her. One soft and hesitant stroking her left breast, another warmer and rougher caressing the right. Then lips pressing against hers from above. She recognized the flavor of Takada-*shachô*'s mouth and opened herself to his probing tongue. Caught in a quivering net of flesh, Lydia thrashed and moaned, reveling in this unexpected abundance of riches. So many people wanting nothing but to give her pleasure, wanting nothing but to watch her come. Only one thing was missing: a hard cock deep inside, stretching her, filling her.

As if she could sense this longing, Ms Inoue reached inside her magic Mary Poppins' bag and brought out her final gift: a firm, perfectly shaped cucumber. Positioning it carefully at the mouth of Lydia's sopping vagina, she eased it inside. Lydia groaned into her boss' mouth and tilted her ass up to deepen the penetration. Bending forward to renew her attentions to Lydia's clitoris, Ms Inoue simultaneously moved the nubby green dildo in and out of her passage, mimicking the motions of a man making love.

At last Lydia came – her shouts muffled by her boss's kiss, her breasts fondled by his attentive lieutenants, her pussy gushing all over Ms Inoue's tongue and hand – forever won over to the Japanese method of working as a group to get the job done.

CHAPTER SIX

I opened my eyes. I had no idea what time it was, but it was dark. A figure sat on the mattress beside me, outlined by the faint glow of the city lights. Who could it be? Masaru back for yet another round? That ballsy Inoue woman who had taken on such a life of her own by the end of the fantasy she might actually manage to stride straight out of my brain into my bedroom?

'Did I wake you?'

I recognized him now, a ghost from the past. Why shouldn't he come now? It was August after all, the month when the dead return to earth in Japan.

'I'm sorry,' Yuji said in a low voice. 'Usually you sleep right through.'

I reached out to him. He slid down beside me and took me in his arms. We found each other's lips in the darkness. His mouth was warm, with hints of garlic and beer. Chinese food for dinner? I took another sniff to catch the incriminating smell of perfume, but I smelled only his scent, male and innocent.

His hand moved to my breast, hesitantly, as if he could hardly believe this was real either. 'Can we, Lydia? I want you.'

He would choose this night, when I was sore between my legs from that cucumber and my lips still burned with the memory of Chieko's kiss. Could

171

he sense my infidelity, smell it on my skin? But I hadn't really been unfaithful to him. That's what I'd been trying to avoid, making love to specters stitched together from memory and dream.

I ran my hands over his bare shoulders and back. My palms tingled. So many layers to nourish my hunger, soft skin, firm muscles, and deeper still, the glimmerings of our history together. A creature more fantastic than any I'd encountered all day.

'Of course, darling, of course. I want you too,' I whispered, no longer worrying about the tenderness between my legs. What mattered was that he hadn't given up yet. And if he hadn't, I told myself, neither would I.

Part Seven

THE SPELL OF THE MOUNTAIN DEMON
(Gunma, 1990)

CHAPTER ONE

'We should get away like this more often.' Yuji smiled as he gazed out the window at the mountain scenery: soaring green cedars, the slate sky of late winter, lingering patches of snow.

I smiled too. It didn't seem wise to point out that it had taken seven months of nagging to get him back up here to the hot spring inn where we'd spent our Japanese honeymoon. 'Sure,' I said, 'now that I'll be raking in the money with my new job in April, we can go to all kinds of exotic places. How about Paris next time?'

Yuji turned to me, the smile broadening. 'And Firenze, too? I think you'd like it there.'

He was playing along – a good sign.

Then he yawned.

'Tired?'

'It was a long train ride.'

I jumped up from the table where we were having our tea and pulled a futon mattress and two pillows from the cupboard. Yuji raised his eyebrows – it was a rather illicit thing to do at an inn in the afternoon – but he joined me on the futon readily enough. In spite of the laboring space heater, the room had a definite chill and we snuggled together, just like those Sundays in his bachelor apartment, another lifetime ago.

'What do you want to do for the rest of the

afternoon? We could hang out in the bath together. Unless you're going to exile me to the women-only bath until midnight like last time.'

'You know I don't like all those men staring at you.'

His light-hearted tone made it sound like a joke, but it struck me that even mock jealousy was another good sign.

'OK, a midnight bath it is. How about a hike before dinner?'

'That sounds good. We haven't been hiking since Big Sur. Caroline's wedding,' he said, his voice warm with the memory. 'How is she doing, by the way? On husband number three yet?'

'No, still with number two.'

'I wonder how long that will last.'

I laughed, but not without a pang at my own disloyalty. Yuji and I could hardly be smug about our perfect marriage, and besides I had Caroline to thank for my adventure back into the working world. *Spare me the whining about the lonely nun's life, Lydia,* she drawled over the phone. *American guys are workaholics, too. Michael works eighty hours a week, but I'm not complaining because sometimes I work ninety. It's just the same as sex. You have to beat guys at their own game.*

As if fate agreed with my cousin, the job search was surprisingly easy. My old colleague, Nancy, was leaving a plum English instructor's position at a women's junior college near Kobe to take over as director of an international school. She recommended me as her replacement, and the president of the college hired me immediately at an attractive salary. I did have a moment of superstitious doubt when I went to sign the paperwork, as if taking a job meant the end of my hopes for a family. I knew that was absurd, of course. Having a reason to get out of the house a few days a week was probably the best thing I could do to put the twinkle back in Yuji's eye.

'Should we get going now?' I said, checking my watch. We'd have to be back for dinner by six.

'In a couple of minutes.' Yuji patted my arm but was unable to stifle another yawn. His eyes closed. He'd been working extra late hours this past week to earn his right to time off.

I didn't mind lying together for a while in companionable silence. Soon enough, we could hit the trail and let the fresh mountain air do its magic on our city-weary bodies.

'Yuji? Would you rather stay and take a nap?' I asked softly when a few minutes had passed.

It was only a formality. I knew by his even breathing that he was already asleep.

CHAPTER TWO

My breath came in frosty dragon puffs as I followed
the winding trail away from the inn, alone. In Osaka
there were already signs of spring, but winter lingered here, as if time moved slower in this silent,
majestic place.

Suddenly I noticed the sound of rushing water
echoing through the trees ahead of me. A waterfall? I
walked with new purpose along the narrow, rock-
strewn path. At least I'd have an interesting sight to
report to Yuji when I got back to the room.

A few minutes later I came to a wooden bridge. I
stepped onto the weatherworn boards and gazed out
over the water. Not far up the mountain there was
indeed a small waterfall, a frothy curtain of silvery
white.

'*Kirei desu ne.*'

I jumped. The voice came from behind me, on the
far side of the bridge. I glanced over my shoulder.
A man of about forty in a camouflage green parka
was seated on the bank of the stream, a sketching
pad on his knees. With his friendly, almost child-like
face and velvety brown eyes, he bore a striking
resemblance to the ceramic figures of the raccoon-
dog *tanuki* that guarded the doorways of noodle
shops, although he lacked the huge, rounded belly
and, on the racier versions, the absurdly oversized

testicles. He was built more like a woodsman, rangy and athletic.

'It *is* beautiful,' I agreed in Japanese, still mildly flattered when someone assumed I knew the language. The man didn't seem like a *chikan*, a pervert. In fact, he had a thoughtful serenity that immediately put me at ease.

'Would you do me the kindness of standing still for just a moment? A human figure will bring balance to the scene, I think.' If there'd been the slightest hint of lechery in his manner, I would have fled, but again his cheerful smile reassured me.

I nodded and turned to face the waterfall, aware of his eyes on my back. My flesh started to tingle – was I that desperate for attention? – but I reminded myself I was just part of the landscape to him. And, as I breathed in more of the pure country air, my body did seem to soften and melt into the air around me.

Moments later the man called out his thanks for my patience.

'You're welcome. May I take a look?'

'Of course, but I'm sorry my drawing is poor,' he said, offering me the sketchbook with a slight bow.

As usual in Japan, he was overly modest about his skills. In a few strokes, he had captured the figure of a woman with wavy foreigner's hair standing at a bridge. The waterfall beyond was closer in the picture than in real life, but artists always took licence with the truth. Then I noticed something else that was factually inaccurate: a weird, gnarled figure hunched below the bridge gazing fixedly at the woman with its bulging eyes.

'*Nani, koré?*' I asked abruptly, in informal Japanese. My own rudeness made my face go hot, but I was indeed curious why this creepy monster was lurking in *my* picture. I should have learned from Chieko not to trust artists with sketchbooks. Why were they always drawn to me? Because they were strangers in their own land, too?

The man's face reddened. 'Ah, yes, I am sorry. That is a *kappa*, a demon of sorts. I was finishing the drawing just as you came by – a foolish bit of imagination. Please allow me an explanation. I study folklore. And teach it too, to ungrateful students at a university in Tokyo.'

'You're a professor?' I said, relieved. Again I'd jumped to false conclusions. My secluded housewife's life was obviously making me paranoid.

'So I am called, although when I come to a place like this,' he gestured to the forest around us with a boyish smile, 'I feel very much the student. I like to come up here during my school holiday. At this lean time of year, just before the spring, the demons and sprites are hungry, and so more likely to appear to humans. This, of course, is good for my research, although the situation is not so lucky for them.' The professor's expression turned thoughtful, as if he were filled with genuine pity for these imaginary creatures.

'Have you seen many demons today, *Sensei*?' My tone was more flippant than I intended, but surely there was no harm in a little flirtation with a professor. I did it back in college all the time.

He smiled. 'I have seen one or two. If one is patient,

they will sometimes show their faces to me. But for you it may be different. The forest is particularly dangerous for a pretty young woman. You must take care.'

Was it my imagination, or did his expression suddenly change, the smile turning sly, the eyes sinister? *Tanuki* were known to be shape-shifters, transforming from one guise to another in an instant.

'Yes, well, I'll be careful,' I said, backing away. 'I have to go now. My husband's waiting for me back at the inn.'

'Is that so? Then I mustn't keep you. Again, my sincere thanks for your kindness.' The man bowed, a quirky but harmless scholar once more.

As I headed back up the trail, I thought again of the weird, spindly *kappa* in the drawing. Of course the professor had drawn him before I arrived, but I could swear the creature was staring at something juicy and desirable on that bridge, as if he'd been waiting for me come along and fall into his trap. I shivered and quickened my steps back to Yuji and safety. It was nothing more than delusion that a famished mountain sprite lurked behind every boulder and tree trunk, watching and waiting for the right time to pounce.

CHAPTER THREE

Yuji's nap did not refresh him for an evening of love. He seemed to fade further with the day's light, as if the exhaustion he had been holding at bay for years collapsed upon him only now on his one weekend of freedom.

He picked at the lavish dinner, forced down one polite cup of *saké* for our toast, and curled up on the futon at the first opportunity, shivering and feverish.

'I'll just rest until it's late enough for us to go down to the bath together,' he whispered, managing a feeble wink, but his eyes never opened again that night.

I didn't have the heart to wake him. But I didn't have room for pity either. Except for myself.

I'd wanted this weekend to be a trip to the past, our past. Yuji was supposed to climb back into his old skin, make passionate love to me in the public bath at midnight, break all the rules, laugh at every social expectation. Afterwards we'd be so mellow, we'd talk about all the difficult things. How we should go to a doctor for infertility tests. How he could try to come home for dinner at least one night a week. How we could save what little we had left. All in all, the most outrageous fantasy I'd had in quite some time.

As midnight approached, I escaped down to the bath to take my familiar brand of solitary pleasure.

The tip-tap of my slippers echoed through the empty corridor, but I knew once I got to the bath, I wouldn't be alone. I never was. Who would I conjure up to do my bidding tonight? An elegant tenth-century courtier intimate with every refinement of the act of love? Or a brawny Heike warrior on the eve of a great battle whose lust for me was fueled by the knowledge that the next day might be his last? Or perhaps something darker and devilish, a hunched, misshapen mountain demon, with skin as tough as bark and a sapling of a cock gushing semen like a waterfall in spring?

I felt a twist of lust, as if rough but knowing fingers were already reaching out from the shadows. I was going to have myself some fun tonight after all.

CHAPTER FOUR

The bathhouse was deserted, the water smooth and glassy. Hot spring baths in Japan usually follow a guiding fantasy, transporting the bather to a rocky grotto, a tropical garden or terrace with the perfect view of Mount Fuji, even if the mountain itself is an image set in mosaic tile. This inn was more ambitious than most. The soaring cross-beamed ceiling, glowing pedestal lanterns, and swimming pool-sized cedar tub brought to mind the cathedral of a cult that worshipped both purity and indulgence. I was more than eager to make my own offering on its altar.

I dutifully soaped and rinsed my 'dirty' parts — under my arms and between my legs — before slipping into the bath with the clean bathing towel I'd brought to cover myself in case I had unexpected company. Sinking in up to my neck, I swirled my hands in lazy circles through the steaming water, inching ever closer to the final goal hidden away in the secret folds between my legs. My other hand cupped my breast, the thumb flicking my nipple languidly. I was in no hurry. I had all night to bring the ritual to its satisfying climax.

Suddenly the sliding door at the entryway rattled on its track and I jerked my hands away, pulling my towel modestly across my breasts.

A shadowy male figure stood in the doorway

staring into the room. His head was tilted to the side, as if he couldn't quite make out what he was seeing through the wisps of steam rising from the water. A moment later the man stepped back into the hall and closed the door.

I sighed with relief. The stranger surely couldn't have seen what I'd been doing to myself underwater. Even if he had, he was gone now, never to be seen again.

I let my hands wander back to their task. Within moments I'd returned to the pleasure zone. I often played with myself in our bath at home, but here in this lovely, timeless place, the sensations were even sharper. The water itself seemed to pulse around me, caressing, teasing, lapping at my pussy, pushing up inside me. I sighed again, this time with longing. As always, my old friend answered the call.

'Good evening, Lydia, my dear, or should I say "good morning"? How nice to be back in this pristine mountain setting. I hope you'll allow me to stay and enjoy myself this time.'

'Come on, you said you'd forgiven me for that. Now, what do you have for me tonight? Something hot and slippery, I hope.'

Before he could reply, the door rattled open once more. Damn.

This time the stranger strode confidently into the bath, swinging a large bottle of *saké* in one hand like a sword. In the other he carried two square wooden *masu* cups, stacked one on top of the other.

It was my new friend, the professor from the bridge on the hiking trail. He nodded cordially in my direction, but didn't say a word as he set the bottle down by the bath's edge and went behind the partition to make his preparations. After some splashing sounds and the slap of water being dashed onto the wooden floor, he emerged without his robe, holding the towel discreetly over his crotch, and stepped into the water.

Mixed-sex bathing etiquette dictated that I shouldn't stare, but I let my eyes graze his body for a few seconds before he stepped into the water. The professor did have a hint of a *tanuki*'s belly, but he was in good shape for a man of his age, although of course I hadn't seen enough naked middle-aged men at close range to make an educated comparison.

'Good evening,' he said nonchalantly, as if we were meeting on the street fully dressed instead of naked in a hot tub at midnight.

'I see you didn't bring your sketchbook this time.'

His eyes twinkled. 'No, but I was under the mistaken impression that I wouldn't find anything interesting here tonight. I did bring some refreshment. Would you care to join me?'

'Thanks, but only a little.' With my other plans on hold, what else did I have to do tonight?

The professor smiled and filled my cup halfway. I returned the favor with a more generous hand. We raised our cups in a *kampai*.

'I was hoping I could meet your husband. Will he be down soon?' my companion asked.

I shook my head. 'He's sleeping. I think he's sick. A flu, maybe.'

'He should watch out for his health. He works too hard.'

'How do you know that?' I blurted out, surprise making me rude once more.

'All young men work too hard. They do not understand what is truly important in life until later. Too late, I wonder?' The professor settled himself against the edge of the bath at a polite distance and took a sip of *saké*. 'By the way, what brings your husband to Japan?'

I laughed. Already the drink was going to my head. 'My husband was born here. He's Japanese.'

'Is that so? Then he must work very hard indeed. It must be difficult for you, too, to be waiting. Always waiting, no?'

'Exactly. That's all I do . . .' The words slipped out before I could stop myself. It had been a long time since anyone, even Chieko, gave me sympathy for my troubles.

'Perhaps you know the saying: *tsutta sakana ni esa o yaranai*.'

I cocked my head. I'd caught the words 'fish' and 'do not give'.

'Don't bother feeding worms to the fish you've already caught,' the professor translated in fluent, American-accented English.

'Don't tell me,' I said in the same language, 'you lived in the States for ten years and you've been indulging my bad Japanese all this time for laughs.'

'Your Japanese is truly very good,' he insisted, eyebrows raised at my accusation. This, of course, earned him extra points. 'And I did spend a few years at the University of Michigan. The winters are very cold there, but I developed a fondness for the local cherry preserves.'

'I'm from the east coast so I don't know Michigan, but I imagine there's a lot of beautiful countryside out there.'

'There is indeed. More *saké*?'

I knew I shouldn't, but it was tasty stuff. I glanced at the name on the label. '*Onigoroshi*? Doesn't that mean "demon slayer"?'

'Why, yes. Your Japanese *is* very good. An appropriate drink for the setting, don't you agree?'

'OK, you talked me into it. I'll take another tiny bit. I have a few demons to slay myself.'

He laughed and poured, a bit more this time.

'And by the way, you're right,' I said, after a long swallow. 'I haven't been eating too many worms recently.'

He nodded agreeably. 'I think you understand in Japan we all must be patient and endure in our lives. That is why we come to a place like this, so we can relax for a short while, and perhaps find a few worms to eat? This is the real Japan. The city is where we worship our false gods. The recent turn in the stock market has shown us how deceitful they are.'

'Don't you think it will bounce back like it did in America?' Yuji thought it was likely to recover once the shock had passed.

'I do not, but I was never a believer in such things. Only here, deep in the mountains, can we Japanese find our soul. So, you see, I must come to this place to get in touch with a part of myself I cannot feel in the city.'

I finished my *saké* and sighed. I wished I knew where I could find my soul. The professor held up the bottle, eyebrows raised in a question. I nodded. A little more demon-slaying liquor might save me from that familiar tug of discontent.

'Here's to getting in touch with hidden feelings. That's definitely why I came here.' I raised my cup with a giggle, confident the professor wouldn't get the reference to my earlier self-pleasuring activities. He'd probably just think I was drunk. Which, it occurred to me, I was.

He gazed at me for a moment, brow wrinkled, then said, 'Yes, I fear I was disturbing you at this effort – of getting in touch with your feelings – when I came in.'

I froze. *Oh, god, he did see. Now what do I do?*

'I don't know what you're talking about,' I lied, blushing.

He nodded, though less in agreement, than acknowledgment of that lie. Our eyes met. Now I did see desire there, or the faint, glowing embers of it. I also saw curiosity, and maybe something close to compassion.

I clutched the bathing towel tighter to my chest, not that such a skimpy thing would provide much protection if I really needed it. OK, so he saw me playing with myself in the public bath. It probably wasn't the first time that had happened in the history of this place, but it was clearly time to put an end to our party. I should get out of the water and rush back to take my place beside Yuji's unconscious body. It was the only proper thing a wife could do if she was prudent, loyal, and happy in her marriage.

And if she wasn't?

Without a word, the professor reached over to refill my cup. I didn't protest. I'd have one more drink to get up the courage to get out of the bath – I was for all practical purposes naked – then I'd march straight back to the room.

'Of course, the mountains are my work as well,' the professor continued. 'I am always watching, observing. And yet I must wonder, as all anthropologists do, if my presence does not change the course of events from what they might otherwise be. That would be a shame indeed.' His eyes flickered.

Through the cottony haze of the alcohol, I suddenly understood exactly what he was asking, which was what I suppose you'd say to any attractive and more-or-less willing member of the opposite sex you caught masturbating in a hot tub. *Should I go away and let you finish in private or stay and help out?*

I studied his face as I considered my reply. The cute, *tanuki* features were only the icing on the cake. What really intrigued me were his eyes, intelligent, attentive, and yes, thirsty. Yet there was something calming in his gaze, too, as if he were stroking me with a piece of soft fur. Sure, I was drunk, but in this case it meant I could see the truth more clearly. He liked to watch. I liked being watched. Maybe the *kamisama* still cared about me after all?

'But I thought your specialty was mountain demons, *Sensei*.' I gave him my best 'suck up to the professor at the department reception' smile. 'Do you do research on women, too?'

'I am open to every opportunity,' he said smoothly. 'But be assured, my intent is never to interfere, only observe what is before me.'

I set my empty cup down at the side of the tub.

I suppose you could call it sorcery, the way my flesh suddenly seemed to soften and flow, transforming me from a good wife – although was I ever truly a 'good' wife to Yuji? – into a silky, sinuous seductress. With a provocative smile, I inched the bathing towel slowly over my chest, rising up just far enough that my breasts floated like white lilies on the surface of the water. My nipples immediately tightened in the cool air.

The professor stared, as if his eyes were bound to the movement of my hands with steel cable. I'd forgotten how much I loved to have a man in my power. I took my breasts in both hands, lifting them in offering. He swallowed visibly.

At first, I was just showing off for him, rolling my nipples between my fingers, licking my thumbs to stroke them over the sensitive tips. But soon enough I let one hand creep between my legs beneath the cover of the water, just as if he'd never come to interrupt me. Except, of course, there was a real man sitting across from me, his face suspended in the ghostly vapors hovering over the bath. From his hooded eyes and faint grimace, I knew he was touching himself, too, lost in his own dream.

Is this how it would be if my old friend took on human form – his eyes dazed by the vision of my pleasure? But now that he was here, I wanted more than his gaze, I wanted to feel him, his hands and lips and cock all at once, claiming me, filling me.

'Will you touch me?' I asked in English, the language of selfishness.

The professor's face twisted into a frown. He wanted to touch me, I could tell, but something held him back. Was it professional ethics or some less lofty obligation like a wife? I decided not to ask.

'It is best . . .' He swallowed again. '. . . If I do not.'

But I thought it best he did.

I rose to my feet, the water gliding from my body like a silk robe. My skin tingled from the mild sting of the wintry air, but inside I was still warm from the long soak, my flesh plumped, glowing, hungry.

The professor's eyes widened and leapt toward me, but his body remained frozen in place.

On impulse, I turned and bent over the edge of the bath, doggy-style, a primal position most men found irresistible. I glanced back over my shoulder. As if drawn by leash, he moved closer. I had, finally, made him an offer he couldn't refuse.

CHAPTER FIVE

Warm hands grasped my hips, sliding over the wet flesh, tracing the curve of my back down over my buttocks. Taking a cheek in each hand, the professor squeezed and stroked and raked his fingers over the skin in soft, tingling circles.

I moaned appreciatively, not sure if I should reach down and touch my clit or wait for him to do the honors. Not that he was in any hurry to move things in that direction. He seemed more interested in exploring the valley of my ass, moving lower and deeper with each feathery, teasing caress. I opened my legs wider and arched up, happy to do what I could to assist his research.

Then the professor began tapping my asshole lightly as if he were playing a little drum. A searing spasm of pleasure shot through my body and I yelped in surprise.

'Shall I stop?' he asked with concern.

'Oh no,' I stuttered. 'Please, I . . .'

'. . . Find pleasure in it?' the professor finished for me.

'Yes.' Could he see how very much I did?

He made a low grunt of assent and continued to stroke my cleft, paying special attention to the ring of muscle around the hole. The sensations were so exquisite, so engulfing, my whole body trembled.

'Is it the custom for your husband to touch you back here?' the professor inquired, his voice husky.

'No. He never does.' I sensed this was the answer he wanted, although in this case, it was also the truth.

'Such a pity to ignore what we can surely call the seat of human pleasure,' he murmured.

A pun? I almost laughed, but was distracted by a new sensation, his hands pulling my ass cheeks wide. I braced for his touch, but felt only warmth, as if a feeble sun were shining on that hidden place for the very first time. I could tell he was staring at me, studying me. Dozens of men had seen my vulva, but this was the first time my ass — in truth, my most secret part — had gotten such professional attention. I squirmed uneasily.

The professor guessed my thoughts. 'Do not be ashamed. You are very beautiful. So clean and pink and beautiful.'

I felt my asshole plump up, reveling in the compliments.

His finger grazed the opening. I whimpered and wiggled like a little dog happily greeting her master. Could it be I had a second clit hiding back there undiscovered all these years?

I'm going to come this way. I'm actually going to come just by having a professor play with my asshole.

'May I kiss you here?'

How could I pass that up?

'Yes, please.'

I gasped at the contact, the pillow-soft warmth pressing against that exquisitely sensitive area. The first kiss was chaste, a smack of lips against my tiny mouth. Then came the tongue, rolling over my ass crack like molten silk. My knees buckled. I clutched at the smooth, damp floor, nearly sobbing with desire.

He circled closer to the sweet spot, his tongue flicking and gliding.

'Now push open,' he commanded softly.

I moaned again in shame and desire. Had I ever done anything more perverse – or more exciting?

'It's dirty,' I whispered, but I felt the body part under discussion flutter seductively. My tongue might protest, but my asshole certainly liked the idea.

And so I pushed, gingerly at first, then harder, opening myself wider and wider, hungry to be seen, filled, loved. My pussy and clit ached in sympathy, longing for his touch. His lips were on me again, and I fought to keep myself open through the hot, ticklish sensation as he kissed me French-style, the tip of his tongue darting into the opening, in and out, in and out. I could feel it in my toes, my teeth, and most of all, in my cunt, which throbbed and drooled with envy.

'Touch me in the front, too. Please?'

The professor pulled away, taking the warmth and softness with him. My body stiffened in regret.

'You are the expert,' he whispered. 'I would not presume.'

I groaned, too desperate to argue that this was no time to be modest about his abilities. But maybe it did make sense to let him concentrate on his specialty while I focused on mine. I slipped my hand between my legs just as he resumed his attentions to my behind. The whole lower half of my body hummed in stereo, front and backside burning, tingling, spinning round and round the twin poles of my finger and his tongue.

Still I wanted more. Surely he did, too? Given his connoisseur's enthusiasm for analingus, butt-fucking would very likely be another of his areas of expertise.

'Please, *Sensei*. Would you make love to me . . . *back there*?'

He paused in his work. 'I would like that very much . . .' he faltered, 'but it is not my role to interfere. I must only pleasure you in a manner your husband does not.'

My husband? Why did he have to bring that up at a time like this? But the image that flashed into my head like a warning was not Yuji's face. Instead, I saw the figure of the starving demon at the bridge, grasping at something warm and sweet, careless of the cost.

I knew exactly how the creature felt.

The professor laid a soothing hand on my back. He seemed to understand. 'I will try my best to make you happy. Remember this is all a dream. The brief dream of a spring night.'

He parted my cleft gently. I opened myself to his tongue, his promises. Because of course, the professor was right. It was just like a dream. My lover had no name. He didn't even have a face now. He was nothing but sensation, a fantasy man like all the others.

And my fantasy man always knows exactly what I want. He knows to tease my crack with cat-like lapping motions while my finger finds its rhythm on my clit again. When I push my asshole open, he understands that I'm begging for more of those quick tongue stabs that fill me with molten pleasure and prickly shame all tangled up together in a delirious brew. He senses from the way my thighs shake, from the helpless mewing sounds in my throat that the pressure is building inside me. So he stops for an instant, then rolls his tongue up and down my ass crack, because he knows it will drive me crazy, but I love it too. He won't touch me anywhere else, but that's exactly what's turning me on − constriction as art − and it is, because my whole being, my whole life, is his tongue buried in my ass. I know my orgasm is near and he does, too, because he's flicking my taut lips back there, up and down, just like I'm flicking my own clit and then, finally, I feel it coming, pounding hard on sharp, burning hooves, galloping up from my asshole, exploding from my throat in a sobbing whinny of ecstasy.

And when my fantasy lover stands and shoots hot spunk all over my back and ass with an otherworldly cry, when he wipes me clean with tender strokes of the bathing towel, even then, after my own pleasure has faded, I tell myself it's a dream. The kind I've had a thousand times before. A horny housewife lets a complete stranger lick her ass in a hot spring bath. It's a fantasy, of course. What else could it be?

CHAPTER SIX

It was all just a dream. And I'll never do it again. Never.

My footsteps were softer, less certain, on the journey back to real life. Denial, regret, fear of discovery. An unfaithful wife was supposed to feel all of these things, and I did. A little.

But what I really felt as I glided down the silent hallway was something quite different. Pure exhilaration. There were other ways to satisfy my desire. I could still come with a man I didn't love. I could be free, for one hour, then slip back into my old life as easily as I slipped back into my *yukata* and left the bath without a backward glance. Yet even then, part of me knew my encounter with the professor was something more: the first step of a journey, a baptism into a new life.

Part Eight

LUSTS OF LEARNED MEN
(Osaka, 1990)

CHAPTER ONE

If you'd told me the day I met Matt McDonald that having mind-blowing sex with him on the floor of our office would signal the end of my marriage, I would have laughed in your face.

To begin with, he was glaringly American, with red hair, blue eyes, and the gawky cuteness of a former child actor who'd outgrown the charm of a snub nose and freckles. His jokes were relentless, if rarely funny, and he seemed to have no doubt that he and his countrymen were the most enlightened and desirable males on the planet.

Even if I had found him the least bit attractive, the fact that he was married to a Japanese woman and had a baby daughter made him completely off limits. At that point in my life I still had principles. I didn't have sex with married men – a category which, I had to admit sadly, included my own husband. Granted, the professor at the hot spring may have been married in his real life, but I'd convinced myself within a week that what happened between us didn't count. He wasn't real. I didn't even know his name.

But I saw Matt often and he was all too real in the worst way. We shared the English instructors' office at the women's junior college, and so we were thrown together every Tuesday and Thursday between classes – me, Matt, and the mountain of ungraded papers, chocolate bar wrappers and opened cans of pre-sweetened vending machine coffee he called his desk. At first I thought he might not have read the poorly translated teacher's handbook they'd given me with my contract — 'All employees will keep his room tidy to show the pure heart of our college' — but I quickly realized he did it on purpose to thumb his nose at the fussy administrators. Japan was a perfect place for a cowardly Western rebel. You could break a dozen rules of etiquette in a day and get that bad boy frisson without anyone really giving a damn, because the Japanese were expecting you to do it wrong anyway.

If all of this wasn't bad enough, I found out on the very first day of the semester that Matt McDonald was a liar.

I walked into the office to find Matt was in conference with a student, which meant he was lounging back in his chair, hands behind his head, one foot propped on the open drawer of his desk.

'It's true, Emiko,' he was saying. 'My uncle owns McDonald's. I helped him invent the Chicken McNugget because I didn't like hamburgers as a child.'

'Eeeeh? Mattoo-*sensei*'s family is very great,' squealed the slim nineteen-year-old seated primly in the opposite chair.

'It doesn't seem like such a big deal when you grow up with it,' he said with a grin. 'Oh, here's the new *sensei*. I'm sorry, New *Sensei*, I forgot your name.'

'*Yoshikawa desu. Yoroshiku onegaishimasu,*' I murmured.

The young woman stood, bowed and rattled off a

more humble version of the usual introductory greetings. Then she added, 'Yoshikawa-*sensei*'s Japanese is very good.'

'Oh no, I have a long way to go.'

'Well, I am late for my class now. Thank you.' Emiko bowed to me yet again and then turned to Matt. 'Thank you very much for your help, Mattoo-*sensei*.'

'My pleasure. And next time you're at McDonald's with your friends, remember me.'

Emiko retreated with a trill of giggles, blushing prettily.

'That's interesting,' I said with some hesitation because, of course, it was possible I was sharing an office with the heir of one of Japan's most popular imports. 'I thought Ray Kroc took over McDonald's around thirty years ago and it wasn't in the family any more.'

Matt snickered. 'Maybe. I wouldn't know. Just to warn you, if you hear some rumors, I didn't go to high school with Madonna either.'

After seven years in Japan, I'd become fairly good at the native custom of adapting my language and behavior to the requirements of each social encounter, and I was confident I knew just how to deal with my new colleague.

'So, Matt, are you always so full of shit or did I just get you on a good day?'

Still lounging, Matt turned his head toward me and gave me an insolent once-over, from my crisp white blouse to my sensible black pumps.

God help me if he found me 'attractive' and thus a

worthy target for his adolescent games. Fortunately, the glint in his eyes faded almost immediately. He probably didn't go for my type either. Too many bad memories of getting turned down for dates back home.

'I do anything it takes to get me through the afternoon. And it's a pleasure to see you again, too, Ms *O-jôzu-desu-ne*,' he drawled, mimicking Emiko's compliment of my Japanese.

'Aren't you afraid you'll get caught saying such crazy things to students?' Not to mention to me. This place was so image conscious, I wouldn't have been surprised if they bugged the office.

'Do you think the little miss is going to check my family background and then report me?'

In spite of myself I smiled. It was pretty unlikely.

'See, Yoshikawa-*sensei*, isn't it a lot more fun when you don't have a stick up your butt?'

An interesting choice of words, I thought, as I flashed on the image of myself bending over the edge of the hot spring bath with the professor's tongue buried inside me. A laugh bubbled up in my throat. I looked him straight in the eye. 'Don't knock it until you've tried it. If done properly, the sensations can be amazing.'

Matt's head jerked back. It clearly wasn't the response he'd been expecting. But the next moment he was grinning again, a new twinkle in his eyes.

This might be fun after all.

I knew that's exactly what he was thinking, although reading minds was supposed to be something you did with Japanese men. Being with Matt took me straight back to the world of Caroline's parties: the smell of beer, tortilla chips and pizza all mixed up with the heady certainty I'd have my way with him – if not someone better – before the night was through.

CHAPTER TWO

My instinct turned out to be right, but Matt and I coasted halfway through the year on insulting banter and junior high double entendres before we actually slept together. The fateful afternoon began unremarkably enough with Matt inviting me out for a beer at the *yakitori* shop by the station.

'Sorry. I've got stuff to do at home.'

'Yuji coming home for dinner?'

'Oh, god, no. I don't even remember the last time that happened.' I bit my lip. That was a mistake. With all of our teasing and bawdy talk, I tried to keep my real life away from Matt.

'Then how else are you going to spend the evening? Eat instant ramen in front of the TV and then pet your kitty?'

In fact, he'd gotten my evening schedule down perfectly. Dinner would be something quick from a package, then I'd probably watch one of those dramas where the neglected wife goes to a love hotel with her husband's best friend, then backs out at the last minute, even though I'm yelling at her through the TV the whole time, 'Go ahead and fuck him for Christ's sake!' And yes, I'd probably have my hand down my pants for dessert.

'But you must have family duties, Matt. Isn't Sachiko waiting for you?'

'She's probably busy with Erika. Besides, she's happy when I stay late because she thinks it means I've gotten a promotion or something. Come on. We can compare notes on the fingerprinting ritual at the ward office, and all the other benefits of life as a foreigner in the Land of the Rising Sun.'

'All right, but don't pressure me to go to a love hotel with you afterwards, OK?'

'Scout's honor,' Matt said, holding up crossed fingers.

An hour and a beer later, he had me in stitches with his imitation of the college president, a pompous little guy as wide as he was tall, who used any excuse for a 'meeting' to practise his English on us.

' "A stitch in time saves nine",' Matt lisped, giving me a sly look that was an amazingly accurate parody. ' "That is common saying in America, no?" '

'Hey, I think you definitely have a future in Japanese higher education.' Beneath the alcohol buzz, I realized I was having a very good time after all.

'Excuse me, would you like another beer?' the chirpy waitress interrupted.

Matt nodded.

'And your wife?' she asked.

He gave me a devilish look. 'What do you say, honey?'

'Just to let you know, we're getting a divorce,' I told her in Japanese. 'And yes, I think that calls for another beer all around.'

Eyes wide, the young woman scurried away.

'Ouch,' Matt said, 'that is a sort of tender subject for me.'

In the interest of collegial kindness, it only seemed right to pretend I was sorry. 'Poor baby. Did you have a fight with the old ball and chain or something?'

'Not exactly. It's worse in a way,' he said, taking a big swallow of his new glass of beer. 'Last night I made the mistake of crawling into bed with Sachi and Erika. They still sleep together, which is great for my sex life, as you might imagine. Anyway, I said to Sachi "who do you like better, me or the kid?" It was a joke, right? But she said, "Of course, I must choose my child." '

I wondered if his prissy tone was an accurate imitation.

'Now I know where I stand. So much for jokes, eh?' he added gloomily.

'They have their limitations.'

Matt studied his beer. 'By the way, that's what I like about you, Lydia. You laugh at my jokes.'

'Wrong again, Mattoo-*sensei*. I'm not laughing with you, I'm laughing at you.'

'Keep it up. You know I love it.' He grinned. 'What about you? Is everything happily ever after with a Japanese guy?'

I blame the beer for what I said next. Two on a nearly empty stomach tipped the balance from bubbly to surly in an instant. 'Oh, I see, is that why you asked me out? To satisfy yourself that my marriage is as bad as yours?'

His eyes turned steely. 'No. I was just trying to be friendly, as a matter of fact.'

I knew he was telling the truth.

I covered my face with my hands. The saucy bitch act was wearing thin, even for me. And now I was making a spectacle of myself with tears which were spilling down my cheeks. Suddenly Matt was on the bench beside me, his arm around me. I wanted to pull away, but I didn't want to make more of a scene either, and then it started feeling nice, the warmth and the smell of him taking me back to another place and time when it was all an adventure.

'It's OK, it's OK,' he said over and over, but of course he was back to lying again, because nothing about it was OK. Not the way he stroked my arm, not the way his touch sent sparks shooting straight to my pussy, not the way I buried my face in his shoulder and whispered – *Let's get out of here* – or the fact that our steps slowed in front of the rent-by-the-hour love hotel half a block down the narrow street from the train station.

'They have these fuck hotels all over the place, but who's having the sex? Not me, that's for sure,' I mumbled. The tears were dry, but the self-pity was still flowing.

'I'm not on the list either.'

We stood there for a moment, staring at the glowing sign advertising the rates for a short 'relaxation' stay or the all-night package.

I don't remember if he took my hand or I took his, but suddenly the ground grew spongy and I was floating again, through the curtains at the hotel entryway, past the picture gallery of the rooms on the wall, down the long corridor to our room. As I stepped inside with Matt McDonald, the last guy in the world

I ever thought I'd fuck, I had the strangest thought: If the waitress saw us now, she'd think we made up and the divorce is off.

CHAPTER THREE

Our first room was ordinary by love hotel standards. Later we'd go for laughs – the camping theme room with a log bed and day-glo stars twinkling on the ceiling, or Matt's favorite dungeon room, with a fake guillotine and a black leather fuck swing. This one just had the basics: a bed, a mirror on the ceiling, a TV with pay-per-view porn, a vibrator by the bed and a vending machine of condoms.

I immediately rolled onto the bed. How easily it came back to me, as if the party slut had been curled up inside me all along, waiting for her chance to come out and play.

Matt didn't join me. He sat down on the edge of the bed, head bowed.

'Hey, got cold feet? Or should say a cold cock?'

He smiled, but I could tell it was just a reflex. 'God, Lydia, I don't know what to say. I think you're very hot. I actually look forward to coming to classes now just so I can talk to you. How's that for a miracle? But I'm thinking if we take this too far, it might get a little weird at work and . . .'

I felt a stab of anger, an ice-cold dagger to the stomach. He'd waited until now to start thinking? Things were already weird, far beyond repairing. I'd dragged Matt into a love hotel and he rejected me. What could be more pathetic than that? The only way to fix it now was to pull him down with me, so he couldn't gloat, he couldn't feel sorry for me. We'd be equals in degradation. Best of all, I knew just how to do it – words. They didn't work with Yuji, but I knew they would with Matt.

'You're not really a bad boy at all, are you?'

'What?'

'You seemed so cool, breaking all the rules. The messy desk. Those crazy stories you tell the students. But at heart, you're just a nice boy. It's OK, though. Everyone pretends in this country. Just like you said that first day, we do what we have to do to get by.'

'Give me a break, Lydia.'

He was angry. I'd touched him that way at least, and it made me bold enough to reach over and fold my fingers over the erection poking up through his khakis. He let out a faint moan of surprise.

'How about this? Don't you think it's a little insincere to be giving me a holier-than-thou lecture on why we shouldn't fuck when you're hiding this big, hard boner in your pants? How long since you've had a good blow job, Matt?'

He exhaled. 'A very long time.'

'So, go ahead, tell me the truth. Tell me you don't want me to kneel between your legs and suck your hard cock until you shoot in my mouth. I swallow, you know. I'm the kind of girl who drinks it all down. But if that's not what you want, then just be honest.'

'I'm not so nice, Lydia.' He shifted on the bed, pushing up against my hand.

'Really now? Are you a bad boy who likes to have his cock sucked?'

'Yeah,' he breathed.

And that's how I first had my way with Matt McDonald, but can you really call it forcing someone when he lifts his ass so you can pull his pants down to his ankles? Or when he lets out a quivering 'ah' when you tell him you're going to suck his cock now, but he'd better not come too fast or you'll have to give him a spanking? Or when he groans as you take him between your lips and arches up into your mouth, and his cock gets rock hard? Is it forcing someone when he says yes, yes, he does want to fuck you, but you make him eat you first, because you want to bring him all the way down into the wet sticky slime of lust with you? Maybe it is, because even after he comes inside you, bellowing and jerking with each spasm, he's still in your power, curling himself around you, whispering, *Jesus, you're hot, Lydia, better than a dream. Much better.*

CHAPTER FOUR

The floating world, that's what they call it in Japan, the neon-lit world of dreams and desire and sex with people you aren't married to, all rolled up together. It really did seem like I was floating that autumn, my feet hardly touching the sidewalk as Matt and I hurried along the narrow streets to the love hotel of our choice, at a different stop along the Hankyu line, every Tuesday and Thursday at dusk.

I quickly discovered that Matt liked me to tie him up. S&M games were popular in Japan – after all, Matt remarked, they even have a whole verb tense called the 'suffering passive' – so the dungeon room was often taken when we arrived after our classes. But almost every room had handcuffs and tethers tucked in the nightstand and hooks at each corner of the bed for bad boys to get their just punishment.

'This is the third day in a row you didn't finish your homework. Do you have anything to say for yourself, Matthew?'

'I'm sorry, Miss Evans. I didn't have time.'

'Didn't have time? What were you doing instead? You were probably too busy masturbating, weren't you?'

'No, Miss Evans.' His reply had more than a touch of rebellion.

'Matthew, I don't have time for games. I want you

to look me in the eye and tell me the truth. I'm your teacher and I'm doing this for your own good. Did you play with yourself last night when you should have been doing your homework?'

His blue eyes met mine. I saw arousal, defiance, amusement, a cocktail of teenage boy emotions that went straight to my head.

'Yeah, OK, Miss Evans, I jacked off ten times.'

I gasped theatrically. 'This behavior calls for extreme measures, young man. First I'm going to tie your hands to this bed. Given your low and lustful character, I have no doubt you will try to diddle your weenie while I administer the punishment.'

Occasionally we'd break the scene to joke about filming a porn series 'Women's Junior College Teachers in Bondage'. Or Matt would urge me try out my new and effective methods of discipline on our students every time they misused definite and indefinite articles. But usually, by the time I had him secured in the leather cuffs, Matt was all earnestness, his face taut, his breath coming fast.

It was only natural then that I did to him some of the things the professor did to me, in another dream. I pushed Matt's legs up and stroked his ass, tickling, circling, spanking him gently now and then, right on the tender flesh, until he moaned helplessly and promised he'd be good.

'Well, Matthew, I suppose you do deserve one more chance, but first you have to finish your make-up assignment. I'm going to untie you now, but you're only allowed to use your hands for one purpose – to play with my nipples while I come on your face.'

'Yes, Miss Evans,' he'd sigh as I straddled him. Thoroughly converted to the path of teacher-pleasing diligence, he'd lick and strum me with his tongue under my careful direction until his face was as slick as a glazed doughnut. By then I was ready to roll on a condom and ride him. I could tell by his grunt of pleasure as I glided onto his cock that he was ready, too.

All that autumn, I kept waiting for the regret to come, but it never did. Even after I boarded the train toward home, I kept on floating in my dream world, watching real life roll by the window like a ribbon. Pachinko parlors with glaring lights and garish floral sprays. A quick, fluorescent-blue glimpse into a cram school classroom, rows of dark heads turned to a young male teacher gesturing at a blackboard. Another love hotel done up like Sleeping Beauty's castle with turrets and lavender neon, inside which, no doubt, other shadowy figures groaned and grunted and tied each other to beds.

As the train slid closer to Osaka station, I told myself stories to soothe my passage back into that other life waiting for me there. What I did after work for a few hours had nothing to do with Yuji. It was a trip to another land, a quick slip-slide into my own past – romping on Caroline's bed with my latest conquest. I didn't love Matt. I didn't even really like him. In fact, I was saving myself from having a real affair. Yuji was probably doing exactly the same thing himself with those hostesses anyway. I was beginning to see the wisdom of my old boyfriend Hiroyuki's claim

– sex didn't count if you did it with a foreigner. It wasn't the same thing at all.

Back in the apartment, I always took a leisurely bath to wash away any lingering scent. Another benefit of my waking dream was that I didn't seem to need sleep. I could wait up for Yuji, welcome him with a light heart, a sweetness I hadn't felt in a long time. Being with Matt made me appreciate my husband more. I could savor the arresting contrast of his white shirt against his golden skin, the smoothness of his chest, the way we fit together just right. To be honest, it thrilled me to make love to two men in one night, to compare the fragrance of their skin, the touch of their fingers on my breasts, the sensation of their cocks moving inside me.

And so the dream went on as I made love to my husband on into the early morning hours. After a while it didn't seem to be a dream anymore. The whole thing was impossible – a fantasy – and yet I was doing it. And getting away with it. Then came the day I woke up.

CHAPTER FIVE

Matt and I were just about to step out of the office one frosty January evening for our usual hotel romp, when I practically tripped over a Japanese woman pushing a little girl in a stroller through our door.

'Excuse me,' I said in Japanese, more surprised by the sight of a child in this 'young maiden's' realm than the physical impact of my collision with the stroller.

'Sachi? I didn't know you were coming to campus,' Matt said over my shoulder. He didn't exactly sound pleased.

Sachiko wasn't fazed. 'I told you this morning we'd be visiting my cousin in Kobe. Erika had so much fun playing with Ruriko, we stayed all day. Since your classes run so late this semester, I thought we would stop by and pick you up. Maybe we can have dinner at the *yakitori* place by the station?'

'Yeah, sure,' Matt mumbled.

'I'm Lydia, Matt's office mate,' I said, extending my hand. Matt had made no move to introduce us.

'Nice to meet you, Lydia. Matt has said nice things about you.' Unlike most Japanese women, her handshake was firm. I was pretty sure she was fibbing about the nice things, but I felt an immediate liking for her. Somehow I'd assumed Matt would go for the cute, dizzy type, but Sachiko had an austere, intelligent face. I let my gaze drop discreetly to her figure, which was more matronly than willowy, not exactly what I would have predicted from Matt's preferences in his students. It took me another moment to realize his wife was pregnant.

'This is Erika.' Sachiko gestured to the little girl who unbuckled herself from the stroller and ran to Matt with a giggle. She was far more adorable than any spawn of Matt's had the right to be. I had to admit, though, that she looked a lot like him, Matt's features reworked into a dark-haired doll.

'Erika-*chan* is very cute.' I addressed this remark in Japanese to Erika herself, who turned and regarded me with knowing brown eyes. I got the unsettling feeling she knew exactly what I did with her father on Tuesday and Thursday evenings.

'Say "hello", Erika,' Sachiko prompted, but the little girl buried her face in Matt's legs. 'I'm afraid she's very stubborn.'

'Just like her dad?'

Sachiko laughed. 'Exactly.'

Matt and Erika regarded us with the same angry scowl.

'Erika wants chocolate,' the little girl cried suddenly, stretching toward a twisted Meiji bar wrapper on the corner of Matt's desk and knocking it onto the floor.

'OK, let's go get dinner,' Matt barked. 'We'd better get Erika out of here before she messes up my desk.'

Sachiko and I exchanged glances. Understanding flashed between us: *How could anyone mess up that mountain of trash?*

As if on cue, we both burst into giggles.

Matt clicked his tongue in annoyance. 'Come on, Sachi. You know they're not wild about teachers' families visiting the campus. Bye, Lydia.' He pushed his wife and daughter through the door, then paused to give me a lingering glance over his shoulder.

His eyes bored into me, but somehow I couldn't read him this time. He certainly wasn't happy, but why take it out on me, just because he wasn't going to get any tonight? Then again, maybe he was.

CHAPTER SIX

When I walked into the office on Thursday, Matt slammed into me like a tornado.

'All right, Lydia, what the fuck did you think you were doing?'

'Excuse me?'

'Tuesday night. Those nasty little games you were playing with my wife.'

'What are you talking about? I introduced myself. I said your daughter was cute. What's wrong with that?'

'You were making fun of Sachiko.'

'I wasn't making fun of her. Hey, if anyone's messing around with Sachiko, it's you.'

He glared at me. His cheeks were splotched with red, and his hands were shaking. I felt my own hands begin to tremble. For a moment I was afraid he might hit me, but instead he scooped up his folders and textbooks and stomped out of the room.

After our first class, he was calmer, even contrite. 'Sorry about that, Lydia. It's just weird for me to see my wife and my mistress together.'

I let out a quiet sigh of relief. Things were back to normal. I grinned at him. 'Your mistress? I don't think so. Mistresses get furs and diamond rings from their lovers. I get to pay half the hotel bill.'

Matt's face clouded again. 'You know, I used to

think your bitch act was kind of cute, but now I realize it's not an act. You really are a bitch.'

He grabbed his class folders and stalked out again, knocking another stack of books and papers all over the floor between us.

It took a moment before I could breathe. My head was reeling and my cheeks burned as if he'd actually slapped me.

Who couldn't take a joke now?

We didn't speak for the rest of the day, or the whole Tuesday after that. I wasn't going to apologize until he did. Sure, I'd been insensitive, but he was the one taking out his guilt on me.

By the end of the third day of pitched battle, my face was aching from the forbidding, humorless expression I was using to shield myself against his stern, accusing glower, but as the Japanese say, *shikata ga nai*, there was no way around it. I only had to make it through a few more weeks until final exams. The president had extended my contract for another year, but unlike Matt, if it really got unbearable, I could always go back to the housewife gig. Still, I liked things better the way they were before.

After Matt stomped out for the last time that day, I flipped off the overhead light and stood at the window in the darkness, gazing out over the lights of the town. In the distance a train slithered by on the elevated tracks, the windows glowing like opalescent markings on a magical snake. How could everything be so beautiful out there and so dark in here? Yuji had turned me down again the previous Thursday night. *Sorry, Lydia, I'm pretty tired*. And I was pretty tired of his heavy, apologetic smile. Without Matt, I had to face the emptiness again. Somehow it was harder this time around.

The doorknob rattled softly. I jumped.

It was probably the cleaning lady, a bent, rounded old woman with more gold teeth than white. It certainly wouldn't leave a good impression to be caught lurking here in the darkness. I reached for my purse and leather shoulder bag briefcase. 'I'm just leaving,' I'd trill. 'Thank you so much for your services.'

But the figure in the doorway was tall. Male. Foreign. Not much into cleaning. It was Matt. He closed the door behind him and locked it.

We stared at each other. His eyes glittered in the shadows. I couldn't read him at all, but I knew I was afraid.

He stepped closer and took me in his arms. At first his kiss was soft, almost tender. This was strange. We rarely kissed and when we did it was more like a bratty dare – I'd spit back his spunk after a blow job or he'd let me lick my own pussy juice from his lips.

His tongue darted into my mouth. A boyfriend's goodnight kiss. Sweet, hesitant. Then his grip on my shoulders tightened and he pressed into me harder, harder still, until I was sure he would leave bruises.

This is like a rape. Except it wasn't.

My whole body was burning with lust and triumph. He wanted me. Someone wanted me this badly.

We sank to the floor behind his desk, crumpling the papers, kicking aside the books. He fumbled with the buttons of my blouse. I let him do it, curled up in his arms like a helpless little girl.

'You're shaking,' he said, almost gently. But then a chillier light glimmered in his eyes. 'Is that because you want it, Lydia? You've gone a whole week without it, haven't you?'

I nodded. It was true, but it was also just a game, wasn't it? A little reversal of our teacher—bad boy scenes. Yet something was different. I wasn't sure exactly what, but I did want it, and I'd give him whatever he asked to get it.

'You want it so bad, you can't wait for the hotel. You have to fuck me right here on the office floor. Isn't that right?'

'Yes,' I whispered.

He yanked off my blouse and pushed my bra straps down. Without unsnapping me, he lifted my breasts out of the cups and began stroking the nipples.

'Nice and responsive as always. I've never met a woman who likes to fuck as much as you do, Lydia.'

Maybe that's a reflection of your bad technique and overall egotism in bed? The words flashed into my head, but I didn't say it. I closed my eyes and yielded to his fingers as they twisted and tweaked the sensitive pink tips. Was he right? Was I the most desperate, sex-hungry female in the whole wide world?

'Let's get these pantyhose off. I'll bet you're sopping wet between your legs. I remember the first day of school, you minced in here in your perfect little teacher suit, Little Miss Priss. Who would guess this is what you really wanted, to be lying back on the carpet with your legs spread wide and a dick up your cunt. It is what you want, isn't it?'

'Yes,' I moaned.

'What if the cleaning lady walked in right now?' he whispered in my ear. 'What if she sees you here on the floor naked? She'll tell the president, and I'm sure he'll be the first to come down for a look at your pink cunt, all spread wide. The early bird catches the worm, eh, Lydia?'

Through the lust, I felt a pang of fear. We could get caught. That part wasn't a game. 'Stop the bullshit, Matt. Come on, let's do it quick.'

'I don't think I like your tone, Miss Priss. First I want an apology for your rudeness.'

The bastard. He knew how to press his advantage. But why not use the sex to work things out between us? Matt wasn't always as clueless as he seemed.

'I'm sorry. I was rude. And inconsiderate. I am sorry, Matt.' I hoped he'd understand I was really apologizing for something else.

'That's a good start. Now I want to hear you ask politely for what you want.'

'Please, I want . . .' the words caught in my throat.

'Yes? I'm waiting.'

'I want you to fuck me, please.'

'Just as I thought. And how do you want me to fuck you, Lydia?'

'Me on top?' It was still the easiest way for me to come and in fact, I seldom let Matt do it any other way. But he was in charge this time.

'Hmm. That has its advantages. While we fuck, I can spank your ass for being such a naughty, horny slut. But I'm afraid we have a problem. I don't have a condom on me. You see, I didn't realize you'd be so desperate you had to do it right here. But I have a

225

great idea. I'll let you suck my cock. After I come in your mouth, I'll have to send you home all empty and wet. Maybe you can pick up a salaryman on the train? Stand right in front of him and wiggle your pussy in his face so he can smell how much you want it. Those guys will fuck anything as long as they're not married to it.'

I stiffened. Now he was pushing it too far, too close to the tender wounds of my real life. Deep inside the lust, a tiny white spark burst into flame, a cool illuminating light. If he wanted to settle the score with sex games, I was more than ready to take him on. He had his apology, now it was time to dust myself off and get back in the saddle. Matt might not know it yet, but he'd be the one moaning for mercy in the end.

I gave another sigh of helpless desire – this one quite calculated – and pressed myself against him. 'I actually do want to suck your cock, Matt. I want to taste you. I love to drink your come. Please let me do it?'

Matt fell for it hook, line and sinker. He snorted and unbuckled his belt. 'You really are every man's dream, aren't you?'

In fact, I did like to suck his cock. I liked the way he babbled and used the Lord's name in vain and acted so damned grateful. This time I rolled out the royal treatment. Tiny tongue flicks and figure-eights over the sensitive skin below the head. Long, ice-cream cone licks from his balls to the taut purple helmet crowning it all. Soon enough I had him sighing and thrashing and pawing at my hair. That's when I stopped.

'All right, cowboy, now it's time for a little ride.'

Matt looked at me, eyes wide. 'Are you nuts? I wasn't kidding. I really don't have a condom.'

'Don't worry. It's no problem unless you have a disease. I'm clean, you can trust me on that. As for the other part, well, I can't have kids. I'm sure of that, too.' I didn't admit that I wasn't really so sure. I planned to ride him to a quick climax, then pull off before he came. Of course, I knew a few drops might leak out, but I did have three years of unprotected sex with Yuji, and a dozen careless encounters with other guys before that with nothing to show for it. The risk seemed small.

Matt narrowed his eyes.

'Come on. Don't you want to feel my bare pussy and spank my ass until I come on your cock?'

His gaze slipped sideways and his mouth moved wordlessly for a few moments, like a fish. It pleased me that he couldn't seem to say the word 'no'.

'Lydia, are you sure?'

I smiled and straddled him, holding the tip of his penis against my very wet, very swollen pussy lips. 'I'm sure. You want in or not?'

He grimaced and pushed up, sliding into me with a low groan. Suddenly, I knew exactly what was going through his American mind. I knew how good it felt to bury himself into my hot, naked flesh. I knew he didn't give a fuck if he wasn't supposed to, if it was wrong, if he might have to pay for it in the end one way or another, because guys never really had to pay, not in any way that mattered.

'God, you're good, Lydia. So hot and wet.'

'I thought you said I was a naughty slut. Can't you make up your mind?' I grunted, quickening my pace.

Through half-closed eyes, I saw his lip curl into a smile that was more like a snarl. A second later, his palm met my ass in a resounding slap.

'Aaah.' The impact sent a jolt straight through me that quickly dissolved into pleasure, foamy fingers of sensation creeping into the hollows of my body.

'You are bad,' he hissed, aiming his second blow directly into my ass crack.

'This is good, this is good,' I blabbered as I skidded over him. The spanking seemed to have released a gush of pussy juice from deep inside me, drenching us both.

'Do you like it when I spank your asshole, Lydia? Do you want me to do it again?'

'Yes. Oh, yes, please.'

Smack.

I winced from the blow, but immediately pushed my buttocks out in offering for more. It hurt, but it felt good, too, so good. Good and bad all mixed together. I was riding him hard, bouncing crazily above him. The blows grew softer, more focused, but each one drove me closer, closer. His other hand reached up to pinch my nipple and I cried out, too loud, my whole torso a rippling column of heat.

'You'd better come soon, Lydia. The cleaning lady will be here any minute.'

The taunting voice, the steady tattoo of his fingers

on my stinging hole, the friction of his belly against my clit, it was all too much. Maybe I wasn't in control now, but I didn't care. I'd planned to snatch my climax by stealth, then sneak away before he knew what had happened, but the spanking had gone to my head, muddling any thoughts or plans, and I bellowed out the news instead, thrusting my hips in rhythmic, tell-tale jerks.

Matt made quick use of the information. Before I knew it he was thrusting back, his face twisted in a grimace of ecstasy. I tried to pull off, but he grabbed my hips and pushed in deeper, shuddering.

I didn't have to wait for the evidence to know he'd come inside me. Under the circumstances, I had to put a good face on it. And hope to god the lie I told was true.

Usually things were clean with Matt. He dealt with the condom, I laid back and dozed in the afterglow. This time I had to hold one of the crumpled papers between my legs to catch his jizz as I dismounted — the homework of some poor girl named 'Michiko' — while Matt gallantly scooted over to get my purse, always stocked with the free tissues the banks handed out on the street corners. The room reeked of sex — grassy semen, the fresh-meat scent of female arousal. The cleaning lady might not have caught us, but she'd probably wonder just the same.

'That was fun,' he said once we'd mopped up. He hooked an arm around my shoulder and pulled me back to the floor. 'It's always good with you, Lydia. That's the problem.'

'Am I missing something? Exactly why is good sex a problem for you?'

He laughed and gave me a squeeze. I had to smile. It was fun with Matt, even I had to admit that. And easy. All it took was one good fuck and everything was back the way it was. Only better.

CHAPTER SEVEN

That night, in the bath, I took extra care to wash myself. I figured most of Matt's calling card had dripped out in a glistening wad on Michiko's composition, but I didn't want Yuji to get suspicious. Not that I expected any more action tonight. I didn't need it.

Kneeling at the faucet like a Japanese woman, I studied my foreigner's face in the low mirror. Temptress. Adulteress. Slut. I was, to be honest with myself, all these things. I'd never looked so beautiful. Maybe it was the mist in the air or simply the result of a good, hard come. Whatever it was, my cheeks were pink and glowing. My lips were plumped in a perfect Cupid's bow. My hair, slick against my neck, only made my face look sexier, more vulnerable. How different from the hollow-eyed, haunted ghost of two summers ago. Now a man wanted me. He couldn't get enough. Every man in the world would want me if they knew how hot I was, how much I loved to fuck.

The bathroom door rattled in its metal grooves. Yuji poked his head through the opening. 'May I join you?'

'You're home early. What time is it? Nine?'

'The client was sick. Probably a hangover from yesterday. No *tsukiai* tonight.' He raised his eyebrows suggestively. 'I might actually get to have some fun for a change.'

'I hope so,' I said, but my stomach tightened. If Yuji and I did it, would he know I'd been with someone else? Maybe if we made love in the bath, with all that water around us, he wouldn't notice if I was a little squishier inside?

He shed his clothes in the outer room and joined me in the bathroom. Instead of kneeling to wash he reached up to the tiny window in the wall and pushed it open. A current of cold air rushed into the room.

'What are you doing? We're going to freeze.'

'It's snowing,' he said, grinning like a child.

I slipped into the tub, exhaling as the hot water wrapped itself around me like a cloak. Yuji rinsed off quickly and joined me. Together we watched the thick flakes twirling outside the window. It was about to get better.

'*Kirei ni natta yo*.' Yuji touched my cheek. 'You've definitely gotten prettier. How did you manage that, when you started out so pretty?'

I laughed. I loved his compliments, when I could get them.

He pulled me closer. 'I like that about you, Lydia, even though you may not believe it. I like it that you do things differently. That you don't follow the rules.'

'So it seems,' I whispered in Japanese into his shoulder as his hands moved down over my back to cup my ass, still mildly tingling from Matt's flurry of slaps. Just then another strange image flashed into my head, the fat little college president nodding over us, pointing to a proverb in his book.

'When it rains, it pours.'

CHAPTER EIGHT

The nausea hit as I was passing by a fish market with Chieko on one of our museum outings during the school break. The smell was so horrible – a sickening brew of rotting fish guts and filthy seawater saturated with mercury and crude oil spills – that my stomach seemed to push straight up into my throat in protest.

'What's the matter?' Chieko asked, putting her hand on my shoulder as I stood hunched over on the sidewalk, holding my trusty Japanese lady's handkerchief over my mouth.

'It's that shop. The fish must be bad or something,' I choked.

Chieko glanced toward the shop and took a delicate sniff, then looked back at me with a smile.

'You're pregnant aren't you, Lydia? Why didn't you say anything? Congratulations. Haven't you and Yuji been trying for a while?'

'Oh, shit.' I hoped the handkerchief had muffled the words, but Chieko's expression told me she'd heard and understood well enough. In fact, it had been almost two months since my period, but that wasn't unusual for me. Being late was more a sign I wasn't meant for motherhood than otherwise.

Chieko took my arm and dragged me off to a coffee shop at the end of the block. She chose a table in the back corner and ordered us both lemon tea.

When the waitress had delivered our order, she leaned forward and said in a low voice in English, 'Lydia, do you have a lover?'

I nodded miserably.

'Is he Japanese?'

I shook my head, unable to meet her eyes.

'Do you want to be with . . . the other man?'

'Oh god, no.'

Chieko chewed her lip for a moment. 'I think this is a difficult situation.'

'That's an understatement if there ever was one.'

'Pardon?'

'I mean, you're right.'

'Yes.' Chieko studied me with concern. 'What are you going to do, Lydia-*san*?'

'Go to a doctor, I guess.'

'I know a hospital in Kobe. They are used to dealing with foreigners. That would be better, don't you think?'

I nodded.

'You know, I couldn't stand the smell of fish either. That's one way to tell,' Chieko confided. 'But after the operation, you'll be back to normal in no time.'

I'd assumed Chieko couldn't have children, but now I realized she was childless by choice. I wondered, fleetingly, who the father of her baby was — Taka or some passing college fling before him? Or was it also recent, the result of an affair, some research for her work?

The paternity of her child, of course, was trumped by a far more pressing question. Who was the father of mine?

The next day Chieko went with me to the clinic for the pregnancy test. The result was positive. After my assurance that my 'lover' would not want to be involved, Chieko insisted she would come along for the abortion too. 'That's what a friend does,' she said, squeezing my hand. She even called to make the appointment for me at the next available slot, the following Wednesday morning, and came up with my lie for Yuji, if it was needed. An all-day trip to Kyoto to see the plum blossoms.

I bowed and murmured my thanks, but part of me wondered if I might not choose real Kyoto plum trees over a Kobe abortion when the day arrived. Chieko seemed certain the baby wasn't Yuji's. I wasn't certain at all.

I spent the next few days dozing in bed, my stomach burning with nausea and guilt. I seemed to have the same dream over and over. I was in a delivery room and a nurse was holding a baby out to me. I studied the child's face, my heart pounding, but its features were twisted in a wail of hunger, and I still couldn't tell for sure. *You'll figure it out eventually*, the nurse said. Her expression was kind, even indulgent.

But the other voices, swirling through my head in dizzying circles, were less forgiving.

First came the low whisper, frightened and pleading: It has to be Yuji's. That's what you want. It's the only thing that will keep you together.

Then a knowing sneer, steeped in mockery: You know it's Matt's. He's so full of himself, it figures he'd have overachieving semen. Two brats to his credit and who knows how many more?

A husky, Caroline drawl: You idiot, you should have had the affair with Masaru instead. You could have the kid, the marriage, and some really hot sex and no one would ever be the wiser.

And then another voice, calm, even reasonable, but most frightening of all: Go ahead and have the baby. Whatever happens you can raise her yourself. That's what your mother did, and you turned out fine. Or did I?

When the day came, I went to Kobe with Chieko. Suddenly, I no longer had a choice to make. But as I lay on my futon, hugging my knees to my chest, still cramping and bleeding and wondering if I could ever scrub that antiseptic odor from my skin, I knew I did have to make a choice. No voices argued or scolded this time. What I had to do was painfully simple. The right thing always is.

Part Nine

THE FAIR CONCUBINE OF
A PROVINCIAL LORD
(Kyoto, 1991)

CHAPTER ONE

The next day I packed a bag and took the train up to Kyoto, with no explanation to Yuji but a brief note telling him I needed time to think things over and would call him soon. Given the circumstances, it might not exactly have been the 'right' thing, but it was as close as I could manage at the time.

In Japanese they call it *iede*, 'fleeing home', a venerable tradition among Japanese wives to give their husbands a little wake-up call. Ideally, the man is so undone by the absence of her care and affection, he follows her – the usual escape route leads to her parents' house – and promises anything to ensure her return. I'd heard, however, that some husbands are so busy with work, they never really notice the wife is gone.

My *iede* retreat was a budget hotel for foreigners in the northern district of the city, the kind of place where you could rent a six-mat room with a futon by the week. Yuji had no way to contact me, short of calling in the police. I'd resigned from my job at the junior college, telling them I suddenly had to return to the States to attend to my dying father. I never saw or spoke to Matt again.

A few dismal and blurry weeks later, I was sitting in the communal kitchen of the hostel, picking at some Sapporo instant ramen, when a peppy young woman from California named Ashley sat down beside me and sent my own life spinning.

'What do you know about working in one of those hostess bar places?'

'Absolutely nothing,' I said with a smile.

'I saw this ad in the paper and I thought it might be a good way to make some money, but I've heard the guys keep trying to touch you when they're drunk. Guys as old as my dad.' She screwed up her face and shuddered.

'It'll be a good chapter in your memoirs, though,' I said.

She laughed. 'I'm just trying to save up enough to get to Bali. Say, you don't speak Japanese, do you?'

'A little.'

'Would you, you know, consider calling the place for me? Just to get the information? Sometimes it's hard to understand their English, you know?'

It was easy enough to say yes to a fellow foreigner in need, but perhaps a little harder to explain why I ended up going for an interview myself the very next day. I even made an attempt to be serious about it. I put on make-up and the one 'nice' dress I'd brought with me. And, of course, I tucked my wedding ring in a pocket of my toiletries case. The woman on the phone had told me 'Club L.A. Woman' was always looking for foreign ladies who could speak Japanese – would I consider stopping by the club as well?

I figured it was a better way to spend the afternoon than staring at the stains on the wall of my room, even though I wasn't planning to take the job if it was offered. I wasn't expecting to be openly insulted either.

One look at me, and the *mama-san* frowned, not even bothering to offer me a seat at one of the tiny café tables. 'I'm sorry, Evans-*san*, I'm afraid you won't do for us. You sounded much younger on the phone. The gentlemen we entertain prefer a "fresh" look.'

I swallowed. I was only twenty-nine. Still girlish, like Mom, but with a worldliness that any man of true discernment would prefer over fatuous Ashley.

'That's unfortunate. I have taught English to Japanese businessmen for several years and am very familiar with the custom of after-hours socializing. I believe this experience would be of great value for such a position.' Especially for a foreigner, absurdly polite Japanese with lots of honorifics and self-effacing humility can serve as a very effective 'fuck you'.

The plump, thirtysomething *mama-san* studied me for a long moment, her gaze lingering on my breasts and legs. 'I'm afraid we can't hire you here, but I do know someone who caters to an older clientele. She is always looking for foreign ladies. If you're interested, I can give my friend a call and introduce you.'

'I would be grateful for the favor,' I said, bowing, although my mind was racing with another reply, another plan: *I'll get the other job and have rich guys dumping money in my lap that could have been yours, you orange-haired bitch.*

And that's exactly what I did.

CHAPTER TWO

Two days later, 'Meg' made her debut at the Club Rousseau. I certainly didn't mind pretending I was someone else every evening. It was just what the doctor ordered. Besides 'Megu' was far easier for the Japanese to pronounce than tongue-twisting 'Lydia'. And it's close to a Japanese word that means 'gift' or 'blessing'. I figured I could use some of both.

To her credit, the *mama-san* at L.A. Woman was right that Rousseau was a better match for me. Not only did I prefer the idea of working at a club named for a French philosopher who coined the idea of the blank slate – start over, fresh and new – but the setting calmed me. Fresh flowers, engravings of French chateaux on the wall, even a bookshelf tucked in the corner so I could read a little Voltaire if I got bored. The other hostesses, two elegant and poised Japanese women who took the foreign names of Marie and Aimée, were both about my age and friendly enough. Best of all, every evening before the customers began arriving, we got to sample the authentic *amuse-bouches* the Mama ordered in from a French restaurant.

Marie, who had a wide-eyed, almost Mediterranean look, was assigned to be my 'older sister' which meant she would sit with me for the first few nights to model the proper etiquette. I was nervous at first and almost giggled out loud when our first client arrived, a fiftyish man whose fair skin, gorgeous cheekbones and dark, soulful eyes gave him the look of a Japanese Louis Jourdan. Did the customers have to be interviewed to fit with the style of the place, too?

Clad in an exquisite, pale lavender kimono, the *mama-san* eased us through the introductions. The regular's name was Kimura, his companion a Taiwanese business partner named Mr Wu. It turned out Mr Wu had lived in Washington, D.C. for several years, and we spent most of an hour swapping memories of my childhood home. Kimura addressed a few polite questions to me in frighteningly flawless English, tinged with Oxford. I mixed a few whisky-and-waters, lit a few cigarettes, and had a surprisingly pleasant time.

The only person who squeezed my knee that evening was Marie, after the gentlemen had left to move on to the next activity of their evening, whatever that might have been.

'Good job, little sister,' she said in Japanese. 'I think you'll do fine.'

'Is it always this easy?'

'Not always,' she replied with a mischievous smile as she ushered me to a new group of customers at the neighboring table.

Some days later, the *mama-san* leaned into the small side room next to the bar that we used to dress and touch up our make-up before the night's work began.

'Megu-*chan*? Mr Kimura asked for you tonight. He'll be arriving shortly.'

Marie and Aimée exchanged a quick glance.

'This is a good sign,' Marie said brightly. 'By the way, if he asks you to dinner, it's OK to say yes. Kimura-*san* is a special friend of the Mama and if he likes you, your level goes up.' She held her palm out flat and lifted it several inches.

'But aren't we supposed to avoid seeing the customers outside of the club?'

'Dinner is OK,' Aimée broke in, adding a final coating of mascara to her eyelashes. Of our threesome, she clearly offered the charms of the traditional Japanese beauty with her oval face, prim mouth and slanting almond eyes. 'Then afterwards, you bring him to the club for a drink. It's like a warm-up for work.'

How did the Japanese always manage to make any job a twenty-four hour commitment?

'But I am allowed to turn him down, aren't I?'

Aimée turned and gave me a stern look. 'Yes, of course, but Kimura-*san* will take you to a very nice restaurant. It is a good chance to study Japanese culture for your research, I think.'

The story I'd given them was that I was working to save money to go back to graduate school in Japan – with a specialty in the seventeenth-century literature of the pleasure quarters in the golden age of the courtesan. So far, everyone seemed to buy it.

'Can I bring you along to the restaurant, Marie?' I said, hugging myself. 'To make sure I don't do anything wrong?'

Marie laughed into her hand, Japanese-style. 'Megu-*chan* is very funny. Go out front now. It's is best to greet Kimura-*san* when he arrives.'

As I walked out to the salon, I took a deep breath and willed my body to soften and relax. My days as a proper housewife were over, probably for good. As smooth as water flowing, I had joined the night side of Japan, where you said 'Good morning' at 9 p.m., and pleasure always came before duty. A world where it was not only OK to tell lies, it was expected. So what if 'the water trade' was based on the commodification of women? I'd turn the tables, let them come to me, fall at my feet, pay fortunes to squire me to dinner with no hope of repayment. Besides, I had a regular customer already. My charming, cultured company was in demand. It seemed like a long time since I had succeeded at something. Maybe I'd finally found the one place in the world where I belonged.

CHAPTER THREE

As March turned to April, I accepted Kimura's invitation to a restaurant that served *fugu*, or blowfish, famous for its deadly poison that would occasionally kill people in the hands of an incompetent chef. It was also extremely expensive, far beyond my budget in my past incarnation as Mrs Yoshikawa. My old life seemed farther away than ever. I'd sent a quick note to Chieko telling her I was OK, and another to Yuji saying I needed a little more time to figure things out, which really meant I didn't yet have the nerve to tell him I could never go back to pretending. In the meantime, I threw myself into a very different kind of make-believe.

In the brighter light of the restaurant, Kimura looked even more like Louis Jourdan in his role as Gaston, the jaded playboy who was saved by a schoolgirl's love. I kept expecting him to break into a chorus of 'Gigi'. But if he had his own reciprocal Hollywood fantasies about me, he kept them to close to his chest.

'Thank you for joining me this evening, Meg. Have you ever tried *fugu*?' Kimura asked in his fluent, if slightly stiff, English.

'This is my first time.' I met his gaze and smiled. 'I do hope it's not my last.'

I was here for one thing: to test out the tricks and

develop the instincts of a hostess. When should I soothe and stroke? When should I tease or provoke? Who Kimura was and what he really wanted didn't really matter as long as I managed the situation with subtlety and skill.

'I've been coming to this restaurant for many years and there've been no fatalities, to my knowledge,' Kimura said.

A kimonoed waitress arrived with our cocktail, grilled blowfish fins floating in *saké*.

We toasted and I took a sip. My lips tingled, then went momentarily numb.

'There is a touch of poison in the fins,' Kimura explained. 'It makes for an interesting sensation, doesn't it?'

I nodded serenely, but in truth my pulse was already racing.

The next course was *fugusashi*, a large platter of raw blowfish sliced so impossibly thin I could see the elaborate blue-and-white pattern of the dish through the translucent flesh.

I lifted a slice with my chopsticks and dipped it in the sauce. The silky texture, combined with the citrus-spiked sauce was one of the most delicious things I'd eaten in a very long time.

Kimura was watching me carefully.

'It's exquisite. The flavor is subtle, but always changing. Like it's still alive.'

He beamed, showing white, even teeth. I also noticed the spray of freckles across his nose, boyish and strangely endearing. 'I hoped you might enjoy it. Of course a scholar of seventeenth-century Japanese history would appreciate traditional Japanese pleasures.'

I shifted in my chair. The lie came easier to me in the softer lighting of the club. 'I'm hardly a scholar. Right now it's more of an interest.'

'Your hobby then?'

I pursed my lips into what I hoped was an appealing French moue. 'The Japanese often use the word "hobby" for *shumi*, don't they? But to me at least, it has a slightly silly connotation — boys with thick glasses who collect stamps or build model ships all day in their basements. But the real meaning in Japanese is something you truly love to do, as opposed to an obligation, right? Perhaps the better translation would be "passion"?'

Kimura listened to my English teacher's lecture with interest. I hoped, at least, he'd now feel I'd done something towards earning this very expensive dinner.

'You make a very good point, Meg. So then you would say Japanese history is your passion?'

'I suppose. I've always been fascinated by the parts of the Japanese spirit that have lasted over time.'

'Kyoto is a good place for that.'

'Yes, I still like to visit temples, but the smaller ones the tourists don't know. Sometimes I'm the only person there and the silence is so thick, I can hear voices whispering.'

'Ah, ghosts from the past. Do they speak to you in Japanese or English?' His eyes twinkled.

'They don't speak exactly. I'd say it's more of a feeling of something lingering.'

A bemused smile played over Kimura's lips.

'You must think I'm a crazy foreigner.'

'Not at all. I'm thinking of a place you might find interesting. Tsumago and Magome, a pair of old Edo towns, deep in the mountains on the old post road to Tokyo. The feudal lords used it to travel from their lands to the capital, but then the railroad was built far to the south and they fell into sleep. As much as is possible, the past still lives on there. Rather like your Williamsburg, I think.'

I leaned toward him. 'Are they far from here?'

'A few hours north of Nagoya. Not far, but more than a day's trip. There are also many authentic Japanese inns, where the lords and their retinues stayed for the night. Perhaps some day I can take you there.'

I hardly knew him well enough to take him up on the offer, but my imagination was already on the road to a land of rustic inns, brawny palanquin bearers, and swaggering samurai amusing themselves with the servant girls who had no choice but to accommodate every desire of the privileged and powerful guests. The vision shifted quickly to a different scene: me lying beneath Kimura, my simple kimono torn open, my legs spread as I submitted to his skillful thrusts.

Pull yourself together, Lydia. You aren't here for sex; it's business.

It was time for a deft change of subject, the verbal equivalent of brushing his hand off of my knee.

'What do you do, Mr Kimura?'

Strangely, we hadn't discussed his work at all, the mainstay of Japanese male identity.

'I am in the import business.'

The waitress arrived with the makings of the hot pot stew — a plate of mushrooms, vegetables and thicker pieces of blowfish, the flesh still quivering in its death throes.

'What do you import?'

'A variety of things.'

'Is it something you aren't allowed to talk about?' Perhaps Kimura's polished façade hid dark, forbidden secrets. Did he smuggle opium? Teenage prostitutes? The hides of endangered species? Or just deforest entire countries to provide chopsticks for the disposable lunches sold at every train station in Japan?

'Oh no, Meg, I could go on for hours about my work which I must do, unfortunately, when I'm at the office. This is my opportunity to forget about those things. I would much rather find out more about you.'

The first portion of fish stew was ready and Kimura busied himself arranging a sampling on a plate for me.

More about me, you ask? Well, Mr Kimura, I've just run away from my husband after I had an abortion. The baby probably wasn't his, but I'm not sure who the father is. In fact, in the last year, I've been so lonely and confused, I've had sex with any man who showed the slightest interest.

The truth probably wasn't the best answer for my current company.

I took a bite of fish to stall for time. It was richer than the sashimi, heady, intoxicating. I tilted my head flirtatiously.

'Don't forget, Mr Kimura, outside of the club, the

rules change. We're equals now. I won't tell you a secret, unless you tell me one, too.'

'Fair enough. But isn't it a venerable Western tradition for the lady to go first?'

I shrugged. I'd already decided to hand him a simple, inconsequential tidbit. 'All right. My real name's not Meg.'

Kimura's eyebrows lifted a few millimeters, the cultivated, Louis Jourdan equivalent of 'Duh, tell me something I don't know already.'

'May I ask your real name then?'

'Lydia.'

'Lydia,' he repeated, getting the 'L' sound perfectly, as if savoring something unusual and very delicious. I would later learn I should have saved this information for the afterglow of our first night together, as a celebration of our new intimacy, but patience was never my virtue.

'It's your turn to share, Mr Kimura.'

'My secret is more of a confession, I suppose.'

'I'll carry it to my grave,' I said, giving him a sidelong glance.

'Well, Lydia, you are not the first foreign lady from Rousseau I've asked to join me for dinner. I do it mainly to practise my English, as you may have guessed, with no further expectations. But in this case, I do hope we will meet again and become friends.'

Friends? If dinners like this are included, why not?

But I only smiled, the best response, Marie told me, because it suggested everything, but promised nothing. Even the exacting Aimée would surely have approved.

The waitress returned to ladle out the blowfish rice porridge, tinted pale gold with egg and thick with bits of fish and vegetables we'd left behind in the hot pot.

I picked up the bowl delicately in my left hand, chopsticks poised in my right. I planned to take a sip or two out of politeness and leave the rest. I tended to get sleepy if I went to work on a full stomach, which wasn't exactly ideal for feigning fascination with the patrons.

'Oh, my,' I breathed, my eyes tearing with pleasure.

'Delicious, isn't it? Porridge is usually a very simple dish, but this is the climax of the meal if you will. Some say *fugu* is an aphrodisiac, but science does not bear out that claim.'

I took another sip of the magical brew to see if I'd been dreaming – if anything it was more delicious, the most thrilling food I'd ever tasted in my life.

'I think the scientists made a mistake. I can understand now why people risk death for it.' My voice came out low and husky. 'Would it be terrible manners if I had more?'

'Not at all, Lydia. Allow me to serve you.' Kimura filled my bowl and set it carefully before me. He himself did not take another serving. He seemed content to watch me, the ghost of a smile on his face.

CHAPTER FOUR

At our very next meeting, I accepted Kimura's invitation to visit the old post towns of Tsumago and Magome in the Japanese Alps, an impulsive act that I'm sure would have pleased neither Marie nor Aimée if I'd told them, which I didn't. Already lies were creeping back into my life.

Throughout the first day of our trip, Kimura and I maintained the fiction of friendship. To all appearances I was on an outing with another fellow history buff, Chieko in male drag. But as we strolled around Tsumago, a village of preserved wooden structures as evocative of samurai days as he'd promised, my thoughts would often take a different turn.

It was hard to avoid the fact we were a couple — of sorts. Unlike Yuji, Kimura was only a few inches taller than I was, but his manner was more enfolding, protective. Japan was an easier place to be when he was by my side. I thought of the phrase *okagesama de* — to be in the benevolent shadow of another's influence. Kimura's attentiveness, his effortless navigation of the waters of Japanese custom, which could still be rough and rocky for me, was a soothing refuge. I knew I wasn't supposed to surrender so easily or enjoy it so much, but I was.

The first awkward moment came when the maid was laying out our futons after dinner. I was, as always, impressed with the innate ability of Japanese hotel staff to read the precise relationship between their guests. On trips with Yuji, the mattresses were placed so the edges nearly touched. Here they were separated by an ambiguous strip of *tatami* straw — No Man's Land — an accurate reflection of the lingering formality between us.

When the maid was gone, we sat in silence, the evening stretching before us. Kimura lit a cigarette.

It was then he suggested we stay another day.

'I'd love to, but I have to be at the club tomorrow night.'

'Could you manage to come down with a bad cold for a day or two?'

'I could, but I'm afraid I'm making it too easy for you. I'm supposed to tease you and make you twist in the wind for a year or so. I'm sure that's how Marie would do it.'

'Please don't worry about these things. We are "just friends" after all.'

'But in America friends are equals. You're indulging my samurai fantasy, and I don't feel like I'm doing anything for you in return.'

'You are teaching me American English, of course,' he replied.

It was then I hit upon another approach. 'I'm not doing so well as a teacher. Your English is excellent, of course, but the problem isn't how you say things, it's what you say. You're always so careful. So . . . Japanese.'

For the first time, Kimura showed visible annoyance. 'Is that so? Do you have a suggestion as to how I might practise American-style content?'

'Take a risk.'

'Ah, I see. Such as?'

'I don't know. Tell me a secret. A fantasy. Something you've never told anyone else.'

He lit up another cigarette. 'I fear I am failing you in this – I can't think of any that would amuse you. I don't collect school girls' panties or eat sushi from women's bodies or any of the other famous Japanese pastimes I read about in your magazines. I'm a rather dull and serious man.'

'Then tell me more about your dull life.'

'The content of this is typically Japanese too. I have a daughter in college and a son who may graduate from high school some day if he ever takes his studies seriously. And of course, I have a wife.'

We locked eyes for a moment. I gave a faint shrug.

'And your parents? Are they Kyoto natives or do you keep them tucked away in a picturesque village near here?'

'I'm afraid not. Both of my parents are deceased.'

'Oh, really? Mine, too,' I said cheerfully. 'I guess we do have something in common.'

He flashed me a look of surprise. 'I'm sorry for your loss. Were you very young?'

'I was three when my father died in a car accident. My mother died five years ago. Of cancer. Although she used to say she smoked to stay thin for her health.'

Kimura squinted at his cigarette then took a deep

drag. 'How do you keep so slim? Not by smoking it seems.'

'No, just healthy Japanese food and a lifetime of neurotic dieting. I blame my mother. That's a typically American thing to do, by the way, it's always mom's fault. Mine never had anything in the house when I was growing up but cottage cheese and rye crackers that tasted like sawdust.'

'Strange how such a rich and powerful country would starve its women.'

'We have our share of bizarre customs.'

Kimura exhaled and stubbed out his cigarette. A moment later, he reached for another.

'In fact, it seems we do have much in common,' he said. 'There was not much food in my home when I was growing up. For different reasons, of course. I think you would not recognize the Japan of those days. We were truly a poor country. And by odd coincidence, I last saw my father when I was three years old as well.'

'What happened?'

'It was wartime. He was sent to Manchuria and died in a Soviet prison camp in Siberia some years after the war ended. Or so we were told. This part of the past is not something we Japanese like to revisit.' He took another drag on his cigarette. 'My mother died young, too. The official reason was heart failure, but I suspect too much work. Too little nourishment. A broken heart.'

And I thought I had a deprived childhood. I managed a soft bleat of sympathy, but my tongue felt heavy, my cheeks hot. Kimura had finally opened himself up to me. Why did I suddenly feel ashamed?

'Our talk is reminding me of a dream of mine – a fantasy, as you called it,' he continued. 'Would you like to hear it?

'Of course,' I whispered.

'My mother loved *ochazuke* – do you know it? A very simple dish of white rice with tea and pickles. But whenever there was rice, she gave it to my sister and me. In this fantasy, I would go back in time and fill the kitchen with sacks and sacks of rice, so she could eat her fill day and night. But that is a child's dream. I suspect you were hoping for something more . . . adult . . . in nature?'

I wasn't sure whether to nod or shake my head. I felt a stinging high in my nose, the way I always did when I was about to cry. I tried to swallow it down, but the tears came anyway.

'*Gomen ne* – I'm sorry,' I murmured, shielding my face with my hand. I'd conjured up the ghosts, and now I couldn't handle it.

Kimura shifted his weight. I thought for a moment he might finally touch me, at least put a hand on my arm to comfort me. Instead, he stood up.

'I see you are tired,' he said gently. 'I believe I'll go down to the bath once more before I retire. I'll do my best not to disturb you on my return.'

Once I was alone, I turned off the light and settled into the futon that lay farther from the door. Not that I could sleep. The historically authentic buckwheat hull pillow was as hard as a rock. Plus, I kept flashing on images of Kimura as a boy, his head shaved to a blue stubble, his skinny legs poking out of tattered shorts. I saw his mother, too, a pretty woman with Kimura's round, almost Western eyes set in a thin face. Eyes brimming with suffering.

These were hardly the kind of thoughts to get me hot and horny and ready for a night of seduction. Maybe that was for the best. I already wanted Kimura to like me. If we added even halfway decent sex to the mix, I'd be feeling something for him before I knew it and I didn't need feeling. I would insist we go back to Kyoto first thing in the morning and then refuse all future invitations. I'd lose my first patron, but there would be others. That was the nature of the floating world.

I was still awake when he returned, although I pretended to sleep. I heard his sigh as he settled on the futon, the click of his lighter, the soft suck of inhalation. I slit one eye and watched the orange tip of his cigarette rise and fall in the darkness.

I didn't need pain, but I felt it anyway, an ache in my chest, an answering throb of emptiness between my legs.

He's here. You're here. Why not numb yourselves with a harmless sip of sweet poison? Besides, I figured if the guy didn't find some other way to relax, he'd probably smoke twenty packs of cigarettes and send us both to the cancer ward before morning.

I shifted on the futon and let out the lilting sigh of a woman suddenly aroused from sleep. Kimura turned his head toward me. There was enough of a glow from the nightlight in the vestibule that I could see him frown, ready to apologize for disturbing me.

'Kazu,' I whispered. It was the first time I'd said his given name out loud.

The frown lifted into a smile.

Without a word, he crushed out his cigarette in the ashtray beside him and crossed No Man's Land to my bed.

CHAPTER FIVE

Back in Kyoto, Kimura continued to visit me at Rousseau, but more often we met outside the club to spend the early evening hours together at a discreet *ryokan* tucked away in the winding streets of the eastern hills. I'd suggested we try out some of the city's love hotels, but Kimura pronounced them 'vulgar'. After a few weeks even the inn seemed to bother his nerves and he approached me with a proposal. A friend's daughter had recently graduated from college and her furnished student apartment was now empty. There would be no key money and no lease, just an informal introduction to the manager as a serious-minded student of the traditional Japanese art of my choice.

That's how I found myself standing in the entryway of a cute two-room apartment accepting delivery of a new set of futons Kimura had ordered from a department store. In the blink of an eye, I'd changed from a more or less respectable wife to a kept floozy straight from a TV drama. Yet my life with Yuji seemed like the made-up story now, less a memory than a bad girl's fantasy of domesticated bliss gone sour.

In the months to follow, Kimura never arrived without more gifts to sweeten our love nest: a box of traditional rice flour cakes from one of Kyoto's finest confectioners; a negligee of ivory lace and satin that reminded me of Jean Harlow; a glossy, and no doubt expensive, book of 'spring pictures', erotic wood-block prints from centuries past.

We usually had a simple dinner first, sushi or noodles delivered from one of the local shops. Then came the real feast. For the appetizer, Kimura liked to caress me slowly, pausing now and then, as if his fingertips were listening to my flesh whisper its secrets. He put the messages to good use. On our first night together in Tsumago, he found out my left nipple was more sensitive and that quick flicks along the right side of my clit were just the trick to send me over the edge. In the discreet inn in Higashiyama, he learned how I mewed when he drew circles in the soft crease of my elbow, and shivered in delight when he stroked my shoulder and pinched my nipple at the same time. Later, in our private hideaway, he grew bolder. He liked me noisy then, coaxing out a melody of sighs when he spanked me lightly on my vulva, then soothed my burning clit with a gentle stroking.

Solicitous as he was, he could be forceful, too, rolling on top of me and trapping my legs between his, his erection pressed between my thighs. He fondled and sucked my breasts for what seemed like hours until I was moaning and arching up against him, the heat of my desire forced inward until my whole body melted, the sheet beneath me drenched with sweat and pussy juice. Only then did he kiss me deeply, a reward for my patient endurance. So hungry was I for any penetration, my lips gaped like a baby bird's and I greedily sucked in the bittersweet tobacco taste of his tongue: the flavor of my father's fingers, the scent of my mother's hair.

The next course of our feast was my pussy. As I might have expected from his ease with foreign languages, Kimura had formidable lingual skills. He started by wrapping his arm under my thighs to hold my legs together while he gave my clit the proper greeting with the tip of his tongue. When he had me squirming and sighing, he eased my legs open, showing off his fancier vocabulary, quick figure-eights and long, silky strokes with the flat of his tongue. For the climax, he pushed my knees up to my chest, then licked and flicked me relentlessly until I came, my body jerking in deep, wracking spasms. This was only my first orgasm of the evening.

Afterwards, he held me, stroking my hair as we planned the main course together. Sometimes it was a new recipe, sometimes an old favorite.

For our housewarming celebration, I got the idea to shave my pussy bare. He claimed I reached orgasm faster, but it may have been his own enthusiasm for lapping and nibbling on my newly-exposed lips and smooth, rosy cleft. It was such a success, it became our custom for him to do touch-ups in the bath before we made love. Nothing warmed me up better than to lie back, my legs spread wide, and submit to the delicate glide of the razor in his hands.

The book of spring prints led to another successful collaboration. Kimura was impressed that I'd chosen his favorite artist, Suzuki Harunobu, as my own. Known as the most elegant of the *shunga* artists, Harunobu's lovers had graceful bodies and wistful, intelligent faces. Their genitals were life-like and always tinted a dainty rose or salmon-pink, not outrageously over-sized and garish like the more famous work of Utamaro. The lovers were often spied upon by serving maids or Tom Thumb voyeurs, or they watched themselves in mirrors as they coupled. Of course, I suggested we act out the scenes, but it was Kimura's idea to take down the full-length mirror in the hallway and prop it by the mattress so we could gaze at our own bodies entwined like an antique dirty picture come to life. My head thrown back as if weighed down by an elaborate coiffeur, my feet in the air and toes curled under in the traditional pose of sexual arousal, the strain of these contortions heightened every sensation, transporting me to a realm of timeless pleasure.

On occasion, our amusements were one-time-only affairs. One evening in high summer, we decided to find out how many times I could climax before I dissolved into a blob of numbed, boneless jelly. The answer was eight. Another time we tied scarves over our eyes – I insisted he do it, too – and found that while blindness put him on edge, it made me more passionate. I found it easier to escape in the darkness.

Finally, as the evening wound down to the inevitable goodbye, we shared a bit of dessert, a form of mutual indulgence I suspect aroused him most of all. Talk.

Kimura said I was the best English teacher he'd ever had, if lying together naked, sipping cognac and telling him my sexual fantasies counts as a conversation class. He especially liked the one about the bisexual orgy with my company president lover and his formidable lady lieutenant, Ms Inoue.

'Your imagination is very rich,' he said, lazily tracing my collarbone with his fingertip.

'I've always liked to dream, too much maybe, but my fantasies have changed since I've come to Japan.'

'Ah, really? How is that?'

'Now there's this sense of breaking free of something, pushing my limits. I must struggle, maybe even endure pain, but beyond that lies ecstasy.'

'That is a rather Japanese fantasy,' he said, amused. After a pause, he added, 'Would you like me to "push your limit" some time?'

My stomach tightened with lust, curiosity, and a touch of fear. 'What did you have in mind?'

'A surprise. But I cannot give you this gift here. Perhaps I can take you on another trip. To Tokyo this time?'

As always, it was impossible to refuse his generosity.

When I thought about it, which wasn't often because I was having too much fun, I knew Kimura and I were as doomed as any courtesan and her paramour from the love suicide puppet plays of old Osaka. We had enough psychological complexes between us to keep a therapist busy for decades. I was the mother he wanted to save, he was the bountiful father I never knew. At the same time, I felt closer to my own mother, for hadn't I stepped into her shoes as the mistress of a wealthy man? I wondered, but never asked, if Kimura's pursuit of the good life was in some way a tribute to his father who had known little of life's comforts in his Siberian hell. When we were in bed together, a whole crew of ghosts hovered in the shadows, whispering, watching. We were never alone, but I didn't mind. I liked having a family.

CHAPTER SIX

The September breeze held a cool hint of autumn when Kimura took me up to Tokyo for the limit-pushing getaway he'd promised. From the very beginning, he seemed to be testing the boundaries of my life, gently but steadily. First, he booked a private compartment in the bullet train, such a breathtaking luxury for me I clapped my hands in delight. Then he took advantage of our near-privacy – the conductor or drink vendor might peek through the door unannounced at any moment – to slide his hand under my skirt and finger me while he nonchalantly leafed through *The Economist*. Equally thrilling was the view of Ginza and Tokyo Bay from our room at the historic Imperial Hotel, a big step up from the dreary youth hostel where I stayed on my only other visit to the city. The calf brains we sampled at his friend's tiny French restaurant in Aoyama were a stretch for me, too, although I passed the test with barely a grimace.

When we climbed into a taxi after dinner, I half hoped we'd head to Kabukicho or the old Yoshikwara pleasure district of Senzoku 4-chome for a tour of Tokyo's decadent nightlife, but he merely directed the driver to take us back to the hotel. Vaguely disappointed, I showered, then lounged in the armchair by the window, wrapped in the hotel's terry robe. I assumed we'd have sex, but instead he seemed more interested in planning the next morning's sightseeing in the historic Yanaka district before we headed back home. Unless Kimura was hiding some very kinky sex toys in his overnight bag, the evening was settling into an almost marital routine.

Then came the knock at the door. Kimura went to answer it, disappearing down the L-shaped entry hall.

I heard a woman's melodious voice, then Kimura's warm, familiar reply. A pang of jealousy passed through me, followed by something closer to terror. My body knew it before my mind did. The stylishly dressed Eurasian woman who stepped into the room was my 'gift'.

With a self-satisfied smile, Kimura introduced us to each other in English. I was 'Meg' and she was 'Naomi'. 'Naomi' certainly was the sort of arm ornament to make any man proud. Her striking face — wide-set eyes, a perky high-bridged nose, full pink lips — was set off by lush, wavy brown hair falling to her shoulders. A belted dress accented her slim hips and, for this part of the world, generous breasts.

The woman smiled and nodded. To my surprise, I felt a twinge between my legs. Perhaps it was the flash of humor in her eyes, as if we were the ones sharing the joke, but part of me took to her immediately.

At first, however, most of me was too stunned to respond.

Naomi immediately dropped her gaze and said in a low voice, 'If you'll excuse me, I'll freshen up for a moment.' She disappeared into the hall. The bathroom door clicked shut.

Kimura rushed over and knelt beside me. 'My surprise gift was not a success, I'm afraid?'

'Oh, the surprise part worked. No one's ever given me a woman before. I'm not sure if I can fit her in my suitcase though.' The tremor in my voice belied the light-hearted words.

He wasn't fooled. 'Lydia, I am terribly sorry if I have offended you. Of course, I cannot "give" Naomi to you. The gift is the experience you will share. Rest assured, she is very good at what she does. But if you are not pleased, I can send her away.'

My stomach was churning with too many emotions to name. I'd never said no to Kimura, sensing that even a hint of discord would damage our fragile relationship, but I wasn't sure I could have sex with someone when the only real bond was money. Of course, Kimura might be insulted if I mentioned it. He obviously didn't share my reluctance, and I could only guess at his other adventures with women in the 'water trade'. In fact, some might argue he was 'paying' me. There was, however, one fear I felt I could share.

I dipped my head in apology. 'It's really so thoughtful of you. It's exactly like something I'd dream up, but I'm worried I won't know how to please a woman in real life. Actually, I'm scared to death.'

Kimura took my hand. 'Believe me, Lydia, I understand that feeling very well.'

Our eyes met. He did understand. I knew it, or rather felt it, an oddly liberating lightness in my chest. What would it be like to understand him? For wasn't that really what he was offering me – my long-time dream of fucking like a man? Tonight it might really happen. Here, floating high above Tokyo, all the rules of ordinary life dissolved into thin air.

My breath came faster. 'What if we start but I can't go through with it?'

'If you want to stop, she will simply go away. I will take care of it.'

So it was just like a fantasy. How could I say no to that? And so I nodded, as if in a trance. Still floating, I let him lead me over to the king-sized bed. I lay down and waited, eyes closed, heart pounding. I heard the bathroom door open, an exchange of words in soft Japanese. Someone drew close to the bed. I smelled perfume.

I opened my eyes. Naomi stood before me, wrapped in the other terry robe, the collar opened loosely to reveal a red satin teddy.

She smiled. There it was again, that sense of familiarity. She knew everything about me. We weren't really strangers at all. When Kimura said she was 'good', I imagined secret sex techniques, but maybe it was this instead?

Naomi sat down at the edge of the bed. Still smiling, she ran her finger along the collar of my robe. She hadn't even touched my skin, but every nerve in my body tingled.

'You really are just like a doll. So small and pretty. I wonder if the other things he told me about you are true?'

What exactly had Kimura said about me in his role as go-between? I was about to ask, but maybe it was better not to know the reputation I had to live up to. I smiled uneasily.

Naomi smiled back, her gaze lingering on my lips. 'Have you ever kissed a woman before, Meg?'

I met her eyes. 'No, never.'

Her amber eyes flickered. She knew I was lying. And she liked me for it.

She closed her eyes and bent toward me. I knew what would come. The soft meeting of lips, the unhurried dance of tongues, the moment that stretched into forever. I was so used to Kimura's tobacco-spiked kisses, Naomi's tasted sweet, like overripe fruit with a touch of mint. She lay down beside me. We turned to each other and kissed again, our fuzzy robes pressed together.

My pulse was racing. The kissing part was easier this time, but I still didn't know the rules. Could I do anything I wanted now – anything at all? In a rush of daring, I slipped my hand under her collar and curled my fingers around her satin-covered breast. It was warm and springy, like a cushion. My palm prickled.

She made a low, humming noise.

Deep inside my belly, my body hummed in reply. But my mind wasn't so sure. Did she really like it? Or was it all an act?

As if in reply, Naomi pulled away from the kiss. She flashed me another knowing smile as she rose up on one elbow and pulled open the belt of my robe.

Without really meaning to, I glanced over at Kimura, sitting in the armchair by the window, cigarette in his hand. His eyes were fixed on us – as one might expect of a man in a hotel room with two women making out on the bed beside him – but his expression surprised me. Behind the glint of lust was a hint of anxious concern, even sadness. I wasn't sure what he was feeling, but I did know I couldn't go on with those wistful eyes watching my every move.

'Kazu,' I said. 'Come here.'

Obediently he stood and walked over to the bed.

'I want you to be with me too. Or is that too selfish?'

He shook his head and smiled.

While Kimura quickly peeled off his clothes, Naomi undressed me and pulled her own robe over her shoulders. Kimura crawled into bed on my other side. Instinctively I turned to face Naomi and pressed my back against him, forming a barrier between them with my body.

'You are selfish,' Naomi whispered, a teasing glint in her eye, but she didn't seem to mind having the front of me all to herself.

She brushed my erect nipple with her finger. I shivered. Her tongue flicked over her lips and she scooted down to follow up with a kiss. Then Kimura began kissing my neck, his hard-on bobbing against my ass. His hand circled around between my legs to tease my cleft with maddeningly delicate strokes.

Surrounded by bodies, one behind and one in front, it was hard not to compare them. Kimura was a hard, hot wall pushing into me. Naomi, still in her silk teddy, was soft and faintly moist, drawing me toward her. Timidly, I reached out to touch her hair, but it was stiff between my fingers, from mousse or hairspray perhaps? What was she thinking as she fixed her hair for the evening ahead — playing out a lesbian scene with an old client's girlfriend?

I moved my hand away. Maybe I shouldn't ask questions. Maybe it was better to lie back and let them do everything, drifting wherever their hands and lips would guide me.

I felt another hand creep between my thighs. Kimura paused mid-stroke, then dutifully pulled away.

'You're so smooth down here, Meg,' Naomi whispered, brushing my lips with her fingertips. Indeed, Kimura had shaved me earlier that day between our room service breakfast and our morning fuck. Then she took my hand and placed it between my own legs. 'I'd love to watch you touch yourself. Show me how you like it.'

I froze. Of course, I'd masturbated for men, but never for a woman, not in real life. But was this 'real life'? How could it be? Heart pounding, I stretched out my middle finger, pressed it into my groove. It felt nice enough, but I didn't usually play with myself in this position, on my side, legs pressed together. I wondered, fleetingly, how Naomi liked to do it when she was alone. With her slim, golden legs spread, one hand diddling away, the other teasing her breast? Or on her belly, thrusting her rounded ass into the mattress? Did she put something inside or push a pillow between her legs?

Suddenly, I was getting genuinely turned on. I let out a soft moan, rocking into my hand.

'This is making me hungry,' Naomi said.

I heard Kimura laugh, low in his throat. In a quick

motion, he pulled me onto my back, while Naomi parted my legs. She tapped my clit lightly with her tongue.

I gasped. Through my veiled lashes I saw Kimura staring down at her, and I watched, too, as Naomi bent over me *down there*, her dark hair spilling over my thighs.

But soon enough, the doubts swooped in. Did she really like eating pussy? Or was I just a body to service to the predictable conclusion, the sooner the better? I was doing a terrible job of fucking like a man. They didn't think, except with their dicks. They took what they wanted, greedily, selfishly. Maybe I could do it too. Maybe I could have it all.

I turned to Kimura. 'I want you inside me.'

He gave a soft grunt of assent and reached for the condom on the nightstand. Naomi paused to check our next move, her eyes smoky, her pink lips shining with my juices. Kimura got behind me again. I lifted my leg and hooked it behind his thighs, giving him a straight shot from the side. He pushed into me with a sigh. Stretched perpendicular across the bed, Naomi parted the top of my pussy lips with her fingers and renewed her attentions to my clit. She was good, but even the stereo sensations of a hard cock in my pussy and a wiggling satin tongue on my clit wasn't enough to still the voices.

What if I took so long to come, she'd start wishing I were a man so she could get her money and go?

'Lydia, my dear, I see you need my assistance in spite of this rather crowded bed. I must say that your lover is a very generous man. I wonder if he isn't a little in love with you? In any case, he's spoiling you rotten, not to mention the benefit to me. You are quite a vision, the three of you, all twisted up in a yin–yang pretzel of carnal depravity. By the way, from my vantage point I must tell you that the crotch of her teddy is drenched. I would have to conjecture that you really are turning her on.'

'Really, old man? Are you sure she isn't just enduring this out of professional duty?'

'Well,' my friend continued, 'the silk is pulled up tight between those pretty legs, just a slender strip pressing up into her crack. I'm sure it's putting pressure on just the right places, her swollen little clit, her tender asshole. It seems Ms Naomi knows how to please herself as well as others.'

I moaned.

The sound seemed to arouse both of my lovers down on the bed. Naomi's tongue flicked faster. Kimura's thrusts quickened. Little did they know I'd brought my own friend to join the orgy.

'After she leaves, I'm sure she'll go home and masturbate. She'll think of your tasty, rose-petal twat and how powerful she felt making you come. You are going to come now, Lydia, aren't you?'

'Oh, yes,' I sighed aloud, gripping Kimura's cock with my secret muscles as I slammed back against him. His hand moved up to my breast and he pinched the nipple just the way I liked it. Naomi was using her finger on me now, not quite the way I did it, but close enough. This was how she turned herself on, this was how she touched herself when she was horny and alone with her own fantasies. I knew her secret now, and suddenly, as if I'd slipped into her skin, I was her, strumming herself later tonight in her bed. I was Kimura too, taking my pleasure as I found it, without asking all of those questions. I didn't need questions anymore. All I needed was to come. And I did, my pussy milking his cock, my scream muffled by her kiss, my whole body lifting off the bed in the bounty of their attention, so dizzying and boundless, I thought for that moment I would never need anything ever again as long as I lived.

CHAPTER SEVEN

'Did you enjoy it?'

Kimura and I were alone, the two of us tucked in bed like an ordinary married couple, his arm around me, my head on his shoulder.

'Yes, but I feel a little strange, too,' I said slowly. 'It's funny because it was your idea, but I'm afraid you think I'm bad.'

' "Bad"? On the contrary, I have always found your enjoyment of sensual pleasure to be a very good thing.'

We lay in silence for a while.

'Kazu, can I tell you something? A secret?'

'Please do.'

'Well, when I first started . . . when I first learned the pleasure my body could give me, a man began to visit me. Not a real man, a voice in my head. He told me he liked to watch me touch myself and he told me I was beautiful. He always said things that turned me on. He had an interesting accent, which I couldn't quite identify. Definitely not American, maybe a bit of British, a bit of French, a man of the world.'

Kimura made the musical sound of the attentive Japanese listener — *yes, go on.*

'Well, I think maybe the man was you.'

His arm tightened around me. 'Lydia, I also feel I have found something I've been seeking for a very long time.'

I felt a tug in my chest, a feeling a little too close to love. As usual, I took refuge in a joke. 'So your spirit really does wander the earth spying on naughty young women?'

' "Naughty"? I prefer a different word. Do you know *kôshoku*, written with the Chinese characters for "love" and "color"? I believe the translation is "amorous". I think that word describes you best. An amorous woman.'

Leave it to Kimura to pull such an archaic word from his overstuffed vocabulary file. But I had to admit it was nicer than oversexed or horny or easy or desperate. Much nicer than telling me I clearly had a neurotic need to earn approval through sex.

Instead I was an amorous woman. I liked the sound of it.

Part Ten

SECRETS HIDDEN IN
A WANTON ROBE
(Kyoto, 1991–1992)

CHAPTER ONE

You could say I'd thrown away my life to become a sex slave to a modern-day Japanese lord. Yet for me, during my months with Kimura, it was more like I'd stepped into the golden, glamorous world I'd imagined as I gazed out Mrs Muller's window, licking strawberry jam from my fingers.

Until one fine October day, when the leaves were just turning and the afternoon sun was tinged with butterscotch tones, a last taste of sweetness before the austerity of winter. Kimura arrived at twilight with the usual packages and a particularly expectant smile. He'd been gone two weeks on a business trip to Southeast Asia, and he was always more passionate after deprivation.

I greeted him with the usual welcome: beer, a plate of dried octopus, the indispensable ashtray, and the futon open and ready in the next room. As I prepared for his arrival, I felt less a servant than a well-seasoned stage manager. My work at Club Rousseau had taught me the subtle power of anticipating my guest's needs.

Sitting cross-legged at the table, tie loosened, Kimura seemed thoroughly at ease. I played the Japanese lady with my legs folded under me. There would be time enough later for lounging wantonly.

'Is that a new dress? It's very becoming.'

'Yes, I went shopping today and I couldn't resist it. But there was one problem. I'm one size larger than I used to be. I've gotten fat. I'm afraid you're going to dump me now.'

' "Dump" you? No.' Kimura stroked my arm. 'I believe you have put on some weight since we met, but in your case, that is a good thing. Women are meant to be soft.'

'*Okagesama de,*' I said, bowing. Thanks to your influence, indeed.

He laughed as he always did when I used Japanese. I suspected he liked the apartment to be English Land. Then he said, 'I think I'll take a bath now.'

I nodded. Sometimes I joined him, but I'd already primped and perfumed myself to show off the new dress for his visit. Once he disappeared into the bathroom, I stretched out my legs and tapped my fingers on the table. Not that I wasn't used to waiting for him. It was pleasant enough to fill my time reading all the classics of the Edo period about libertines and amorous women or wandering the shopping streets disguised in sunglasses and a hat in case I happened upon anyone I knew from my other life. I certainly liked having no obligations but a night or two a week of sensual indulgence that left my throat raw from the cries of ecstasy.

But I had to admit I'd been feeling restless recently. My eyes settled on the shopping bags sitting at the entryway. What had he brought me this time? Something silk from Thailand perhaps? I felt the childish urge to peek. I knew I could easily fake surprise when the formal presentation was made.

There were two bags this time, one large glossy shopping bag and another smaller one resting behind it against the wall. I knelt by the entryway step and eased the smaller bag from its hiding place. It was from a portrait studio, and the contents weren't wrapped, just two heavy cardboard folders.

It wasn't a gift, I knew that immediately, but I pulled out the pictures anyway, my hands trembling with the danger of it.

I opened the first folder. A young woman in a long-sleeved maiden's kimono stood rather stiffly, holding a fan, her mouth lifted slightly in what I'd called an *'omiai smile'*, appealing, but serious enough to show her worthiness to shoulder the responsibilities of a wife. She had Kimura's rounded, Western eyes and was cute, if a little plump. I should, of course, have put both pictures back right away. Instead I opened the other folder.

Now the girl stood behind an older woman who was seated on an upholstered chair, wearing the formal, crested kimono of a married woman. The mother had more of a classic Japanese prettiness — a round face, eyes drawn with a master calligrapher's sweeping hand — but what struck me even from a picture was her aura of refinement and elegance. There was probably not a single cell in her body that could be called 'vulgar'. She was also pleasingly rounded, not to say fleshy.

I was in the presence of the women of the Kimura clan. Wife and daughter. The real ones. As I looked into their dark, faintly smug eyes, I felt a twist in my stomach that was very much like self-loathing.

The door of the bathroom clicked open. It was too late to hide, too late to pretend. Kimura stood above me in his blue-and-white robe. The room went cold, tinged with the flinty odor you smell before the thunder comes.

He said nothing. He just looked down at me holding the portraits on my lap. The air was so heavy now my chest hurt and I could barely breathe, much less speak. I slipped the portraits in the bag and set it back against the wall. I should have learned my lesson from the Matt fiasco – a mistress keeps well away from the wife – but apparently I hadn't.

'I'm so sorry,' I whispered, resisting a very genuine urge to bow. I knew he'd think I was mocking him. 'I thought it was my present.'

'That's in the other bag,' he said. There was the slightest hint of amusement in his voice.

I grasped that filament of warmth like a lifeline. Maybe if I promised to be good and never do anything wrong again, he would forgive me? But for the moment, it seemed, all I could manage was to sit frozen in miserable silence.

'Lydia?' he said finally. 'Shall we go to bed now?'

It seemed like a good sign. But even lying naked in his arms, I had a sense he was standing above me, looking down.

'Let me do something for you tonight,' I whispered, although I wasn't quite sure what that would be. Blow jobs made him anxious. The only time he let me do it longer than a minute, he had to smoke a cigarette to get through the ordeal, although I was showing off my best tricks.

'I do have a request tonight,' he said. 'I would like to do something . . . simple. Like our first night together in Tsumago.'

In some ways, our lovemaking that night was very much like Tsumago. We did nothing fancy or edgy. He seemed to expect little of me but to lie back and receive his homage. This time, however, my flesh was exquisitely sensitive to his touch, each caress hovering on the edge of pain. Several times I even had to fight back tears. Again my body seemed to know it was our last time, even though it would be many months before my mind caught on to the truth.

Later, he held me and stroked my hair, rubbing a lock between his fingers, as if appreciating the fine, silky texture for the first time. 'I'm sorry I brought the pictures here, Lydia. It was my mistake.'

He spoke slowly, his voice filled with genuine regret.

CHAPTER TWO

At first I didn't do anything too embarrassing in public. I didn't stalk him or call his office constantly or chop off my little finger and send it to him like the spurned courtesans of Edo times would do in a desperate bid for attention.

Privately, I was a disaster. I lay in bed all day brooding, replaying the scene in my head. He'd been around long enough to know the chemistry between us didn't come along every day. We belonged together, love suicides from ages past now reincarnated for a second chance. How could he just cut me dead without a word of goodbye?

In my less hysterical moments, I decided it made sense he had to punish me for a while. I deserved to be punished, for that and so many other thoughtless things I'd done in the past. But if I waited stoically and elegantly, thus proving I could be trusted to keep my proper place in his life, he would forgive me.

Instead, a few weeks later, a nervous-looking young man appeared at my door on behalf of Kimura-*shachô* with a request that I find another place to live as soon as possible and an envelope of 'parting money' to help with the move, although I could stay a while longer as necessary.

Still I didn't call or beg or make a scene. I quietly lost ten pounds in a month and stepped up my evenings at

Rousseau. Kimura had stopped coming there, too, but I told myself I hadn't lost him yet. A part of him was still with me, watching me, as he always had.

But everything else in my world changed, as if someone had snapped on the overhead light in a room lit by candles. No longer was the club a place where charming sophisticates engaged in witty repartee with women of wit and experience. Suddenly the men's faces grew ordinary, even homely. They sprouted moles I hadn't noticed, their lips mumbled the same uninspired pleasantries over and over. Marie and Aimée took on a robotic look, their smiles frozen, their eyes glazed.

When the *mama-san* introduced me to an old friend of hers who was in Kyoto just for the evening, I did my best to charm him and show anyone who might be paying attention that I hadn't lost the skill. I even agreed to continue our conversation after closing time at the lounge at his hotel, which led to an invitation up to his room. In bed, I made the expected sounds and movements with far more enthusiasm than the quality of his performance merited. I'm sure the *mama-san*'s friend had no idea he was engaged in a live sex show, pumping away above me for the benefit of my audience of one, seated in the armchair in the corner taking it all in, his face taut with jealousy.

See, Kimura, I can do this with anyone. What happened between us meant nothing.

I accepted the tip — not payment, of course, just a small contribution toward the pricey dictionary of seasonal images for *haiku* we'd discussed — without blinking an eye. Accepting cash was much the same as accepting lingerie or fine dinners in the name of friendship. Except it was more honest.

CHAPTER THREE

My chance for a spurned woman's revenge came in December, the season of the endless round of parties to send out the old year. I was being courted by another older man at the club, but I was doing it right this time, stringing him along with smiles and fluttering eyelashes. My reward was an invitation to an exclusive party known for its suggestive entertainment. An annual event that would surely be of interest to a scholar of the floating world my new friend, Mr Suzuki, promised.

The party was held in a spacious *tatami* room in a traditional restaurant, nothing out of the ordinary except for a folding screen of plain, translucent rice paper set up on a dais at the front of the room. Rows of low tables were laid out perpendicular to the stage for the audience, mostly groups of older men accompanied by a younger assistant or two and the requisite female companion to keep the liquor flowing. By the time I arrived with Mr Suzuki and his two younger colleagues, Nagai and Uchida, the company was already well lubricated and boisterous.

We found a place at the centre table and poured *saké* all around. Soon after, the first performance began on the stage: a shadow play between two figures dressed as a samurai and a courtesan. The actors struck poses and uttered long, sing-song speeches in archaic Japanese, rather like kabuki, although I guessed from the occasional bursts of laughter and bawdy shouts of appreciation that the content was X-rated.

Try as I might to feign interest, my mind and my eyes began to wander to the smooth, strong-looking fingers of young Nagai's hand resting on the table. I wouldn't mind performing a little play opposite those actors, I thought, pleased that my libido at least was finally recovering from the shock of the past fall. Of course, there was that wedding band gleaming on his left ring finger, but maybe if I pretended it wasn't there, he would too? Unfortunately, Suzuki was paying the bill which meant by definition I had to treat him as the most interesting man at the party.

A bustle of movement over by the entryway interrupted my lustful reverie. I glanced over at the latecomers, a slim, confident man and a woman in a dress of shimmering gold fabric that hugged her willowy body, an eye-catching costume that struck me as a rather Western choice for a holiday party. It took me another moment to realize I knew this couple. Kimura and Aimée.

He scanned the room, looking for acquaintances, I assumed, while Aimée secured them a place at the far table. I held my breath, hoping for a polite nod, or even better, a specter of a fond smile.

His eyes swept smoothly past me without the slightest flicker of recognition. The message was loud and clear. I no longer existed. I was erased. Forgotten. Tossed in the trashcan like last week's issue of *The Economist*.

But I was going to show him I was very much alive.

I leaned toward Nagai with a conspiratorial smile. 'The play is interesting to watch, but I don't really understand what the actors are saying.'

'It is a little difficult for me as well. It's very old-fashioned Japanese,' he said cordially.

'What do you say in Japanese – *furu-kusai*? "Stinking of the old"?'

'Yes,' he said, his eyes widening. 'You know Japanese very well.'

'No, I still have so much to learn.' I moved closer. 'Don't tell Suzuki-*buchô*, but I don't really like this old-fashioned stuff. I'd rather have *okonomiyaki* and beer.'

'Me, too,' he admitted with a quick glance at his boss.

I decided Nagai would do just fine for my purposes – polite, suggestible, and easy on the eye. He reminded me of the college boys sauntering down Kawaramachi Street, the ones I used to pick up in coffee shops and discos, except in the years I'd been away his jeans and sweater had turned into a business suit.

I peeked over at Kimura and Aimée. She was pouring *saké* for him, holding the flask just so, but I'd had enough practice that I could hold my own on that score.

'More *saké*, Nagai-*san*?'

He dipped his head in a quick bow and held up his cup, then returned the favor.

I finished mine in one gulp. He filled the cup again.

'Thirsty?' he asked with a smile.

'I'm trying to forget the old year. That's what

bônenkai means, right? Did you have a good year, Nagai-*san*?'

'So-so,' he said.

'Mine definitely had its ups and downs. Let's forget together, *ne*?' I filled his cup and tapped him playfully on the arm, allowing myself another glance across the room.

Aimée leaned toward Kimura, her hand resting on his sleeve. They could have been a mirror image of Nagai and me, except for the lingering look that passed between them. Perhaps they were sleeping together – or they used to or they would soon – but that wasn't what sent a sharp stabbing pain through my chest. I could tell from their mellow, knowing smiles that they were friends in a way I could never hope to achieve, intimates in the true sense of the word.

I grabbed a fresh flask of *saké* and downed a few more cups like kamikaze shots. If I was going down, I'd do it in flames and take them all with me.

I turned to Mr Suzuki. He knew the host of the party, who might be willing to include an impromptu interlude in the evening's entertainment if the scene would amuse his guests. I leaned close and whispered my scandalous proposal in his ear.

CHAPTER FOUR

'Please lie down, Mr Nagai.'

I pointed to the low table I'd ask them to set up on the stage behind the paper screen. Nagai sat down at the edge and stretched out obediently. I hiked up my skirt and straddled him. The stagehand adjusted the lights so our shadows would project to the best advantage.

Nagai had tried to get out of his very special English lesson, but Suzuki slapped him on the back and insisted. '*Omoshiroi darô* – come on, Nagai. It'll be an interesting experience.'

Then he appealed to me. 'My English is poor.'

I smiled, just drunk enough to be wickedly clever. 'Don't worry, sweetie, it's about to get better.'

And now it was show time.

'In honor of this splendid party,' I announced in my best wedding-speech Japanese, 'I would like to demonstrate a very special way of learning English, a Japanese way, which I'm sure you all know. It's called "learning through the body". However, first, I would like to thank my kind assistant for his help.'

I grinned down at Nagai, who gazed back at me, his eyelids drooping from the gulps of *saké* he'd swallowed before he came behind the screen with me. I saw a glimmer of fear there, too, but I wasn't going to let a little thing like that interfere with my plans.

After all, aren't we all afraid? Aren't we all being used?

'Let's begin, shall we?' I switched into English, with a touch of the cultivated continental accent. 'First, we'll study some names for the parts of the body.'

I took Nagai's hands and placed them over my breasts. There was some laughter from beyond the screen and a whistle. 'These are called "breasts". But did you know that in English we call them by many names? Tits. Hooters. Knockers. Boobs.'

I moved his hands to my ass. He was loosening up a little and a woozy smile played over his lips. 'These are buttocks. Bottom. Bum. Booty. Ass . . . hey!' Nagai had goosed me. 'Behave yourself, sir, this is a serious English lesson.'

More laughter from the crowd and a few kabuki-style cries – *Go, Nagai!*

'We mustn't forget what's up front.' I rose up on my knees. 'This is a vulva. That's all the good parts together. Sometimes we say pussy or cunt or clam. I understand the Japanese sometimes say "peach". I think that's nice, because peaches are very delicious.' I swayed seductively, but at this point it wasn't even an act anymore. I actually felt a surge of power rising up between my legs, not just the warmth of Nagai's body, but something deeper, more primal.

'And what's this big hard thing?' I brushed Nagai's erection through his trousers. He closed his eyes in embarrassment or pleasure, I wasn't sure. And frankly, I didn't care. Only Kimura mattered.

'We call this a penis. Or cock. Or dick.'

There were more cries of approval. I hadn't had such acclaim since I starred in my high school's production of *A Midsummer Night's Dream*.

'Now for the verbs. We have kissing.' I bent over and grazed Nagai's lips with mine, then arched back smoothly.

'We have caressing.' Again I put his hands on my breasts. This time Nagai gave them a soft squeeze, his thumbs brushing the nipples. 'That feels very nice. You are such a good student,' I cooed. 'And now, one of my favorite things. The sucking.'

I slipped off the bench and knelt over his crotch, bobbing my head up and down over my clenched fist. This was a favorite with the crowd, too, by the sound of it.

'And last, but not least, the fucking. Anyone out there have a condom handy?'

Several voices cried out for a condom and one came flying over the rice paper screen. I picked it up. It was warm, probably from someone's wallet. 'I think it's best we continue this lesson at another place. Maybe a love hotel?'

There was more laughter, and shouts of 'Here, do it here. Let's study English.'

Wobbling a little, I looked over at Nagai and dipped my head in a bow of thanks.

He sat up, a slightly stunned expression on his face, blinking and rubbing his neck.

I noticed the wedding ring again, but I shook off the pang of guilt. It was nothing personal, nothing that would interfere with his real life. Besides, he'd be the envy of his colleagues. What Japanese man hasn't fantasized about being overpowered by a sexually voracious foreign woman? We'd stepped into a porno comic for a few minutes, and now we were going to step out.

It was time for the real climax: my chance to see the expression on Kimura's face. I grabbed Nagai's hand and pulled him along to take our bows.

The applause was gratifyingly enthusiastic and I bowed low, my eyes darting across the room to the place where Kimura was sitting.

Or had been sitting. All that was left were two abandoned *saké* flasks and cups, a well-used ashtray. He and Aimée were gone.

CHAPTER FIVE

I thought it best to leave the party on an up note, so I said goodnight to Suzuki and made my way to the door, dodging a few grabbing hands along the way. As I left the banquet room, a young man called out 'Miss Megu?' and slipped an envelope into my hand. After he left, I checked the contents – a generous stack of ten-thousand yen notes, my performance fee. Not bad wages for a novice thespian, even if I didn't get the real payoff I was hoping for. I stuffed it in my purse.

I stopped at the ladies' room down the hall. I wasn't so pleased with what I saw in the mirror. My mascara was smudged and my lipstick uneven, and I looked generally disheveled. Not that it mattered, I was going straight home, but I pulled out my hairbrush for a touch up.

The door swung open and Aimée walked in. She didn't smile or greet me, she just stood there, floating behind me in the mirror, looking very elegant in a stylish coat with a fur collar.

'Where's your escort?' I said in Japanese, giving my hair a few more unnecessary strokes with the brush.

'He stepped out to buy cigarettes,' she said in a cool voice. 'He said this year's entertainment was too vulgar for him.' She said the word 'vulgar' in heavily-accented English, drawing out the sounds: baa – ru – gah.

'Fuck you both,' I murmured under my breath.

'I probably won't be seeing you as much in the New Year, Megu-*chan*,' Aimée said. 'The Mama has hired a new foreigner. A very pretty young girl from London.' She placed special emphasis on the 'young'. 'Kimura-*san* is very happy to have a new English teacher. The Mama always calls him first with the news. I must give you credit, though. You lasted longer than most.'

I met her eyes in the mirror. 'You brought him here on purpose. You knew I'd been invited to this party. I'm not sure what game you're playing, but you can stop right now.'

'Game?' Aimée's eyes glittered. 'For foreigners, it's a game. Or a joke. The clever ones like you call it a research project. For me, it's life.'

'Fuck you,' I said to her face and stomped into the bathroom stall. I peed noisily without flushing the toilet to mask the sound, another fuck-you message, in case she didn't get my meaning the first time.

When I came out, she was gone. And so was the envelope of cash from my purse, which I'd forgotten to take into the stall with me.

CHAPTER SIX

It was strange to walk into Rousseau wearing jeans and a sweatshirt. Odder still was the look on the Mama's face when she saw me, a momentary ripple of distaste disturbing her usual calm.

'Megu-*chan*,' she said, 'Mr Suzuki will be stopping by later to see you.'

I apologized for the short notice, but told her I was coming to resign instead. I was going back to America sooner than I expected.

She didn't try to talk me into staying, not even for the evening. In fact, she seemed relieved. I'm sure Aimée had told her about my new sideline as a sex show performer, and even I had to agree it didn't really fit with the tone of the club.

I stopped by the tiny dressing room to pick up my things — make-up, a few accessories.

Marie gave me a subdued 'good morning'.

'Sorry to hear you're leaving us,' Aimée said, her brow faintly furrowed in an excellent imitation of regret.

'I'm prostrate with grief myself,' I said in English, figuring she'd get my tone if not the words. I switched into Japanese, 'Say, Aimée-*chan*, you didn't happen to see an envelope of mine the other day?'

'Why, yes, I did find one just lying around. You

shouldn't be so careless about important things.' She reached into her purse and pulled out the envelope.

I snatched it from her. I could feel money inside. The contents were apparently untouched.

I bowed to Marie and thanked her for her guidance over the past year, then picked up my last pay envelope from the barman on the way out. In the elevator I counted the crisp, clean bills from the club, then checked my 'thank-you' envelope. The amount was the same, but the immaculate ten-thousand-yen bills had been replaced with new ones. Or rather old ones, creased and handled. Dirty.

I had to admire Aimée's knack for the eloquent gesture. But she was wrong if she thought I minded dirty money. I could easily beat her and the Mama at their game, if only for a round or two.

Fishing Mr Suzuki's business card from my *meishi* wallet, I stopped at the next public telephone and called his office. His receptionist put me through. I felt a little like Aimée, anger boiling my voice down into syrupy softness.

'Suzuki-*buchô*? This is Meg. I'm very sorry, but I won't be at Rousseau tonight. In fact, I'm starting my own business. An English conversation school. The other night, I decided I enjoyed teaching so much, it was time for a career change. I could schedule you in for a private lesson this evening, if you like.'

A few minutes later, I'd booked my very first customer. On my way back to my apartment, I bought two slices of apple tart from a café – the closest I could get to bona fide American apple pie. Then I stopped in at a pharmacy and bought a large pack of condoms.

CHAPTER SEVEN

My 'English school' wasn't so different from the club. I kept the lighting low and intimate. On the table I'd arranged china plates of apple tart, coffee and snifters of cognac, a remnant of Kimura's bounty. Flirtatious talk kept the mood light and easy. But there were a few differences, too. For one, I was dressed casually, in jeans and a blouse. For another, I was sitting on Suzuki's lap and he'd just unbuttoned that blouse and was tracing the lace trim of my bra with his finger, softly, slowly.

Mr Suzuki had nice hands, I decided, the fingers thick and competent-looking. Over our much slower courtship, I'd become genuinely fond of him. I liked his narrow, leathery face, his gravelly voice and his world-weary air. Beneath it, of course, beat the heart of a boy from the snow country along the Japan Sea. He told me once that my easy blush reminded him of the girls in his home village who always had rosy cheeks in the wintertime, a compliment that touched me more than the standard praise of my beauty and charm.

Now I was feeding Mr Suzuki sweet tidbits of truth about American culture. Yes, we had the saying 'as American as apple pie', but Americans nowadays preferred ice cream or chocolate chip cookies or brownies. American men liked desserts. Japanese men did not, or so I was told.

Mr Suzuki agreed, his hand cupping my breast, the thumb stroking my nipple until it poked up through the shimmering pink fabric. Indeed, he said, he preferred a salty taste. And what about tastes in lovemaking? Could I teach him the differences there?

I realized I was hardly the expert since the only American I'd been with in quite a while seemed to prefer either being tied up and spanked, or wrestling me to the floor of his office and spanking me. Not typical behavior of all my countrymen, although again I couldn't say for sure.

'It depends on the couple, of course,' I said. 'But in the honeymoon period there's lots of kissing and lovey-dovey words. American women like it when a man says "I love you".'

'Not such a popular saying in Japan.' Mr Suzuki's hand glided over to the other breast.

I resisted the urge to reply, 'Believe me, I know.' Instead I said, 'Americans aren't so good at unspoken communication. They like things loud and big. For example, American men like big breasts. The bigger, the better. But as you see, I'm more Japanese in that department. By the way, what you're doing right now feels very nice.'

'Yes, very nice for me too,' Suzuki agreed. He nuzzled my neck, a favorite Japanese erogenous zone.

'Americans have a custom of comparing foreplay to baseball. Maybe you've heard of it? First base is kissing. Second base is the sort of thing you're doing now – touching and teasing the breasts. Third base is below the waist.'

'Here?' he asked, his hand dipping between my legs to stroke me gently through my jeans, right over my clit.

I sighed and snuggled closer. 'Yes, there. Although for my generation, third base is usually oral sex. And of course, a home run is "going all the way". That's another interesting expression, isn't it?'

Mr Suzuki agreed that it was, and he was learning a great deal from my lesson. My new venture was proceeding quite smoothly indeed.

I suggested the bath might be a good place to review important vocabulary and Mr Suzuki saw the merits of my 'learn through the body' approach, sliding his soapy hands all over me in what I had to admit was a very pleasant massage. Then we retired to the bedroom to explore verbs.

We didn't kiss, but there was some more caressing. By the time we got to 'third base', Mr Suzuki was more interested in making love than oral sex, which was fine with me. He rolled on a condom, rolled on top, and came in a few minutes, which was also fine with me.

The end of the lesson was cordial, if a bit awkward. I scribbled the apartment's phone number on the back of one of his business cards, apologizing that I hadn't had my own official ones made up yet, but I hoped he would consider another lesson. He thanked me for my instruction with a bow and promised he would call again soon.

I poured myself a second glass of cognac to celebrate. Not only had I picked the Mama's pocket for an evening, but in under two hours I'd earned the same as two weeks'-worth of lessons at an English conversation salon. A couple more of these and I could buy my plane ticket back to San Francisco. Caroline had extended an open invitation for me to stay with her and I'd always wanted to live in California. With a few more lessons after that, I could tide myself over until I found a job although, frankly, any real job seemed pure drudgery.

Why not keep going? Unlike those dismal encounters I endured to torment Kimura's memory, I was the boss here. I'd get creative and develop a menu to cater to every flavor of Japan's longing for America. I could offer the celebrity package – get a platinum wig and sing 'Diamonds are a Girl's Best Friend'. Or maybe ask Caroline to send a cowboy hat and bolo tie and offer a Texas barbecue dinner followed by a rodeo ride?

Prostitution. The word was dirty. But what I'd just done wasn't dirty, I decided, it was clean. Surgically clean. Romance was what muddied things between men and women. The heart and the groin were separate for a reason. Wasn't that really the secret to fucking like a man?

Smiling, I raised my cognac in a toast to my promising career as a clear-eyed prostitute–tutor and a very prosperous New Year to come.

Part Eleven

BALLAD FOR A WOMAN
OF THE STREETS
(Kyoto, 1992)

CHAPTER ONE

After the second cognac, I was no longer quite as optimistic about the year ahead. My life was a mess. I had no job, no lover, not even a friend to turn to for help.

Maybe it was my partially my fault, I thought, pouring myself another drink with a wobbly hand, but that wasn't the whole story. Yuji, well, he might come across as the innocent party, but he'd lied when he told me he'd be there for me. As far as I was concerned, he left me long before I left him. I was too ashamed to call Chieko. Even if she did forgive me for disappearing on her, I didn't have the guts to tell her about all the things I'd done in the past year. Caroline might be able to handle it, but it would be too early in the morning in California. I was definitely in a bind. Lolling back on the sofa, I flashed on the image of my naked body all tied up like a Christmas package in bands of black velvet ribbon.

That's when I thought of Masaru. He lived in Kyoto, not very far away, and he knew all about prostitutes. He probably even *liked* prostitutes as people, so he wouldn't mind staying friends with me after what I'd done. It certainly wouldn't hurt to call him. If his wife, Ryoko, answered, I'd hang up immediately, chug down the whole damned bottle of cognac, and never wake up again.

The *kamisama* must have been feeling generous that day, because Masaru was the one to answer the phone in his rumbling Japanese.

'Masaru? It's Lydia.'

There was silence on the other end of the line, then a soft, Japanese-style 'heh?' of surprise. 'Lydia? Where are you?'

'I'm in Kyoto. Can you meet me tonight?' I gave him the name of the train station nearest my apartment, not a bad place to rendezvous by car.

'Yes, I can meet you.' He spoke quickly, as if he were afraid I might slip away.

'And please don't tell Yuji. Or Ryoko. I don't want anyone else to know.'

He didn't answer right away and I wondered, panic rising, if I'd made a mistake.

'OK, I won't say anything. See you soon then?' Now the words came slower, as if he were trying to humor a crazy person. Maybe I was crazy to call him, but at least I'd have someone to talk to.

Masaru was as handsome as ever when he drove up in the red sports car he'd kept from his bachelor days. But the look he gave me when I climbed into the car was not so familiar; it was as if he were seeing a ghost and not merely his friend's fugitive wife, half-pickled in Remy Martin.

'Thanks for coming, Masaru. I really appreciate it. Can we go somewhere quiet to talk? Or maybe just drive around a little?'

His expression softened, and I saw a touch of the old spark in his eye.

'I know a good place,' he said, and shifted the car into gear.

'And thanks for not telling anyone. I hope I didn't put you to too much trouble.' It struck me only after I hung up that I was asking for more than his silence. He'd have to lie to Ryoko to come see me.

He smiled. 'That's OK. I want to help, if I can.'

I leaned back in my seat and gazed out at the neon lights of the shops, the golden squares of window in the apartments and offices, Kyoto in her evening dress, so beautiful and mysterious. I'd wanted to tell him my troubles, maybe ask for advice, but the reality of my life suddenly seemed dreary and pathetic. I've always liked dreams better.

'This reminds me of high school,' I said drowsily. 'Whenever I went cruising with my friends we'd joke about driving all night until we got to Florida. Where do you think we'd end up if we drove all night?'

The idea seemed to amuse him. 'It depends on which direction we go.'

'You're driving, I'll leave that part up to you. I brought refreshments for the trip. Want some?' Grinning like a teenager on a joy ride, I showed him the cognac bottle in my shoulder bag.

He glanced at the bottle, then at me, with obvious concern. 'No, thanks,' he said.

So he was going to be judgmental after all. I was tempted to blurt out that it wasn't my fault his absurdly repressed culture made it so you had to be drunk before you could be honest with yourself or anyone else, but before I could speak, he sweetened his refusal with another smile, as if he was genuinely glad to see me.

I smiled back. 'By the way, where *are* we going?'

'A quiet place to talk, of course,' he said, raising his eyebrows with more than a hint of his old impudence.

And I responded with the same pang of illicit desire. I still didn't know where we were going, but he'd given me just the answer I was hoping for.

CHAPTER TWO

Suddenly we were inside an apartment. Actually it was more like a museum. The Western-style furnishings had an old-fashioned, almost Victorian squatness I'd only seen once years ago when I was invited to the old family mansion of a wealthy student.

'You don't live here, do you?' It wasn't where he lived the last time Yuji and I had come to visit anyway, but a lot of things had changed in the past year.

'No, it's my uncle's second apartment. I think he used to keep a girlfriend here, but those days are long gone for him.'

'You use it for your girlfriends now?'

Masaru didn't answer.

'Here, have a drink. You know it's rude not to join me. Let's drink to the new year.' I pushed the cognac bottle into his hand.

He glanced at the label. Clearly impressed it was the good stuff, he got two snifters from a cabinet and poured for both of us, a generous glass for him, less for me. I finished mine in one burning swallow, then wandered off into the living room and poked my head into the bedroom in the back. It had a Western-style bed with a headboard upholstered in velvet, a definite nod to bordello chic.

I glanced back at Masaru. He stood stiffly,

watching me, cognac in hand. He seemed more nervous here, even formal. And why not? The place felt
haunted, as if at any moment Masaru's uncle's
'second wife' might appear in her stylish Nakamoto
kimono, tripping past on her way to meet her *danna*
at Gion's grand geisha dances in cherry blossom time.
But I'd had enough of ghosts. I wanted flesh, hot,
hard and male.

'I'm feeling a little dizzy,' I said, nodding toward
the bed. 'Do you mind if I lie down for a minute?'

'Make yourself at home.'

I dropped my coat on the floor and crawled to the
far side of the bed. The bedspread had a slightly
musty smell. Masaru had followed me as far as the
doorway.

'Lydia . . .'

'If you want to talk, come over here.' I patted the
bed beside me. 'Don't worry, it's just as friends. I
won't attack you.'

Masaru hesitated, then took off his jacket and lay
down next to me. Of course, I immediately pressed
myself against him and rested my head on his shoulder in a more-than-friendly way. He wrapped an arm
around me. Our legs twined together, and his thigh
pushed between mine, as if we were long-time lovers.
I was surprised at how easily he gave in. Unlike me,
he wasn't drunk enough to use that as an excuse.

'Have you been in Kyoto all this time?' He stroked
my arm, a slow trip from elbow to shoulder and back
down again.

'Yes. I was having an affair with my father.'

He snorted softly. Why didn't men ever believe you when you actually told the truth?

'Let me tell Yuji I saw you. He's very worried about you.'

I pressed my face into his chest. 'Just tell him I'm dead. I don't exist anymore as he knew me. Maybe I never did.'

'Come on, don't say that. We'll talk about it tomorrow when you're sober.'

'The marriage is over though. That will still be the same tomorrow.'

Masaru didn't answer. Had he known it, too?

'Masaru, can I ask you a question? Did Yuji ever cheat on me? Please tell me the truth.'

'I can't say for sure, but I don't think so.'

'That makes it worse, you know. I'm a bad person, Masaru. Very bad. I think I just came to Japan to use people. That seems to be all I know how to do.'

'No,' he whispered, touching my hair, 'you're not a bad person.'

'I'm selfish and impatient. I'm bad even for a foreigner.'

'You should've married me. I understand you better than he does.'

I looked up at his face. He didn't seem to be joking. His expression was dreamy and rather complacent.

'You? You turned out to be the most traditional one of the bunch. *Omiai*, taking over the family business. You run a fucking kimono store of all things.'

'Hey, if I had something to fight for, I wouldn't have given in so fast.'

'It's too late now though, isn't it? You couldn't

leave Ryoko and your business and come to America with me, could you?'

He paused. 'Is that an offer?'

Masaru's hand moved to my breast. He stroked the nipple through my blouse, and it stiffened. I let my hand wander lower. He was hard. Such a calming, reassuring feeling, although it should have scared me – when did sex with a man ever lead to anything but grief? But the idea of Masaru pining over me, his one true love, for all these years lifted my spirits. Just for a moment.

'Come on, you'd never really do it. It's just another fantasy. But it's funny, I had an idea for my own business just today. A service for guys who want to have sex with a foreigner without any of the troubles. The American Honeymoon Package, apple pie included. What do you think?'

He decided to take it as another joke. 'I could be your first customer.'

'I can't take money from you.' As soon as I said the words, I wondered if in fact I could.

'That's OK, it's an old family tradition to pay pretty ladies for sex.'

'Are you going to tie me up?'

Masaru's reply was to roll nimbly on top of me and spread my legs with his knee. A classic move that always set my heart pounding.

He smiled down at me. 'Sure, I'll tie you up if you want me to. I'll pretend you're a whore. I'll do anything it takes to get what I want.'

'What do you want?' I asked, although I had a pretty good idea.

'To feel you come in my arms.'

How could I argue with that?

The next thing I knew he was kissing me, a sweet kiss, soft lips brushing mine, then a slow and easy tongue. It was almost enough to make me forget, but something about the very tenderness, the familiarity, the fact that it actually did mean something to me, made it suddenly unbearable. I twisted away.

Of course he looked baffled. Even I had to admit I was sending mixed messages.

Could I tell him the truth? Could I confess that he was actually going to be my second customer tonight, and though I'd been lusting after him for years, I was so drunk and depressed, I'd be more likely to start crying in his arms than have an orgasm?

I settled for an easy lie to put a chill on the proceedings for most guys, especially the Japanese.

'I really want to do this, Masaru, but, well, it's not the right time of the month.'

It took a moment for the news to sink in, but then he sighed and rolled off to stare up at the ceiling. 'It's OK. I've waited five years. I can wait a little longer.'

Ah, yes, waiting. That's pretty much all I'd done, too, first for Yuji, then Kimura, languishing away in that cute little apartment, now turned brothel. The very thought of going back to that place made me sick to my stomach. Then I had an idea.

'Hey, I have a big favor to ask. Do you mind if I stay here for a few days? I need to be out of my apartment. The sooner, the better. I was a bad girl and Dad disowned me.'

'Sure. I'm happy to help out.' He started to say something else, but stopped himself.

'And please don't tell Yuji anything yet. I'll call him soon, I promise.'

Masaru nodded. 'I'll stay out of it.'

As if he wasn't up to his dick in it already, but under the circumstances, it didn't seem wise to point out the contradiction.

CHAPTER THREE

For our first proper date a little over a week later, Masaru took me to a dark, smoky *izakaya*, the ideal place for two adulterers to blend into the shadows. We didn't say much at first, except to discuss what to order: sweet potato vodka cut with hot water, mushroom caps stuffed with minced chicken, eggplant and pimento and rice balls grilled to crunchy perfection.

By the second *shôchû*, our lips were looser. 'I remember the first time we met, I thought you hated me,' I said, swaying toward him.

'Really? You got that wrong. I remember thinking you were very good-looking. Not just the way the Japanese think any blonde *gaijin* is attractive. I knew even an American would call you pretty.'

'I thought you were cute, too, but you gave me this look, like you were angry at me.'

Masaru's shoulder brushed mine. 'Nah, I was scared of you. You know, Lydia, when the light hits your blue eyes the right way, there's a flash, very sharp, almost like a knife.' He tilted his head and looked into my eyes. 'Yes, like two knives.'

'That does sound scary. But now that you know me, you realize I'm really meek and harmless.'

Masaru smiled, an ironic smile, which was almost American except for that slightly crooked canine tooth that gave him a fetchingly wolfish air.

I took another swig of my drink. 'So, did you have American girlfriends when you were in the States?'

'Yes, a few.'

'Did they have blue eyes?'

'The first one did, Jenny Jarrett. That was in Seattle, the homestay in high school.'

'She taught you more than English, right?'

He nodded, his eyes soft with memories. 'How about you?'

'My first time? Oh, your old friend Caroline gets credit for that. I had a boyfriend, but he was really just a friend, and Caroline decided I had to lose my virginity to preserve the family's honor. Rather Japanese of her to take on the responsibility for her inexperienced cousin, don't you think? So she threw a party for me, invited lots of guys and I picked my favorite. She let me use her room and everything.'

'You're not kidding, are you?'

'You'd know.'

He blushed and fiddled with his glass. 'That was a difficult time for me. Lots of stress, you know? I really wasn't planning to have you walk in on us.'

'Well, it definitely made an impression.' In fact, right now, nestled next to him in this murky hideaway, it was the only thing I really remembered about my wedding day. Warmed by the *shôchû*, I leaned close and added, low in his ear, 'I can't tell you how many times you tied me up and fucked me in my fantasies.'

Masaru gave me a sidelong glance, his eyes narrowed. 'I should tell you about a few of mine. Or maybe it would be better to show you?'

He laced his fingers through mine. The moment he touched me an electric jolt of pleasure shot straight to my pussy, with shivery aftershocks warming my thighs and the backs of my knees, setting my toes tingling with desire. It's a magic that only happens with men you want to fuck and haven't yet. Although I was definitely enjoying the sensations, if I had my way, Masaru would surrender this power before the night was through.

He seemed to have the same idea. 'Want to go back to the apartment?'

I thought he'd never ask.

While he paid the check, I slipped into the restroom to take care of another natural urge. The stall was occupied, so I peeked into the mirror. I fluffed my hair, but decided not to touch up the lipstick – Masaru would probably want to minimize any evidence for the wife. I did look good, though. Even after all these years, the *kamisama* were still providing for me, just when things were looking glum.

But, as I squatted over the old-fashioned toilet, I decided maybe the *kamisama* were having a little joke at my expense instead. My period had started early, for real this time. Damn.

I was too high on *shôchû* and hope to let it bother me for long. Masaru and I were creative and motivated, there were plenty of other things we could do. Maybe I could even get him so worked up he'd brave the great taboo. I'd certainly had plenty of other unlikely things happen while I was in Japan.

CHAPTER FOUR

The moment we got inside the apartment, Masaru pushed me back against the door and kissed me hungrily, as if someone might walk in on us at any moment. His fingers worked the buttons of my coat and he yanked it over my shoulders. I grabbed his ass and pulled him close. Our bodies were well suited for a stand-up fuck in the entryway, which in Japan is the consummate in-between space, not quite private, not quite public. I'd been in the country long enough to feel a mild thrill that we'd be doing it with our dirty shoes on, too. So far, I liked his fantasy a lot.

I fumbled for the zipper of his jacket, then went for his trousers. I could give as good as I got. Maybe I'd even kneel and suck him off here, like a cheap whore in an alleyway.

I should've known Masaru would do me one better. Still kissing me hard – my lips were already throbbing – he grabbed the collar of my blouse in both hands and pulled. My cry of surprise mingled with the sound of cloth tearing and buttons flying.

'Look what you did. Fuck you.'

'Yeah, that's the idea.' He met my eyes. I felt the dare in them.

I started to laugh, the kind of low, throaty laugh I could only manage when I was very turned on. I was never very attached to that shirt anyway.

Smiling, he hooked a hand under my thigh and lifted it to his hip. If we were naked, he could easily slip inside. As it was we were dry humping, a slow, deliberate call-and-response, he glided forward, I pushed up to meet him.

He let go of my leg and started unbuckling my belt.

'No, not here,' I said, though not without regret. Next time I definitely wanted to try impetuous, boundary-busting, do-it-right-there-in-the-*genkan* sex, but it wasn't the best setting for owning up to my little lie tonight. I struggled away from him, kicked off my shoes and jumped up into the apartment proper, my ruined shirt hanging open as I headed through the dim hallway toward the living room.

Masaru was close behind. He grabbed my hand to pull me to the bedroom, but I slipped away again.

'Let's play American high school. Make out on the sofa. You can pretend I'm Jenny.'

He fell back onto the couch with me readily enough, but as he slipped an arm around me, he murmured, 'Why pretend? I want to be with you.'

I laughed again. I liked the way he kept me off balance, blending the sweet and the sharp. I certainly didn't want to ruin the mood by pointing out we'd been pretending our heads off all evening, never once mentioning Yuji or Ryoko, as if they didn't exist.

'I think you'll like this game,' I said, turning and swinging my leg over his lap so I had him trapped in my signature girl-on-top straddle. 'I did some wild things back in high school.'

He leaned back and smiled, but it was no surrender. He was watching, waiting to see how I'd use the power when it was my turn, how I'd twist and shape it with my hands and my lips and my thighs. I realized I was panting and already damp with sweat. I had made a plan: some slow kissing followed by a bit of mock high school girl reluctance to let him touch my breasts, which would transfer nicely to a real reluctance to let him in my jeans. Then I'd cap it off with a make-Marybeth-damn-proud blow job that would either get him so horny he'd fuck me anyway or at least would soften his disappointment into forgiveness.

But I hadn't counted on the challenge in his eyes and the way it stirred me, not just *down there*, but in my chest and my skull, my whole body tingling with possibility. I knew then I was going to do things with this man I've never done with anyone before.

But first it was enough to do things I'd dreamed of on those Sunday afternoons as we stood together in my kitchen: simple, but forbidden things. I touched his face, so lovely in the neon glow filtering through the lace curtains. I tipped forward to kiss him, not our first kiss, but for me the first deliberate one.

He closed his eyes, yielding for the moment. Thoughtful comparison – or *monoawase* – is a Japanese custom that dates back to the days of Prince Genji. Through the senses, the connoisseur detects the differences, grand and subtle, among samples of fine incense or a flight of artisanal *sakés* from different regions of the country. Now I breathed in Masaru's fragrance, milder than the ashy, tobacco scent of my older lovers. Now I tasted him, slipping my tongue between his lips. Beneath the tang of *shôchû* and soy sauce, I detected long-ago echoes of chocolate, brown sugar, butter, America.

I moved my hands lower, over his shoulders to the buttons of his shirt. I knew what I would find beneath the cloth wrapping. The vision of his bare, bronzed torso was burned into my memory. But now I could glide my hands over the smooth, golden skin, test the nipples for sensitivity – very little, it seemed – gauge the firmness of muscle, the heat of his flesh.

Masaru made a soft sound of appreciation, his head still tilted back as if he were sleeping, but his hands took on new life, sliding my shirt from my shoulders, unhooking the clasp of my Japanese-made bra with practised skill. He brushed my nipples lightly with his fingertips. I gasped at the contact, then moaned as my hips instinctively rocked into him.

He rolled my nipples between his finger and thumb as if he were adjusting a radio, then pinched them gently.

I was pushing against him rhythmically, the way I did when I masturbated with my pillow, an old exercise from the *No Hands* program. Why not come this way now? Once he'd pleasured me, it would make it all the easier to go the blow job route. Masaru seemed happy enough to be used as a rubbing post for a bitch in heat. I'd never seen such a contented smile.

This is what you've really been looking for, Lydia, a guy who can meet you halfway.

I tried to still that voice, whispering things more forbidden than anything we'd said or done so far. Yes, we did have a lot in common. We were both in the thrall of the foreign, both dangerously hungry for sexual thrills. We'd both married the wrong people for the wrong reasons. But that didn't mean we were meant for each other. It didn't mean we could turn a bridge of clouds into rock-solid stone.

Perhaps Masaru sensed my distraction, for at that moment he slipped his hands under my ass and nudged me up on my knees. Now he was kissing my breasts, using his tongue in the most beguiling way. I shuddered and arched up for more, my high school girl's resistance all but forgotten.

Masaru's lips still suckled, but his hands dropped again to the zipper of my jeans. Instinctively I reached down and pushed him away.

He looked up, surprise melting into a roguish smile. 'You still want to be in high school or can we grow up and use the bed?'

It was time for the truth.

'Oh, Masaru, promise you won't hate me.'

He cocked his head in an unspoken question.

'The other night I told you it was the wrong time of the month. But now it really is.'

He frowned for a moment, then realization dawned.

'You know, I was drunk and I hadn't seen you in so long and I wasn't even sure it was real.'

He gave a soft grunt of assent. He didn't seem too mad.

'I could do something else for you.'

He considered the offer for a moment, then shook his head. 'I don't want the first time to be like that.'

His voice was soft, romantic even, but there was no

doubt the mood was broken. There'd be no more sex games tonight.

I plopped back down on the sofa and wrapped my shirt around me. He took my hand, but I'd have to say the silence between us was not exactly comfortable.

Finally he said, 'Lydia, maybe it's none of my business, but are you still seeing that guy you called your "dad"?'

'Oh no, that's so over,' I said, and suddenly I did feel lighter, as if a weight had been lifted from my chest. Kimura, Suzuki, the whole scene at the club — had that ever been part of my life? 'I'm not involved with anyone now.'

'What about me?'

I sighed. 'Come on, you're just playing around. I'm part of your merchant family heritage, just like this weird apartment.'

'That's not how I see it,' he said.

I didn't have the nerve to ask him how he did see it, but it sounded promising for the future. In fact we did make a date for the following Friday and after he gave me a lingering goodbye kiss, he said in Japanese, so smooth and warm it made my knees melt, *'Kondo dakun da yo.'* Next time I *am* going to have you. Then he added with a grin, 'Sorry about the shirt.'

Later, I lay in bed stroking myself to juicy bits of memory from the evening past, the bruising kisses in the hallway, the glimmer in his eyes as I started fucking him through our clothes, the intoxicating arrogance of his promise to 'have' me.

I knew what that meant, of course — and the

submissive little masochist in me was fiercely turned on by the idea — but would I 'have' him in return? Could he leave Ryoko for me? Not likely, but not out of the question either. For the time being, I'd probably be more of a *nigosan* or 'second wife', which, if you got past the sexist stigma of it might not be such a bad thing. Why not let someone else take care of the laundry and the thank-you notes and the birthing and the diapers and all of those other messy feminine duties? That left the dinners in good restaurants, wild stand-up sex in the entryway, and the romantic confessions for me. It was every kid's dream come true. I wouldn't even have to eat my vegetables to get dessert.

But first I had to make a break with my old life, for both of us. By next week, I decided, I would be 'clean' for him in more ways than one.

CHAPTER FIVE

I called Yuji the next morning, when I was sure he wouldn't be home, and left a much-rehearsed message on the answering machine.

'Hi, it's Lydia. I'm sorry. About everything. I know that's not enough, but I was thinking maybe we could talk. Or not, it's up to you. I'll come to the apartment on Sunday around three, OK? If you're not there, I'll understand.'

And then, somehow, I was actually standing in front of the apartment, ringing the doorbell, wondering if I should use the Japanese term, 'I'm home', or go with 'Sorry to disturb you', or say nothing when I stepped up from the entryway into the living space proper. That is, if Yuji even answered the door.

He did.

He looked the same, maybe a little thinner, but good.

We exchanged nervous, reassuring smiles – *we'll both be polite, it won't get ugly* – but his eyes were guarded.

As I walked back to the living room I noticed the wedding picture was gone, but everything else about the apartment was pretty much the same as the day I left almost one year before.

We sat down on the sofa, separated by a few feet of cushion.

I looked down at my hands. In the past year, the veins had become more prominent, the wrists bony and fragile. They weren't a young woman's hands anymore.

Yuji waited in silence. Of course, it was my responsibility to explain.

'I'm sorry,' I said in English, a strange choice of language perhaps, since Japanese is so rich in apologies of every nuance and they all would have been proper in this case.

Yuji didn't reply for a moment. A very long moment. Then he said, in careful English, 'I thought when you left that you were saying maybe we could try again in a different way. But when you stayed away so long, I knew you were telling me something else.'

I couldn't have put it better myself.

'Yes. Well, this is hard to say,' I stuttered. Another Japanese expression that was perfect for the situation. 'I had a boyfriend for a while. That's over now. But . . . but I don't think I can go back to the way it was.'

He nodded.

'I'm sorry your father was right about our marriage being full of troubles.'

He lips lifted into a fleeting smile. 'What are you going to do now?'

'Go back to America,' I said. It seemed to be what everyone expected to hear.

He nodded. 'We need to talk about what you want to take . . .'

'Don't worry about that. I don't want anything.'

He reached for my hand. 'We'll work something out.'

It was easier than I expected to touch him. There was no twinge of lust or regret. This bond was softer, two people comforting each other over a misfortune beyond their control. As we sat there together, the heat in his flesh seemed to fade, like the colors fade as evening falls and drifts into night.

'Your boyfriend,' Yuji said, not meeting my eyes, 'was he Japanese?'

'No. American. You don't know him.'

His shoulders relaxed and he exhaled softly.

I knew it would be the answer he wanted, less a lie than a gift, smoothing the edges, softening the blow. It was the least I could do for him now.

CHAPTER SIX

The next stop on my 'clean up my old life' tour was my final trip to Kimura's apartment to clear out the rest of my things. I planned to put most of it out for the next day's garbage collection, but I did pack up the silk Jean Harlow negligee and some books.

When the phone rang, I answered, expecting it would be the manager to make arrangements for me to drop off the key.

'Am I speaking with Megu?' The male voice on the other end was deep and pleasant.

My heart skipped a beat. 'Yes.'

'My name is Tanaka. Mr Suzuki told me about your new English school.'

'Yes,' I said, in proper Japanese style, trying to keep my breath even.

'I also saw an example of your English lesson at the party a few weeks ago. I enjoyed it very much.'

'Thank you. It's very kind of you to say so.' In spite of myself, I smiled. I had a fan.

'I understand that you're giving private lessons.'

'Yes.' I sounded calm enough, but my pulse was racing. As I stood there clutching the receiver, a strange vision seemed to open before my eyes: Meg's English Tutoring Services, a thriving enterprise, with a strong client base built on referrals from satisfied customers. I'd be the envy of my friends from college, who were struggling to get their own consulting companies off the ground back in the States.

The voice interrupted, 'I was wondering if I could schedule an introductory lesson in the near future?'

Instinctively I glanced toward the door of the apartment. The hallway seemed to stretch, the entrance foyer shrinking to a shadowy, distant realm. Time collapsed too. In an instant the doorbell would ring and the man on the telephone would be standing outside the door, waiting for me to walk the long path to open it and let him in. What would I find on the other side? Would the face be as smooth and assured as the voice? There were some types of men here I didn't like at all – the pompous ones, the skinny ones with darting eyes, bad breath and stringy hair, the ones who got nasty when they drank. You could call me a slut – most people probably would – but I'd always chosen my partners, always found something in them that answered my fantasies of the moment. But Megu-*sensei* would have to give her 'lesson' to whomever or whatever stood waiting out there.

My hand on the receiver was moist with sweat. I tried to play the hostess, polished and polite and exquisitely attentive to my listener's feelings, but the words came out quickly, desperately. 'Yes, well, yes, but unfortunately I have to go back to America for a while. A family matter. I'm leaving very soon, but I can take your number or let Mr Suzuki know when I'm back and perhaps we can arrange something then.'

'Ah, yes, I understand.' The voice was noticeably cooler. The man quickly said goodbye and hung up.

I put the receiver back in the cradle, still clutching it as if it were glued to my skin. I'd slammed the door on that one. If I really did want to start up a 'language school', I'd blown a good opportunity to cast the net wider. Even if this Tanaka — a name as genuine as Meg, no doubt — were ugly, the voice was nice enough. I could have closed my eyes and faked it. At least I could have left him with a better impression on the phone, charmed him and tantalized him and made him curious enough to call back.

How else could I pass the time in my new life as Masaru's second wife, waiting, always waiting for him to tear himself away from his public duties?

I turned and caught a glimpse of myself in the mirror hanging in the hall. But the figure gazing back from the mirror wasn't a woman. It was a freak with a pointed nose and sky-blue, space alien eyes. No wonder people stared at this bizarre creature.

I would never be Japanese. I'd spent so many years in this country, most of it earnestly trying to learn the language and customs, but I was no closer to getting what I really wanted.

The creature in the mirror was still staring at me. Her pale lips were deathly still, but I knew what she was asking.

'What do you *really* want?'

Answers bubbled up, like water from a hot spring, voices I'd denied for a very long time.

I wanted to stop apologizing all the time for not doing things right. I wanted to be more than just a small part of someone's life, jammed into a tiny room, waiting for my treat. I wanted to stop floating and step onto dry land and figure out if I could still walk. Most of all, I wanted to do something I could feel truly good about for a change.

I knew exactly what I had to do, although I'd been trying to avoid it. I had to go cold turkey on this Japan fantasy and get my ass back to America. But I still had one important conquest to make before I left. I picked up the phone and called Masaru at his office.

CHAPTER SEVEN

'Well, Lydia, this is it. Your last night in Japan. All in all, it's been quite an eventful stay, wouldn't you say?'

The mid-priced business hotel near the airport was a dreary place. There wasn't much else to do to pass the evening but masturbate with a little help from a friend.

'Yes, I guess it was. I appreciate your help, by the way. You were always there when I needed you.' I slipped my hand into my panties. My finger settled into the groove just to the right of my clit.

'Believe me, it was my pleasure, my dear. Now this is a rather ambitious souvenir you're taking back with you – an entire palace? Rather like the *Tale of Genji*. Didn't the Shining Prince keep each of his wives hidden away in a separate wing of his mansion? I see you've copied him rather nicely with your Chamber of Springtime to keep your collection of juicy young men and the Cloister for Lovers of Autumn to house your jaded connoisseurs of a certain age.'

'Yes, I never know what type I'll be in the mood for, but you know who I want tonight.'

'Indeed I do. He's waiting for you in the Pavilion of Summer. I promise I'll keep a low profile and only peek at the proceedings through a discreet hole in the paper door.'

My chosen lover for the evening is certainly worth spying on in his dashing *yukata*. In real life, Masaru favored jeans and Nirvana T-shirts for off-duty relaxing, so he'd probably be annoyed to be decked out as Japan Boy, but this was my fantasy.

When he sees me he sits up, his eyes gliding appreciatively over my slinky, translucent negligee. He beckons to me Japanese-style — a waving gesture that looks rather like an American 'goodbye'.

Obediently I sit on the *tatami* beside him. Without a word, he dips his finger in his glass of chilled *saké*, anointing each nipple with a few icy drops. They stiffen and poke through the silk, so tender they almost feel sore. Masaru circles the tips with his forefingers, the friction of the wet cloth bringing a sigh to my lips.

He watches my face carefully as he teases me. Apparently unsatisfied with the intensity of my response, he picks up the glass and pours the entire contents slowly over my breasts, soaking the whole front of the negligee.

I gasp, gooseflesh rising all over my body. My pussy tightens in a spasm of anticipation.

'You've ruined it,' I protest timidly, for I'm not sure I'm allowed to speak.

His eyes bore into me, amused, taunting. He grabs the front of the slip and tears it down the front, leaving two jagged, gaping halves.

'No, *now* I've ruined it.'

My cheeks burn as if he'd slapped me, but I don't dare to complain. I bow my head submissively and see that my chest is heaving, already dotted with the telltale flush of sexual arousal.

'Where do you want to go tonight, Lydia?' he asks. It's more of a command than a question.

I know the answer, but my tongue is suddenly thick and clumsy with shame. I want too much. I've always wanted too much.

Masaru hooks a finger under my chin and lifts it so I'm gazing into those penetrating eyes once again. 'Around the world, of course. Isn't that right, my little traveler?'

I nod, blushing.

'Then let's get started on our journey. The magic carpet is right over there.' He nods toward the single futon spread out by the decorative alcove. The hanging scroll is very unusual but well chosen, an erotic spring print of a courtesan, her legs bound to her torso with rope, her lover's giant cock poised to enter her ruddy, swollen vagina.

'I know you want me to tie you up just like your cousin, but that wasn't real *shibari*. I was going easy on her since it was her first time in Japan. I get the feeling you can handle something a little more authentic.'

Masaru opens the carved wooden chest by the alcove and pulls out a thick coil of golden rope. My heart stops. This is the real thing. But when I'm able to breathe again, I notice the bonds are fragrant with the calming perfume of fresh *tatami* straw, the sweet, intoxicating smell of old Japan.

'I'm anxious to get on to the fucking part, so I

won't do anything too elaborate tonight. Just a little *kaikyaku kani*, the open-leg crab tie. Do you know it?'

I shake my head. The rest of my body is shaking, too. Masaru pulls the rope slowly and carefully through his hands as if it is living flesh, as if he is making love to it.

'You'll find out soon enough what it is. Come sit on the futon. Oh, and take off those rags. I always suspected you'd look much better naked.'

I slip off the tattered negligee and crawl over to the futon. Masaru commands me to sit very properly — like I'm at a tea ceremony — and wraps the doubled rope around my waist. It's much softer against my skin than it looks. Masaru's forehead is creased with concentration, but a faint smile plays over his lips as he pulls the loose ends through the loop formed by the centre point of the rope and ties it fast.

'Lie back and bring your knees to your chest.' His voice is quiet, but chilly. A voice to be obeyed.

My breath is coming so fast I think I might faint, but I manage to follow his command. He wraps the rope around my leg several times, binding my thigh to my shin, then he ties it crosswise underneath my bent knee, so my left side is immobilized in a come-and-fuck-me position. Already I'm wet. Very wet.

'Hold your wrist against the inside of your knee.'

Trembling, I extend my arm between my legs. He wraps more rope around my wrist and secures it to my knee. With practised speed he gives the same treatment to my right leg and wrist, then pulls the remaining rope around the back of my neck and ties it to the left leg to make a harness.

Now I can't close my legs. I can't move them at all. I'm frozen, totally exposed and helpless. My heart is pounding and my throat is painfully dry. My pussy on the other hand is drenched in a flood of hot juices. It trickles down my slit, pooling under my ass. The mattress is going to be soaked. And yet, even in my daze of lust and fear, I can't help but notice the beauty of the golden rope criss-crossing over my pale skin, the smooth, but implacable knotting. Constriction as art indeed.

Masaru stretches out on the futon, his face between my legs, to study me. 'Did you shave yourself just for me, Lydia? How thoughtful to let me see everything. Your pussy is so pretty, like shiny folds of pink satin. Push open now. I want to see where my dick will go exploring in a minute or two.'

Of course I obey – I must – but not without a soft moan of shame.

'Are you embarrassed, Lydia? Embarrassed to let me see your naked cunt all wet and spread wide?' he asks, head tilted in mock concern.

I nod, unable to speak.

'Let me do a little more tying. Just to make you feel more comfortable.' He picks up the negligee, tears off two strips of silk and knots the end together. Then, with casual cruelty, he rolls me back almost onto my shoulders and slips one end through my rope belt. Jerking the band up into my ass crack and pulling it taut over my clit, he secures it to the front of my belt. Now my whole cleft is throbbing, burning. I'm throbbing everywhere, pain and pleasure all twisted up together.

Masaru gives me a wink. 'I don't think you'll be able to trick me out of fucking you this time, Lydia.'

He lies on top of me, resting on his elbows, his firm belly pressing against my cunt. Instinctively I push up against him. My clit is so hot and swollen, the pressure alone makes me sigh.

'Humping me like a little dog and you're not even in heat. Do you think you can come this way, just by rubbing yourself against me?'

'Is that what you want?' I ask, my voice quivering. The silk is chafing my tender spots but it's highly arousing, too. I very likely can come this way, and soon.

'Actually,' Masaru says, narrowing his eyes, 'I want something else right now. I want to tell you how I really feel about what you did to me the other day.'

Now there's a dream come true, a Japanese man opening up to me about his true feelings. Unfortunately, given what I did, I know things might get unpleasant.

'Please, Masaru,' I beg, 'can't we have sex first? After all, this is my fantasy.'

'Yeah, well, deal with it, Lydia, because it's hard for me to play along with this little S&M scene when I'm so pissed off at you. You lure me out to a restaurant and all of a sudden you tell me it's over, you've moved out of the apartment, and you're going back to America at the end of the week. What could I do? We were in public, my hands were tied.'

A fantasy lover with an attitude? This wasn't going the way I wanted at all.

'Look,' I say, 'I know it wasn't the bravest way to do it, but I didn't trust myself. I knew you'd get me into bed if we were alone. I really want to do it with you, but I owe it to Yuji . . .'

'He'll never know, I promise.'

'Maybe, but you'll know and that will change things. It'll be better for him – and you – if I'm not so selfish for once in my life. You'll still be friends when I'm long gone.'

'That's another thing I want to talk about. Why can't you stay? I know we can work something out.'

'I don't think so. If I did the mistress thing again, I'd have to keep trying to be Japanese. I've given that up. I'm a greedy foreigner. I want all of you. And I can't pretend it doesn't matter that Ryoko's going to have a baby this summer.'

Masaru squeezes his eyes shut and takes a deep breath, just like he did in the *robata* grill when I said goodbye for real. He is obviously in pain, torn, trapped. I know exactly how he feels.

I want to touch his cheek tenderly, comfort him somehow, but of course my wrists are tethered to my legs. And so I try another way to soothe him. It might work better this time around.

'Isn't it sort of romantic, though?' I say softly. 'Like an *enka* song – the years of yearning, the one brief night of unconsummated love in your uncle's apartment, the duty that wrenches us apart so that all we have is memories and tears. A very Japanese ending, don't you think?'

Masaru groans. 'Great, now my life is a whiny *enka*. Did I happen to mention I hate *enka*? That sappy fantasy of traditional Japan crap doesn't work for me. I like happy American endings.' He looks straight into my eyes. As much as I want to, I can't look away. 'We would have been great together, Lydia. I would have made you feel so good.'

I feel tears rising, just as I did then. 'But this feels good too, to do the right thing for a change.' I try my best to smile. 'And I'm always looking for new kinds of pleasure. Aren't you?'

Something in his expression shifts and softens, and he manages a smile, too. A sad one.

'But, hey, in here we can do anything we want,' I say, switching to hearty American good cheer. 'Do you still want to go around the world?'

He shakes his head. 'No, I'm too depressed for anal sex. By the way, can I untie you now? It's not really my thing.'

I laugh and nod.

He loosens the ropes and unwraps the silk strap between my legs. When he feels how wet it is though, he grins, an encouraging glimmer of the old Masaru. He runs his hands over my newly liberated wrists and legs.

'Does it hurt?' he asks sweetly.

'A little. But it feels good to be free.'

Our eyes meet. Without a word, I know what he wants. I want it, too. I rest my hand on his chest and push him slowly back to the futon. Like a precocious child who's already learned the act of unwrapping the present is the best part of Christmas, I tug the belt open and part the sides of his *yukata*, inch by tantalizing inch.

He's not hard. Yet. But that's the way I want it. I like to watch soft cocks raise their sleepy heads, twitching, yawning, stretching. I run my fingers along the crease where his groin meets his thighs, draw circles on his belly above the wiry pubic hair. He catches his breath and his cock stirs. Gliding my fingers up and down the shaft, I caress him to full attention. Masaru has the perfect cock, long enough, thick enough, slightly curved to the left to add personality. But even perfect beauty can use some accessorizing now and then. I take the strip of silk, still damp with my juices, and wrap it around his hard-on. Closing my fist around him, I stroke him until he arches back and moans. I pull the silk away and he moans again, a sadder sound this time.

'It's not over yet,' I whisper.

Kneeling beside him, I bend to suck his cock. On the first glide of my moistened lips from tip to root, he swells and hardens still further. Sure, it felt good to be noble and sacrifice my carnal pleasure for the sake of his friendship with Yuji, but to be honest, nothing feels as fantastic as this – my hungry mouth filled with something so hard and insistent, yet exquisitely sensitive. My pussy clenches with desire, and I reach between my legs to masturbate.

Masaru touches my shoulder lightly. 'Lydia? I can't wait anymore.'

I can't either. I turn and straddle him. We're both wet enough I can slide right on to his cock.

His expression – eyes squeezed shut, lips parted in a silent cry – looks like pain, but I know this time it's something else.

I begin to move, grinding my clit against his belly. He leans up to take my nipple in his mouth. His right hand reaches around to tease my ass cleft, his left reaches up to caress my other breast. He's an octopus, a thousand-armed Buddha, and the man of my dreams, filling every empty hole, even my heart.

His finger starts tapping my asshole, sending sparks shooting up my spine. I can't hold back anymore. I start to buck, slamming so hard into him, my knees bounce up off the mattress with every stroke. I'm going to come. And it's going to be good, I can tell, the kind of orgasm that starts as a hot pulsing in your cunt, then spirals up through your chest like a tornado, then climbs higher still until your skull bursts open, so that for a moment you really are suspended in air like a cloud.

When I hit the ground again, Masaru was gone. My old friend had vanished, too, without even a 'goodnight'. And I was left alone in a single bed with a hand that smelled of pussy and sore thighs from holding my legs in that crab position I picked up from leafing through a bondage book one lazy afternoon back in Kyoto. It was nothing more than the typical aftermath of a hot time in bed with the horny babe I know and love best. So why was my face suddenly all wet? Why the hell was I crying?

After so many years in Japan, I should have known this was the only way to tie it all together. After all, I still had one more night in this enchanted land, where yearning is always sweeter than fulfillment and the best-loved stories end in tears.

Part Twelve

A HUNDRED MEN WHO FOUND A PLACE IN MY HEART
(San Francisco, 1992)

EPILOGUE

When I finished my story it was past eleven and the fire had died to glowing ash. Brad was stretched out on his side to my right, elbow bent, cheek resting on his hand. Tim sat cross-legged on my left, his eyes fixed on me, a faint smile on his lips. I was leaning back on the throw pillow, hands behind my head. Both of them were close enough that if I wanted to I could easily reach out and turn the slumber party into an orgy with an inviting squeeze of Brad's shapely arm, Tim's solid thigh.

But always the question: what *did* I want?

The expressions of my students, too, were hard to read in the dim light. They said they wanted the real story, but maybe they'd gotten more than they bargained for.

Still, this was America, where it was always best to keep the mood light.

'Well, class, any questions?' I glanced from one to the other.

Neither of them spoke for a time. A long time. Were they contemplating the futility of human desire with newly enlightened hearts? Or were they too shocked and horrified to speak? Suddenly I realized that either way, I was glad I'd told them. I felt lighter, cleansed. Even if they weren't ready for the truth, I was.

Still, it was a relief when Tim's beeper went off again, breaking the silence at last. He checked the number and sighed.

'You can use the phone downstairs in the kitchen if you like,' I offered.

Tim bobbed his head nervously, which struck me as a rather Japanese gesture, and within a minute he returned to tell us he had to be going, although he had enjoyed the evening. It had been very educational, he said, eyebrows lifted in a touch of irony.

Brad watched him go with a mischievous smile. 'Do you think those two lovebirds will get back together?'

I wasn't sure – happy endings aren't as common as we wish – but I smiled anyway. After all, with Tim gone, it meant one less temptation for me.

I turned on my side to face Brad. 'Don't let my example scare you off while you're over there. I'm sure it's a very different experience for a man.'

Brad cleared his throat. 'By the way, while we're talking about truth, I just wanted to let you know that I'm probably not going to Japan. I've always been ambivalent about the move, so I started looking for another job. In a way, I've been coming to your class under false pretenses. Not that I haven't learned a lot from you, *Sensei*.' He grinned, then added, softly. 'Really, I have.'

'So you're not going? When do you plan to break the news to the management?'

'Soon. I'm still working out the details with the new company. I know my boss won't be happy. But hey, it's my life.'

I certainly couldn't argue with him there. Could it be that I actually admired the boy for his selfish opportunism?

Or maybe he wasn't such a boy. In the next moment he was asking if he could see me again, for coffee or something, since he wouldn't be flying off to distant lands after all.

I laughed. 'You want a date with an old lady like me?'

I couldn't tell for sure, but I think he was blushing. 'Brad, I should be honest with you, too. I'm thinking of abstaining from sex for a while. Maybe forever. Of course, I hope we can still be friends in a spiritual sense.'

Now Brad laughed. 'I hope you haven't made your final decision quite yet.'

I was doing fairly well at keeping my twitching lips from stretching into a smile, but unfortunately for my future as a saint, I made the mistake of looking into his eyes. It wasn't the first time a man's gaze went to straight to my head like liquor. It definitely wasn't the first time sexual excitement beguiled me with visions of things that didn't really exist. But it had never gone as far as all out hallucination.

There, right before me, Brad's face suddenly began to ripple and shimmer like the haze hovering over an asphalt road on a hot summer day. The flesh began to melt, the features stretching and shifting into a new face, poignantly sharp for a moment, then dissolving back into blankness again. First, I thought I glimpsed Hiroyuki, his dark hair framed by my pillow, his whole countenance shining with pure delight. With a blink, it was Dr Shinohara's sculptured, monkish face, the eyes softened into desire yet content with contemplation. All at once, I wanted to thank them, for gifts I felt I only just opened this very night. But before I knew it, they were gone, and Matt was gazing down at me with heart-twisting sorrow, then Mr Nagai was looking up, his *saké*-hooded eyes not quite masking the flicker of raw fear. Gratitude turned just as quickly to regret, and I would have apologized if I could have. I had used them, I could admit it now, and that's never what I really wanted.

The next face lingered a moment longer than the others, as if to make sure I saw who he was. Better still, this time he saw me too. Kimura smiled, fondly, and my chest ached with something like love, but maybe it was just recognition of pain, loss, longing. The smile blurred, the eyes lengthened and swooped upward and it was Masaru, his face tilting back against the sofa for my kiss. I almost called out to him, but the vision receded and it was Yuji floating before me, love and sadness all tangled up in his eyes.

Was this all I had left of them? There was no twinge of arousal, no flash of naked limbs intertwined, no memory at all of ecstasy, theirs or mine. Just the string of moments when a man stepped out of the rushing crowd and saw me as more than just America and let me have a glimpse beneath the finely crafted mask of Japan.

'Hey, Lydia? Are you OK? You looked really out of it for a minute.'

I blinked. A fair-skinned American face loomed over me. It was Brad, back to his original form.

Without thinking, I reached up and touched his cheek. It was warm, solid. Real.

'Who are you?' I whispered.

The question didn't faze him. He seemed to know the right answer was simply a smile.

At the end of her story, the Amorous Woman told the young gentlemen that the confession of her sins in their presence had cleared away the clouds of delusion so that her true heart could shine forth like the moon. Now, in my heart, I knew my vow of eternal celibacy was a little extreme. Maybe if I stayed away from married men, pornographic shows and taking money for it, I could slip in a little sex if the chance for a real connection came along?

Brad leaned toward me and I closed my eyes, knowing – and not knowing – what would happen next. But one thing was certain. This was no Japanese *enka* song. The ending would be different.

I was in America now, where the best is always yet to come.

L♥VE

You'll love *Scarlet* magazine!

Scarlet is a hottest monthly magazine for women featuring the sort of frank and informative features other women's mags wouldn't dare print – and it's packed with exclusive erotic fiction from the world's sexiest writers!

For **only £29** you'll receive **12 issues** of Scarlet and your next Orion book **free** worth £7.99

So what are you waiting for? Turn over the page to find out how you can take advantage of this great offer.

3 easy ways to take up this great offer:

1) Online at www.scarletmagazine.co.uk/orion

2) By phone on 0870 220 6398 and quote code ORBOOK

3) By post. Fill in the form below with credit or debit card details or attach a cheque made payable to Scarlet Publishing Ltd and post it off to the Free Post address below. It's that easy!

FREEPOST RLZY-XZJG-ABRH Scarlet Publishing Ltd, 800 Guillat Avenue, Kent Science Park, Sittingbourne ME9 8GU

✂

NAME AND ADDRESS	I WISH TO PAY BY:
	☐ Cheque. I enclose a payment of £29 payable to SCARLET PUBLISHING LTD
Title _____	☐ Visa / Mastercard / Switch. (Issue number_____)
First name_____	Card number ☐☐☐☐ ☐☐☐☐ ☐☐☐☐ ☐☐☐☐ ☐☐☐☐
Surname_____	Start date ☐☐☐☐ Expiry date ☐☐☐☐
Address_____	
_____	Signature _____ Date_____
Postcode_____	Email _____
	☐ No, I would not like to receive news of other products and services from Scarlet.
	☐ No, I would not like to receive news of other products and services from carefully selected companies.